Blue Monday

By

Ron Brassfield

© Copyright 2001 by Ron Brassfield. All rights reserved.

No part of this book may be reproduced, stored in a retrieval system, or transmitted by any means, electronic, mechanical, photocopying, recording, or otherwise, without written permission from the author.

ISBN: 0-75965-599-5

This book is printed on acid free paper.

1stBooks – rev. 08/22/01

1.

The halogen beams of police and firefighters illuminated shafts of swirling smoke rising from charred rubble—all that remained of Wild Bill Hiccup's Drink 'n Drool.

To Pamela Travers, to see the smoking ruins of this place, to walk through its ashes, was just about worth the long drive in the middle of the night. When her family had lived in the county, her father had always longed to shut down this disgusting dive, with its *"Girls! Girls! Girls!"* neon sign flashing across the boondocks. The scummy establishment had been the cause of many a police call, nearly always a walk into danger for the minions of the law. Its nihilistic, rough trade clientele of biker gangs and permanently disenfranchised ex-miners frequently brawled with lethal weapons. Usually, they were drunk, and arguing over who had paid the *"girl!"* the most, and who therefore deserved her sexual favors for the night. Pam had heard her late father grumble, more than once, about brown-bag money and the failure of the courthouse to shut this place down once and for all. Now it looked as if fate had, at last, taken care of that job.

The gravel parking lot was nearly empty. Sheriff Montrose shone the beam from his club-length flashlight over the shattered remnants of a battered and charred Acura, a Lincoln town car in a similar, dismal condition, and the debris covering them. Now being removed, bit by bit, by fire department personnel and volunteers rousted out of their own cozy beds, the sheriff explained to Pam that these metal shards were fragments from a military Bell helicopter—a type used in search and rescue missions.

"Figure they come down from the Mountain Home Base," he drawled. "Now, *why* they flew down here and *what in the world* took them out, nobody at the base'll say. But—I think I might have an answer laying back at the hospital—if we can only pull that answer out."

"Sheriff!" called one of the county rescue workers from inside the burned-out shell of Wild Bill's.

Montrose went inside, cautiously, shining a light long enough to allow Travers to stand in the doorway. "What is it, Ted?" asked Montrose.

"What's left of a Cobra, Sheriff."

"That's a king-hell *combat* fighter," Montrose muttered.

"*Was*. Now, it's just pieces of junk," Ted intoned.

"Can you give me a lift to the county hospital, Pam?" Montrose asked.

Travers shrugged, and they climbed into her car. It had covered a lot of miles during this dark night.

She had been dreaming an exhilarating dream of flight when the phone rang, waking her at 1:30 AM. Her eyes blinked, adjusting from magnificent vistas of the cascading sections of countryside far below, to the bleary, static, rectangular vision of her clock radio's glowing LED. The phone again rang, a once silent companion turned rude mechanical intruder. It had to be a wrong number at this hour. She lifted the receiver and listened.

"Pam? Hello? This is Sheriff Montrose down't Mountain City. Are ya there?"

Travers had never thought to hear this voice again. Randy Montrose was an old crony of her dad's when he was alive and on the police force in the state to the south. Now a Sheriff, Montrose was suddenly calling her after eight years. He didn't want to give her much information over the phone, he said.

She felt her father would have wanted her to respect the sheriff's wishes. She grudgingly agreed to make the trek south from Boise to meet him.

And so she had driven, down along Highway 51, through the Shoshone Reservation into Elko County, blaring Whitney Houston on her CD player and eventually catching glimpses of the shimmering waters of the east fork of the Owyhee River. Now she again fixed her eyes on the road, grim and wordless, as she drove Montrose to the hospital. She braced for whatever she was going to see there, telling herself she had surely seen as bad or worse in her daily line of work.

"I've got a live soldier upstairs, a survivor named Lieutenant George McIntire," Montrose intoned as he and Travers strolled through the hospital corridors. "He caught a bullet in the arm at Wild Bill's," he added, as they boarded an elevator. "Now, I don't know yet who pulled that trigger, but I got a suspicion it might've been this two-ton lug we hauled in to the burn unit." Montrose twitched slightly.

"I assume he was burned in the fire from the copter crash," Travers replied.

"Nope, didn't look like it. We found him a half-mile down the road, in the wreckage of a *truck* that blew up. In fact, it was the bartender's pickup."

"Good grief."

"I haven't got to the good part, yet. The reason I called you. Finding those two guys was strange enough. But, wait'll you see who we found *with* 'em."

On the second floor, they walked to a guarded room. Another deputy also stood guard over the next room. "Go on back to the station house, Jake," Montrose told his deputy. "I ain't goin' nowhere for awhile."

"The pictures gonna come out good, you think, Sheriff?" asked Jake.

"Well, I hope so, but the drug store ain't open for another few hours," replied Montrose. "I dropped the roll of film in the chute, though. Now get along and round up them suspects."

"Yes, sir." The departing deputy nodded to his colleague standing guard at the next door.

Montrose opened the door, switched on the light, and entered the room, along with Travers. There, lying on the bed with his wrists strapped to the side rails of his hospital bed, lay a handsome young man with red hair and vibrant, completely blue skin.

Travers nearly swooned. She wondered if she were still dreaming, after all.

"How long has—*he* been here?" she asked the Sheriff.

"'Bout five hours now," Montrose replied, checking his wristwatch. "He's already had a couple o' sedative shots, though the nurse said *one* would keep him out for twelve hours." The sheriff opened the wardrobe and pulled out an olive drab military undershirt and fatigue britches. "He was dressed in these," he commented, eyebrows arched upward. "What d'ya make of 'im?"

"I don't know," she said, leaning in close. The youth was burned, bruised and abrased in places. "Is this—real?" Travers stammered, lightly touching the youth's forearm.

"It don't wash off, if that's what you mean. They've checked him out. He's got a mild concussion. No broken bones, though. Nothin' that won't, most likely, heal."

"But, he's—blue."

"Right."

"Okay. That's strange, all right. But why call me down to see him?"

"Wellll, I figured this kid might tell us somethin'. But in a case like this, well, it might take a well-trained professional to know how to ask the questions right, know't I mean? I mean, puttin' the suspect in the right frame of mind to cooperate, don't you know." Montrose cleared his throat. "I've heard some talk about the work you're doing in the prison system."

Travers tensed. If word of her techniques had reached the Sheriff, her entire program was in danger. If it were shut down, she felt it would be a tragedy for the criminal justice system in Idaho.

Travers had been something of a prodigy in psychology studies. Her grades had allowed her to skip her senior year into college, and thanks to intensive work-study, she had her doctorate before her twenty-third birthday. She was considered within the professional community to be immensely dedicated, with a pioneering mind and an intensely disciplined attitude.

Two years into her prison work, the low rate of recidivism she had developed among her parolee "patients" had proved this assessment correct. None of her colleagues knew that her "special" applications were a winking arrangement with Warden Whitsell—for now. She saw no harm in them, and hoped that one day they would be commonly accepted in penal systems nationwide.

Meantime, Idaho's prisons were exploding with inmates. The Republican-dominated legislature continued to pass ever-more punitive laws, mandating longer sentences for every imaginable offense. The sparsely-populated state had over 4,000 prisoners in its penal system, more than three-quarters of whom were imprisoned for non-violent offenses. Most of these were minor drug users, and an occasional dealer, but people were also serving years-long sentences for such

Idaho-specific felonies as passing bad checks under $50.00, or driving on suspended licenses. With each new felony placed on the law books, the guard union made additional large donations to the incumbents' re-election campaigns.

Idaho had attracted her due to its severe legal system, but Travers now found her workload wearing. She had followed a series of critical articles in the Boise *Spokesman-Review* and regretted that the schools had lost a quarter of their money while prison construction allocations had tripled. With little money for rehabilitation and vocational training in the system, Warden Whitsell was hard-pressed, squeezed between the skeptical press and citizens' pressure groups on the one hand; legislators, police and prison guard unions on the other.

And now, she realized that the small light she and the warden were shining into the system was in danger of being snuffed out. So she decided to ignore the implications of Montrose's statement. She looked earnestly at Montrose and attempted a diversion.

"Could he be—an alien? Were those helicopters shot down by a UFO?"

At that moment, the blue youth groaned and stirred. Drowsily, he shook his head, then opened his eyes. Travers gasped. Their irises were large and yellow-orange, and in their centers, he had the slitted pupils of a cat!

2.

"Are you—real?"

The breathless question came, this time, not from Pam Travers or Sheriff Montrose, but from the blue lad who lay strapped to the hospital bed, covered by a sheet up to the chest. He gazed, open-mouthed, at Travers, who seemed to tower above him. Travers, brow knit, looked again at Montrose. The Sheriff chuckled, despite himself.

"Seems to be the question all around," he quipped.

"What's your name?" inquired Travers of the blue youth.

"They call me Will Monday," was the reply. "Who are you? Where am I? Why've you got me tied down?" he asked.

"Did you not steal a man's truck?" inquired the Sheriff sternly.

"You're—you're a lawman, aren't you?"

"Yep. 'You have the right to remain silent. Anything you say may be used against you in a court of law. You have the right to an attorney. If you cannot afford an attorney—'" Montrose began the familiar recital of the suspect's "Miranda" rights.

"You're arresting me?" cried the blue lad. "Oh, no, you don't know what you're doing! Let me go!"

"'If you cannot afford an attorney, one will be appointed for you.'"

"You don't get it. I'm running for my life. If you put me in jail, they'll get me for sure."

"Now, in jail, under lock and key, that's about as safe as it gets," the Sheriff admonished. "It's only until your hearing, probably just a day or two. Ain't like there's a big backlog o' cases in Mountain City. An' I figure the judge, and the whole rest o' town, 'll be eager to get a look at you."

"No, I've gotta get outta here!" The blue youth struggled against his bonds, thrashing in the bed.

A strange thing happened as he struggled—the canvas straps began to smolder.

"Calm down! Please!" begged Travers, even as her mind raced. Was he somehow generating that much friction in his struggle? It made no sense.

Lying in the darkness of the next, guarded room of the Elko County Hospital, Lieutenant George McIntire stirred slightly. He was sedated, numb, but aware that he was bandaged across the chest and down his immobilized left arm.

In this moment of cogency, he remembered dressing for the daily martial arts session and wondering what was to become of his charge, Will Monday.

Will could sometimes beat him in sparring, these last few months. Middle age was creeping in, slowing McIntire at last. There was no denying it. At the same time, he felt pride in his pupil; Will was becoming a better fighter.

But, he had also developed a restless and surly mien. Major Avery fussed about his attitude, but then, Major Avery always fussed. McIntire worried that Will was relapsing to the state he had found him in four years prior, when he was brought into the Project to build the boy's flagging morale.

In their session that day, McIntire decided he wanted to provoke a reaction. The two circled each other warily, though Will had a dull and distracted cast to his gaze. At a moment's length, McIntire gave him a piteous look and lowered his arms.

McIntire turned to leave the floor. "You win," he shrugged.

"Hey!" called Will. "I thought we were sparring."

"No. I told you, *you win*," McIntire said, as he stopped and turned around. "I came here to teach you to live. It looked for a while as though you'd learned something. But you've defeated me." He turned his back on the lad again.

"How *can* I live anymore—in *this place*!?" cried Will, in anguish.

Ah. Here it came. "How can you *not*? How often have I told you, you have to accept your true nature. That world out there won't give you any room."

"It's a lot bigger than this world in here," protested Will.

"Is it? Or is that just your illusion? Look. You are *not* a normal human being," McIntire reminded him. "You can *act* like them, but you can't *be* like them, or *look* like them—any of them, and Lord knows they don't get along with each other as it is. And they won't accept you. Period. So I tried to teach you the inward path. But I can't actually change you from the inside. Only you can do that."

"*I can't win!*" Will cried.

"Remember how I taught you to put yourself in the place of your opponent? You have to know his fear and his desire, win from the inside out. Right now your opponent is Will Monday."

"You always give me some *in-yo* riddle! Is that the last thing you're going to say to me?" Will stood there, the confusion growing on his face.

McIntire stopped. Turned. "Stop dreaming you're someone else," he said flatly, and proceeded once more on his way.

At last, the long-suppressed rage which McIntire knew lurked there, longing for release, scrawled itself across Will's expression.

And, with a raging scream, Will raced to attack his mentor.

The rest was a blurry memory of the adrenaline rush of finely-trained reflexes coming into play. As they fought with renewed ferocity, Will made the mistakes of a novice, the many mistakes of a fighter who misdirects his energies, primarily the error of giving in to anger. After a flurry of thrusts, parries, and glancing strikes, McIntire had him on the mat, with a sweep of his heel. He twisted Will's arm behind him and pinned his neck tightly to the mat.

"You're getting ahead of yourself, kid," he gloated. "Your enemies will love you."

Suddenly, McIntire felt a shocking flash of extreme heat which made him recoil in pain from his pressure hold on Will's back.

Will screamed in rage, springing to his feet and executing an astonishing roundhouse series of kicks that sent McIntire leaping back and fending for all he was worth.

McIntire reversed course adroitly, to leap in at the first opening. He placed a heel into Will's left plantar to buckle his knee to the floor, where he pinned it with his foot.

Will screamed and tried to wriggle free, but McIntire held firm.

"I thought I'd taught you some discipline," the Lieutenant grunted, resisting Will's efforts to break free. Will braced his hands flat on the floor, and McIntire could feel his every muscle tensing.

All of a sudden, it was as if a magnet lifted them both from the floor and pushed them ten feet apart. They both skidded across the floor. They looked, wide-eyed, across the gulf at each other.

Disturbed, they yet rose as if nothing unusual had happened. The gymnasium, so full of tension a moment before, had found peace. At length, McIntire managed to look Will in the eyes again.

"They do care for you, in their way," resumed McIntire, quietly.

"And that's as good as it gets," replied Will.

Ruefully, McIntire nodded.

3.

Will Monday apparently had decided this would be his last training session with George McIntire. Through the simple expedient of exiting the complex, and climbing into McIntire's car with the keys—*how did he get out the front entrance? how did he get the keys?*—he opened the blast doors with the remote control unit on board and drove to the surface. After all these years, his first real glimpse of the outer world would be colored by the waning sunlight through the windshield of McIntire's Acura.

McIntire remembered how he had knocked and called at Will's door at chow time, then gone on to the kitchen to sit down to his meal. Gradually, he had realized Will was very late. He strode to Will's cabin, knocked again, and threw open the door. Finding the cabin unoccupied, he raced to the monitor room. Major Avery slumped there in his seat, his feet propped up on the console next to a half-eaten sandwich. *The Andy Griffith Show* played on the monitor before him.

"Christ on a crutch!" exclaimed McIntire. On another screen, the security station for the nuclear complex, above them on the surface, was being breached by a gate-crasher. McIntire saw his own Acura, traveling sixty miles per hour, buck roughly over the speed bumps, and smash through the stop rail at the guard post.

"Get Gentry on the horn, now!" barked McIntire, shaking Avery awake.

"What the hell? I'm the superior officer here," Avery balked, groggily coming awake.

"Will just tore out of here, *in my car*!" McIntire shouted.

"Okay, okay. Where *you* going?" Avery asked, petulantly.

"Mountain Home!" barked McIntire. He had to reach the air base as quickly as possible, in hopes of having a search party locate his automobile while it was still visible from the air.

McIntire could think no more of the day's events. He realized he was in a civilian hospital. He knew that when he came to again, he was likely to face a lot of questioning. Even so, he was in no shape to attempt an escape at this time. He lapsed back into unconsciousness.

Next door, a young nurse rushed into the room where Will was strapped into bed, hypodermic syringe at the ready as prearranged with the Sheriff.

"Careful, don't touch him!" warned Montrose.

Hesitantly, the nurse made a quick dab with an alcohol-soaked cotton swab, between the bars onto Will's upper arm, and jabbed him with the hypo.

"You don't understand. They're gonna get me," grumbled Will, as he began to drowse under the powerful anesthetic injection.

The nurse trembled slightly. "Some hot stuff, huh?" she murmured, watching as the last wisps of smoke dissipated into the air.

"Like I said, keep it to yourself," warned Montrose.

"Who'd believe me?" asked the nurse, stealing an intrigued look back at Will on her way out the door.

"So, c'mon, Pam, what d'ya think?" Montrose asked Travers again.

"He sounds like an acute paranoid, but look at him. I mean, who knows?"

"So, in short, he's blue, has cat-eyes, 's crazy as a loon, and hot as a firecracker." observed the Sheriff drily.

"At least he's got a name," muttered Travers. "We need to speak with that soldier," replied Travers. "At least we already know *that* much about your Lieutenant, uh—"

"McIntire," said the Sheriff. "Even if we can wake him from heavy sedation, which seems to be pretty easy with *this* young fellah for sure, I 'spect all we're gonna get is name, rank, 'n serial number."

"Well, we better try while we can," responded Travers.

"You know it," Montrose replied, lowering his voice. "I'd hate for all this to get swept under the rug, and me know no more than I do now. That's why I was hoping you'd break a little something out of your black bag, like maybe some sodium pentathol. You'd do it in the pen, wouldn't you?" He winked.

Travers stared at Montrose. Her methods were supposed to be a secret, but obviously they were not completely so. She spoke carefully.

"Those men are convicts," she told him. "Him, I don't know. I came down here tonight because my dad respected you. Not to bring some kind of 'truth serum' or 'black bag.'"

"I'm friends with the head administrator—" Montrose began, when they heard the muffled voice of Montrose's deputy issue an order to halt. Montrose and Travers hurried out to the hall.

There stood five men in dark suits, with four orderlies wheeling a pair of gurneys behind them. The leader, around sixty, with grey hair and steely eyes, flashed a wallet in the face of the deputy who fidgeted with his holstered gun. The deputy gawked at the badge, which bore the insignia of the National Security Agency.

"You have something that belongs to us," said the intruder. "We're here to pick it up."

Montrose squinted at the badge. *"NSA?"*

"General Morgan Gentry," uttered the man crisply, "That's all you need to know. Tell your deputy to step aside."

Montrose nodded, and the nervous deputy stepped aside. The General's men wheeled their gurney into the room.

The General then turned to the slender, thirty-something man at his side. "Major, make a sweep here. Anything that's touched him; any blood or urine they've taken; anything, down to a cotton swab or a tongue depressor, round it up!"

"Yes, sir," said the other man, who saluted and deployed the three others.

"Exactly what's goin' on?" demanded the frustrated Montrose.

"Something that's out of your jurisdiction, Sheriff," replied Gentry. "By the way, you should have kept your eye on the guy they brought in downstairs."

"The two-ton lug in the burn unit? He sure ain't goin' nowhere."

"He already did. And not with us."

The "orderlies" rolled out of the room with a sheet completely covering the body lying on the gurney, presumably that of Lt. McIntire.

"We know that man was alive," interjected Travers. "We know his name, his rank—we can check on him."

"He'll be *fine*. What's important for you to remember is that *he was never here*. Him—and especially *the other one*," responded Gentry.

"And if we do remember?" Travers queried.

"It's worth your life," Gentry calmly replied.

Travers and Montrose shared a look of alarm.

"Major Avery," continued Gentry, "make sure he's ready to leave."

"Yes, Sir," replied the taciturn Major Avery, who, like Gentry, was dressed in a dark business suit. With a glance at Travers, he opened the door and stepped into the room where the young man was being held.

"We know you, Sheriff," said Gentry, "but who's the young lady?"

"An old friend."

"Name?" Gentry snapped.

"Travers," she replied.

"Travers? Of the Idaho prison, up in Boise?"

"How'd you know?" gasped the startled young woman.

Gentry grinned, slightly, now looking at her as if with recognition. "Do you believe in Fate, young lady?"

"Just now, I'm not sure what I believe in," Travers muttered.

The orderlies returned with their gurney, and entered the hospital room where the strange young man lay sleeping.

"Sheriff, I know you're a good man. I just hope we don't have to return to your peaceful little town," said Gentry to Montrose, advisedly. He turned to Travers. "Doctor, we're going to have to talk some more."

The orderlies and Major Avery rolled by, with another covered body on their gurney.

"I'll call you, Pam," the Sheriff promised, with a stern look at the General.

Montrose tipped his hat slightly. He motioned to his deputy to join him. The two lawmen departed, down the hall.

4.

Dawn broke as Sheriff Montrose arrived back at his office. Good. He was knotted with frustrated curiosity, too wound up to sleep as yet. At least the light would allow him a better look at the site of Wild Bill's.

When he stepped inside the police station, he nodded with satisfaction that his deputies had brought in the night bartender and several of the regular riff-raff who had helped define the character of that blighted spot on the county's moral standards.

"Sheriff, good ta see ya," bellowed Dan, the tall bouncer, who still wore his black club T-shirt with the business emblem on the chest.

"Never thought I'd hear you say that, Dan," replied Montrose, as he looked over the rest of the sorry lot who sat about the anteroom of his jailhouse.

They were, aside from Bud the bartender, a threesome of Dan's fellow outlaw biker gang members. Resplendent in tattoos, earrings, and leather boots, were the retarded, leather jacket and jeans-clad Cletus, the bearded, cagey, denim-covered rake, Chainsaw, and his drinking buddy, Belcher, with his Mohawk-style hair, rat-tail running long down the back, beer gut half-covered by a leather vest, dirty undershirt.

"Wha'ja find out, Sheriff?" asked Bud, eagerly.

"Not near as much as I'da liked to," sighed Montrose, sitting down at his desk. "What about you boys, you got anything to say 'bout what happened out there last night?"

"A blue fairy come in and burned it all down," babbled Cletus. "A *flamin'* fairy," he added. "*H-yuk! H-yuk!*"

"Somebody mind tellin' me somethin' that makes sense?" snapped Montrose.

"Hell, what he's sayin' ain't that far from the truth, Sheriff," rumbled Dan. "Weird as it sounds."

"Wait a minute. I'm gonna brew some coffee." Montrose got up to start preparing his coffee maker. "I guess you boys could use some, as well."

To murmurs of general assent, the sheriff tried to prepare both the coffee and his sleepless mind so as to evaluate the tales he would hear from the motley crew cowering in his jailhouse. This was the first time the sheriff had seen them ready to cooperate with the authorities.

"Well," Dan commenced, "me and the boys, Cletus, Chainsaw, and Belcher, stepped outside about sundown last night to get us a breath of fresh air. The show was just gettin' good on stage, but Cletus needed, well, relief, and the men's room was locked."

"Contessa had her top off already?" asked Montrose, implying it was truly degenerate to reach that point in a strip show as dusk was only falling.

"Yeah," Chainsaw picked up the narrative, "but I never had properly thanked Dan for the favor of his friendship, so I thought I'd go out where it was more quiet-like, so's to properly express my gratitude."

"Belcher, I suppose you went along so as to cut loose, too?" surmised the Sheriff, getting coffee cups from his cupboard. Belcher looked down, mildly embarrassed, and chuckled.

Dan resumed. "But we's just outside a second or two, long enough for Cletus to get it unzipped over't the corner of the clubhouse, when we heard peelin' rubber from up by the mountainside..."

The red Acura hewed to the road's edge as its driver pushed the safety envelope for the sake of speed, navigating closely around the mountain. The fact that he was on a downhill slope was no solace for the driver, who could feel the sputter of the engine. The gauge showed that the car contained exactly as little gasoline as the driver had money.

He coasted the auto as far as he could, stopping at last in the midst of a gravel parking lot nearly full with parked vehicles. He read the flashing neon signs and knew that he had, indeed, arrived in a new and unknown world. *"WILDS BILL HICCUP'S DRINK 'N DROOL,"* they proclaimed in pink, tubular lighting. *"GIRLS! GIRLS! GIRLS!"*

Ahead of him, he saw several wild-looking men loitering at the edge of the porch of Wild Bill's. Their eyes turned toward him as he rolled to a stop amidst the sound of crunching gravel.

He wondered why they were so calm. Then he realized that, in the dusk, and behind the windshield as he was, their perception of tones was not nearly as sharp as his own. Yet, he dared hope for a moment that the General would be proved wrong, that the natural-born people would accept him. Maybe he could even meet the "girls."

He got out of the car, and heard clear sounds of riotous merrymaking from inside. His pulse quickened as he walked toward the men.

"Dibs on the Acura," Chainsaw was saying, as the men laughed. Chainsaw drew near the approaching stranger, who appeared as little more than a silhouette against the backlighting of the yard light, out by the roadside. "Got a light, citizen?" he asked, producing a cigarette from the pack he unrolled from his T-shirt sleeve.

"No, sorry," replied the silhouette. "Where are we?"

All four men laughed at this one. Belcher was in mid-guzzle of his Pabst when he heard the question. He spewed an eighteen-inch beer geyser before engaging in a strangled laugh.

"We're in the middle of nowhere, citizen," replied Chainsaw. "Where people go to 'get lost', get it?"

But the stranger merely muttered "Okay," under his breath while they laughed. He was already inside Wild Bill's as their laughter subsided.

"Hey. You better tell that spindlehead about the cover charge," grumbled Cletus to Dan, the bouncer.

"Damn straight," said Dan, realizing he had left his post. He dashed up to the door and stepped inside, with Cletus and Chainsaw loping in behind him.

Inside the club, there was no need to pursue the interloper beyond the opening in the banister that funneled patrons past the the entry checkpoint into the saloon. The kid stood there, in his fatigues outfit, transfixed by the sight of the shapely Contessa on stage, twirling her brassiere over head, gyrating her feminine asssets as the packed house of animated degenerates whooped and hollered. Grizzled, drunken men, and some women, laughed and cheered her on, beer sloshing from swinging mugs and streaming down stubbled chins.

"The show ain't free, Sonny," growled Dan, seizing the young man by the shoulder to turn him around. At his first good look at the youth, however, he stopped cold.

As the sheriff handed him his cup of coffee, Dan was saying, "'Course, first thing I thought was this was some kind of refugee from a circus act, or somethin'. Now, I seen from behind this kid was red-headed, but then when I got a better look and seen he was blue-skinned, I 'bout *shit*. Then, I saw his *eyes*. You seen 'em, didn't ya, Sheriff? I figured he hadda be wearin' some kinda contact lenses, but I couldn't figure out why he'd wanna do that."

"Yeah, I don't know," explained the sheriff. "But, I'm with you so far. Go on."

"I'll tell ya what I seen outside right about then," chimed in Belcher. "I'd hung around outside 'cause I figured Dan'd be haulin' this fool back out any second, and maybe we could have a little fun with him."

"You mean, a stompin' party?" asked Montrose, drily.

Belcher looked down again. "Nothin' like that happened, Sheriff. It was a lot worse than any stompin' party. First of all, I seen this Lincoln tearin' around the hillside, like that Acura had, an' it skidded into the parkin' lot, slingin' gravel from here to yonder. I seen these two weirdos get out o' the car, and I had this crawly feelin', like somethin' real heavy was about to go down."

Two dark silhouettes emerged from the Lexus. At the sight of them, Belcher's blood suddenly ran cold. The driver was a tall, spindly man dressed in a long trenchcoat and a broad-brimmed hat. Emerging from the other side of the car, a bulky muscleman stood up and reached for a pistol in a shoulder harness. The man in the trenchcoat waved, and his hulking companion loped around to the side of the building. Belcher sidled back into the barroom. They might have some real trouble on their hands.

5.

"It sure was embarrassin'," lamented Dan.

"Hell, you couldn't have known the kid was a judo master, Dan," said Chainsaw in Dan's defense.

"Well, I ain't never been flipped like that before. Broke a table plumb in two. Got myself soaked in beer..."

"I stood up for ya, Dan," fawned Cletus.

As the mortified Dan sailed through the air, Cletus hit the release button on his switchblade knife and proceeded to thrust toward the blue kid's bent back. But the kid twisted around quickly enough that Cletus's first swipe tore just the sleeve of his jacket. Cletus darted forward and took another couple of swipes, but the blue kid leaped back and to one side, dodging them as well.

Suddenly, realizing he was backed against a patron's chair, the blue kid turned, grabbed the seat right out from under the man, and swung it around in time to intercept Cletus's lunging blade in its back board. Then, he yanked back the chair, drawing the switchblade from the startled Cletus's grasp.

Belcher entered at that moment, grabbing Chainsaw's arm and warning, "We got trouble."

"No shit, Sherlock," snarled Chainsaw.

Belcher gasped. It was his first good look at the blue kid. Not only that, the kid had just taken Cletus's switchblade. He set the chair down, yanking the blade clear. He folded it back into its shaft, and handed it back to Cletus, as if it were no threat at all. But the angry gleam in the kid's animal eyes flashed an unmistakable warning that he wouldn't repeat his gracious performance.

"Let's *git* 'im!" growled Chainsaw.

"But—" Belcher began. No use. Chainsaw was leaping forward. Belcher had to join in—it was their code. Each of the two toughs grabbed one of the blue kid's arms in a lock. They took him down, his knees to the floor. Now they could begin the rough-up.

Except—the fabric they clutched was smoking. They suddenly felt as though they held a tight grip on a hot iron. They let go, screaming.

In the course of the struggle, the whole mass of patrons had become aware of the fracas, and a chorus of screams went up as the blue kid leaped back onto his feet. Not only was he the wrong color for a human being, he had just humbled four of the most feared punks around with little effort. The sight of two of them, smoking at the hands and screaming in pain, triggered a mass panic.

"I was gettin' up off the floor when I seen what had happened," Dan continued. "The kid looked as surprised as anybody else. He stood there lookin' down at his arms like he'd never seen 'em before."

"Meantime, the place was emptyin' out," added Chainsaw. "The strippers was freakin' out. The customers, *everybody* started stampedin' for the exits. One asshole even jumped out the back window."

"Wait!" cried Will, leaping onto the stage to pursue the three strippers, who were fleeing backstage. "I won't hurt you!"

But the strippers trotted out the door beside the stage and joined in the fleeing throng. The sight of the panicking crowd's fear dealt a crushing blow to Will's heart. It was just as bad as the General had always said it would be. But, could the General have known that he would *burn* people who touched him? That had never happened before.

In despair, he watched as the crowd thinned out the back. From outside, he heard the sounds of auto engines starting, the thumps and bumps of collisions as the patrons jostled to get out of the parking lot.

"So I guess none of you knows about how those helicopters came along, and everything went *ka-blooey*?" Sheriff Montrose seemed disappointed that the story trail had apparently petered out.

"No, Sheriff," said Bud, the bartender, "that's the part I come to tell you about. I was around for pretty much all of it."

"Well, then, do go on," encouraged Montrose.

On the porch, the wiry man stood to one side, allowing the yokels to flee. Better if there were no witnesses to his activities. When the last seemed to have gone, he stepped inside.

Will slumped, despondent, on the edge of the stage. Music played to an empty house inside as the wiry man entered. There appeared to be no one else around. Unnoticed by Will, the hulking muscleman was silently poised half-inside the back door.

The wiry man doffed his hat. "Will Monday, there you are," he said cheerily. "You've been strangely hard to track."

Will leapt from the stage, startled at the sight of this bizarre stranger who knew his name. He backed away from him a couple of steps, then noticed him motion slightly with his forefinger.

He turned and glimpsed a hulking figure behind him, with leathery vest and shoulder holster, arms closing to grab him. He ducked, barely in time to evade their closing grasp.

With his pursuer poised to spring, Will vaulted over the counter, into the bar. There he discovered the huddled figure of bartender Bud, shivering in fright. He dropped the single-barrelled shotgun he had been holding close.

"Don't hurt me," pleaded Bud.

Will yanked his thumb toward the bar's open end. Bud lost no time in scrambling out of the enclosure, rounding the corner toward the front, only to freeze in his tracks when he saw he would have to pass the other two strange invaders.

The wiry man withdrew a strange headset from the folds of his coat and donned it. A lens covered one eye as he adjusted what appeared to be a knob on the earpiece.

Turning his gaze onto Bud, the wiry man scoffed, "It's only a bad dream. Go!"

Bud was embarrassed to find himself actually tiptoeing toward the front door, smiling and nodding all the way, like an old Stepin Fetchit caricature.

The menacing figure lowered the swivel microphone and hissed, "Vee. *Persuade* the naughty boy."

"Vee" took a run at the bar. Just as he vaulted toward its interior, Will raised the shotgun and squeeze the trigger, discharging its blast right into the huge man's chest. Vee toppled back to the floor.

Will looked to the wiry man. His only reaction from the nightmarish figure was a mild shake of the head.

"I just cleared the door when I heard the whirring of them helicopters," Bud went on. "I looked up and seen 'em clearing the mountaintop. They was sweepin' searchlights all 'round, and I was caught in a beam right off."

"How many helicopters, Bud?" asked Montrose, taking notes on a pad.

"I'm pretty sure they was three."

Montrose nodded.

Back inside the bar, time stood still for several seconds as Will and the wiry man heard the clip of the helicopter blades. Beams of light stabbed into the windows from outside. Will turned his gaze back to Vee, who was standing up from the floor. No blood. The special vest he wore had protected him from the shotgun's blast.

The wiry man issued another command. "Vee! He's ours. Take them out!"

Vee dashed outside, past the bartender, who was tracking the flight of the choppers as they flew over the tavern. As the trunk of the car flew open, V lunged inside. A switch clicked, and a charging rheostat whined. Vee stood up, hefting a portable missile launcher over his shoulder.

The helicopters had circled the plain beyond Wild Bill's, and now were doubling back. Bud remembered the Bell 406 personnel model from his Army days; there were two of those. But, what chilled him was the sight of the Cobra flying along with them. There were normally no combat exercises conducted in the area. Yet, what else could explain these helicopters now buzzing the plain?

One of the Bells drew closer. Then, Bud realized what was happening on the ground. The muscle man held a Stinger hand-held missile launcher, modified for one-man operations, at the ready. Then—he fired it!

With a deafening blue and orange explosion, the Bell was shattered, right above Wild Bill's. Bud cursed himself for a fool for having paused to identify the aircraft. He dashed for the grassy slope at the side of the building. Shards of heavy, flaming metal debris rained all around. The main bulk of the helicopter crashed right into the storefront, taking the inner quarter of it down in flames. Flying shrapnel missed Bud by scant inches.

Bud raised his head. Smoking scraps of metal stuck in the ground around his body, lit by the flaming bawdy house. Bud spat out a mouthful of grassy sod.

Riding in the other Bell, bathed in the light of the explosion, Lt. George McIntire shouted to his pilot. "Son of a bitch! Get this mother, *down*! *Now*!"

The pilot acknowledged the order and began descending to the plain. The Cobra gun ship that had come along in case of trouble, however, surged toward the devastated site.

Inside, Will and the wiry man both hugged the floor, hands over head, as Bud had done outside. They clambered to their feet, each assessing the other. The wiry man had lost his headset in the flaming rubble. He still clutched his pistol, however. He snarled at Will, "Choose, William. Come as you are, or come along bloody."

Suddenly, 35-millimeter rounds from the Cobra ripped ceiling to floor in a dual enfilade from the back to the front of the sundered building. The wiry man promptly collapsed once more into a tight ball, huddling on the floor.

When the withering fire passed by on either side, he lifted his head, trembling in outrage and gut fear. He raised his pistol and strode about madly, looking for Will. There was no one around. The spreading fire now engulfed the front door in flames.

Outside, Bud crawled though the tall, waving grass several yards in the direction of his lone pickup truck . It had been left unharmed, so far, at the far front corner of the parking lot. Preparing to rise and make a dash the remainder of the distance, he paused to be certain Vee was preoccupied.

The spitting sound of the big guns had Vee's attention firmly fixed on the rushing attack of the Cobra. Bud glanced back toward the Lincoln, where Vee rummaged in the back of the vehicle once more.

"Sayonara, sucker," Bud muttered.

Just then, Vee stood up with a rifle-like weapon, the likes of which Bud had never seen—something like a high-tech bazooka.

The Cobra's bullets had smashed through the ruined edifice of Wild Bill's, and were chewing through the Lincoln itself when Vee pulled his trigger. Instantly, he became a Jovian figure, with undulating electrical energy surging from his weapon to strike at the Cobra.

The wiry man ran out of the building in time to see the sparkling electrical energy inundate the gun ship. The stricken Cobra hurtled forward with sheer momentum until it crashed in a sickening, fiery cataclysm against the rocky mountain face across the roadway.

"*Ahhh*-hahahahahahah!! It's the New Millennium!" the wiry man cackled.

"*Hold it, Mister*," growled a voice. The wiry man whirled about to see Lt. McIntire and his pilot step from around the corner of the blazing building. They held Uzi submachine guns on shoulder straps, pointed right at himself and his musclebound minion.

The wiry man and Vee went for the handguns in their shoulder holsters. McIntire and the pilot unleashed short bursts of fire from their Uzis. The impact of their spitting bullets knocked Vee and the wiry man backward, to the ground.

"The big guy was the one the Rescue Squad took in to the burn ward," commented Montrose, frowning. "They didn't say he'd been *shot*."

"Well, he was, but, it didn't matter, Sheriff," said Bud, sipping his last slurp of coffee.

6.

"So, the soldiers separated," Bud continue. "They searched opposite sides of the place, which was burnin' up pretty good about now. The one, I seen later was a lieutenant, he ordered the other man. But, I felt this hand on my shoulder, and, sure enough, the blue kid had crept from around back o' the buildin' and he's huddled there in the grass with me."

"Were ya spooked?" asked Montrose.

"Well," Bud said, looking around anxiously at the bikers the youth had bested, "I wasn't too comfy in my trousers anymore.

"It did seem the real deadly hombres were the ones the soldiers had just cut down. Still, it wasn't like I had a scorecard, exactly."

"What'd'ja do?" queried Montrose.

"I give the kid an honest answer," replied Bud, "when he asked me..."

"Is that your truck?" Will motioned toward the one remaining able vehicle in the lot. The Acura he had arrived in and the Lincoln were both ruined, half-buried under burning debris.

"Y-y-yeah," stammered Bud.

"I've gotta have it," insisted Will.

On the verge of weeping, Bud pulled the keys from his pocket and handed them over.

"Take care of her, okay?" he asked. "I only got two more payments."

The blue youth paused a few seconds, as if searching for reassuring words. "My last twenty-three games of *Death Race 2000*, I scored *all real high* rounds." He obviously meant these statistics to sound reassuring, though Bud's expression still bespoke his anguish.

Will plucked up the keys and scurried toward the pickup.

Prowling the tall grass near the rear of the destroyed building, McIntire whirled at the sound of the engine starting up. He raced around to the burning storefront to see the truck winding onto the roadway, gears grinding. Bud stood at the shoulder, watching, shaking a fist and stomping the gravelly earth. "Damn freakin' *freak!*" he cursed.

"A blue kid?" McIntire demanded, as his pilot sprinted back up to rejoin him.

The crack of a gun sounded. The pilot lurched forward, face-first into the gravel lot. McIntire whirled, too late to avoid the fiery impact of bullets in his arm and shoulder. He half-dove, half- toppled to the gravel, and lay stock-still.

Bud fell to his knees in terror at the sight of the burly Vee and the wiry man, standing once more, smoke crawling from their gun barrels. They strode forward triumphantly. The wiry man stood over the fallen lieutenant and snarled, over the muffled sobs of the bartender, "Haste makes wasted, Lieutenant. Did you think I wore *this*," clutching the lapel of his leathery trenchcoat, "because it's *cold outside*? I will have *bruises* all over my ribs, though." He kicked the fallen, bleeding Lieutenant in the ribs for emphasis.

The wiry man nodded curtly. He and Vee darted off toward the plains behind the ruins of Wild Bill Hiccup's.

From sheer curiosity, Bud followed, making sure to lag well behind. He watched from afar as the wiry man climbed into the cockpit of the remaining Bell helicopter, and Vee stepped onto the skid, clinging to the side door handle. The rotors whirled to life, spinning faster and faster, until the whirlybird lifted off from the ground and flew in the direction Will had driven.

"That's the last thing I knew, until I saw the flash from the explosion 'round the ridge a way," Bud summed up.

Sheriff Montrose had arrived at the scene soon after that, to find the flaming bar collapsing, the ambulance unit just arrived. Charred bodies and rent vehicles tangled in rubble and debris everywhere were testament to a blazing catastrophe. None of them knew what had happened to Bud's pickup. The gas tank seemed to have exploded.

"You boys stay out of trouble, hear?" said the sheriff to Dan and the others. He affixed his signature, in addition to their own, on a sworn statement. He expected he would file it away, never more to be seen. He would probably have to speculate until his dying day about the true meaning of the night's events.

At that same moment, a van with darkened widows drove down Highway 225. Will, lying in the back, nightmarishly relived the ordeal in his own mind.

He had been at the wheel of the truck, desperately trying to control its unaccustomed bulk and feel, unable to outpace the helicopter which swooped low overhead. There was a loud thunk in the truck bed, and the next thing he knew, an arm like a tree trunk smashed the rear glass and caught his head in a vice grip.

The truck wheeled off the road, and rolled over and over, buffeting him about, causing the arms to release him. When he recovered his wits enough to feel the smarting of his bruises, he tried the door and rolled out of the upside down pickup truck.

He picked himself up stiffly from the ground. All his joints seemed intact. He reeled a few steps away from the truck. To his horror, he saw that the behemoth who pursued him was limping along after him. He felt a white-hot rage of frustration at this burly stranger who would stop his flight for freedom. Fists balled up, Will had bent to scream his rage at the oncoming figure.

The last thing he recalled was a fiery blast of white heat and light.

Then, the darkness. And after that, the woman. The policeman...

Will stirred, groggy, coming to for the third time since his—since the—what had happened, anyway?

The world swam into focus in his tortured view, and he saw General Gentry hovering above him. He would have much preferred to never see this stern gaze again—especially after being caught in this boneheaded, impulsive escapade.

He certainly hadn't proven to McIntire he was growing adept in the arts of *in-yo*, the ways of the *Ninja warrior*. Mac had told him he could become truly formidable in time, in a league with some of the hired muscle McIntire had encountered in his military career as a counter-espionage intelligence agent. It was supposed to bolster his confidence. It evidently had, up to a disastrous point.

"How'd you get out here, Will?" demanded Gentry.

Will reflected glumly that he hadn't lasted much over two hours in the open. He wondered if the gunner in one helicopter had known he might have killed Will with his gunfire into the burning bar. Then he realized, that gunner himself must be dead, that he had borne witness as two military craft—*looking for him*—had crashed, killing he knew not how many men.

"Mac—?" he attempted. The word simply hung on his tongue, uncomfortably on the verge of blossoming into a complete syllable, but not quite daring to cross that gap before Will's vocal chords tightened.

"You're both lucky," Gentry said, gruffly. "McIntire was hurt—but not killed. We picked him up from the same hospital where we got you."

The hospital ! It *had* been real. And there, he'd met a pretty young lady *in the flesh*. He had actually spoken with her!

"You didn't answer my question, Will," intoned the General. "You stole *keys*, a *remote unit—why*, Will? Didn't what we told you down through the years *ever sink in*, boy?"

"I—I just—"

"No. Save it," snapped the General, brooding. "We'll have an inquest in a few days, once McIntire's recovered a little. You think it over, very carefully."

"I - I understand, Sir," said Will, not at all sure that he truly did.

After silently brooding a few more moments, the General added, ominously, "Whatever you meant to do, you sure did one thing tonight. You've changed your world forever."

7.

Pam Travers sat at her desk, a reproduction of Antonella de Messina's *The Martyrdom of St. Sebastian* overlooking her back. The suffering saint, painfully pierced through multiple times with the arrows of his nemeses, looked mournfully toward Heaven.

Several hundred convicted child molesters had inexplicably passed into the system in the past year; they were called "trendies" by many prisoners for this reason. She was reviewing the file of one of these now.

A guard escorted in the prisoner. Travers glanced, for a fraction of a second, at the reflection in the mirrored far wall. The hunched and writhing Clyfford Wilznowski, in his thirties, with his elongated face and protuberant, aquiline nose, was called "Weasel" by the other inmates. Weasel took his seat before Travers's desk. Upon a nod from Travers, the Guard departed.

"Mr. Wilznowski. How are you today?" asked Travers, brightly.

"Fine, Pam," replied the con, with a slight smirk. He rose, casually, to stretch.

"That's 'Dr. Travers' to you. The chair, please." Travers pointed to the chair opposite her desk.

Weasel ignored her and sniffed up his collar, looking at his reflection in the mirror. "It's been a while, Dr. Travers. Been too busy for me?" He turned and shuffled slowly toward the desk. "Still no ring on your finger. That's a shame."

"I haven't met anyone with the right values," Travers said, rising just as his hand darted for the top button on her blouse. Anticipating his move, Travers adeptly caught his wrist and swiftly bent it back under his forearm.

"Owwww," grimaced Weasel as Travers walked him back to the chair.

"Don't make me call the guard. Sit," she insisted, pushing him down. She returned to her chair behind the desk, leaving Weasel rubbing his wrist.

"Now what do you say? With a smile," Travers chirped.

Weasel, putting on a smile, replied, "Thank you, Doctor."

"That's better," Travers replied. "Cigarette?"

He took her proffered cigarette, and a light. Travers started her tape recorder, and discreetly flipped a wall switch beside her desk. A vent fan began running overhead, drawing the smoke of Weasel's cigarette upward.

Travers engaged the prisoner in small talk about the goals they had established in previous sessions, and what milestones he had reached in his life as a prisoner since then. In due course, the con relaxed, then appeared to grow bored as his cigarette diminished in length. Smoke continued to waft upward from it. His face grew a bit more slack with each puff, until at length, he spoke in a dreamy, languid voice.

Travers moved a pen rapidly across the surface of a pad of paper she held in her lap. A mini-tape recorder ran on her desk, audio-recording the session.

"Now, Clyfford, what do you see when you come out of the house?" Travers asked softly.

"Men are loading their couch up on the truck. I think that's the last piece of furniture. Yes. They're pulling away. The little girl is on the truck with my teddy bear. Riding away. I hate that little girl."

Travers spoke in soothing, hypnotic tones. "No. When they leave, you go in the house, and find your teddy bear with your other toys. It's okay." She went for a while in a similar vein. "Now, it's later. You're five years old. You find the little girl who lives next door has no toys of her own. She's littler than you and not as strong. Now that you are a big boy, you decide to give her your teddy bear. Your teddy bear makes her very happy. And that makes you happy, too." Weasel smiled and nodded at intervals, living the dream within his own mind. At last, Travers said, "Sleep, Clyfford."

Clyfford Wilznowski slumped with a lax smile and closed eyes in the chair. Travers rang the guard. This time, two guards with a gurney showed up, hoisting the convict between them and placing him on the gurney to make the return trip to his cell.

In their wake, Gentry stepped in to the office, having been watching through a one-way window.

"Damn remarkable," exulted Gentry. "You know how to handle yourself."

"Thanks."

"What'd you use on him?"

"It's a derivative of curare."

"And you mix it yourself, from raw ingredients?"

"Yes," confessed Travers, looking down, uncomfortably aware of the illegality of what she was doing.

"And what would you say you get out of these sessions?"

"The regressions give me access to key moments in the subject's life," Travers said flatly. "No matter how trivial they may sound to us, like the stolen teddy bear incident, such moments imprint a stamp, an attitude, toward a subject that can determine later behavior patterns."

"So, you figure if you remove the stimulus, you remove the response," Gentry summed up.

"Yes, in a nutshell. But, we can't replace something with nothing. We have to steer the outcome. It's easier to implant a memory the *opposite* of what happened than something totally unrelated. Completely fabricated false memories have a very weak effect, or none."

The General studied her with a smug smile. "So, what did you get from *this* session?"

"I've been working with Clyfford for six months. He's a convicted rapist. You don't make someone like him overnight. But, one by one, I've isolated the incidents in his life that instilled his deep-seated hatred of young women, his desire to dominate them, violate them. This had to be one of the earliest. Soon, I think he'll have released all the resentments. Then, we can work on reforming him to get along in society."

"Like surgical psychological strikes," Gentry observed.

"Right. I don't try to radically remake anybody—I just change a few minutes of their lives—forever."

"And you've done this with others before now. My agency noticed your low recidivism rate here. Now I understand how you do it—I think. Gentry placed his fingertips together, composing his next statement carefully. "Now, I'm a man in a situation just at the moment. I need someone who has certain very rare skills. The pool of people I could usually choose from, I can't afford to approach just now, for certain reasons. So, I've come to you. How would you like the chance to serve your country, Miss Travers?"

"I've got plenty of work cut out for me right here, General. I'd be happy to lend some advice..."

"That won't work in the matter of our friend, Mr. Monday. You're not supposed to have ever seen him. But you have. And so have others. And, there are certain people who will know where to find him, and they will if we can't contain this information. He needs a new home—quick—a whole new, different kind of life, understand. We can't stay to the course we've had him on. And we can't take the chance he'll talk about his old life once he gets going in his new one. You can see how I'm interested in your work, don't you, Doctor?"

Travers swallowed. She suspected anyone who learned too much about Will Monday might end up wishing they had not. Yet, Gentry knew what he knew about her. And, he was leaning into her space.

"I'm gonna have to ask you to miss a little work," he said.

"I can't afford to do that."

"I've talked to your Warden about this. I think you can."

"The alternative would be—?" she asked.

"A wise man once said, 'nothing that's whispered in the closet shall not be shouted from the mountaintops.' I've found that out the hard way. Believe me, it's not a lesson you want to learn—unless your interest in the justice system goes a *lot deeper* than I think it does," Gentry said, raising an eyebrow.

"I don't want to seem unsympathetic, or to say what you're doing here is not important," Gentry continued. "But, it is illegal. In the best of all possible worlds, maybe it wouldn't be, who knows? In the real world, I think we're all prepared to choose the least of evils, aren't we?"

"I—I guess..." Travers fought a panic inside.

"Your warden has some paper work waiting for you in his office. Go fill it out, and we'll be off."

Gentry's eyes contained not a speck of sympathy.

8.

The general and the prison psychiatrist drove in an official "maintenance van" with darkened glass windows. Their trip lasted hours after her workday was over, and they did not have the smoothest of roads for the whole tour. Finally, on a lava-encrusted field, broken and melded by industry, a light water nuclear power plant sat near the Lost River Sinks. Travers noticed, as Gentry drove them up to the guard station, that the gate on the opposing side was tied together with ropes.

"Home, sweet nuclear plant," grinned Gentry to Travers, who sat in the passenger seat.

He handed the guard at the station a special ID card, which the guard slid through a reader terminal, which apparently granted approval to admit them to the facility. The guard handed the ID card back to Gentry. The gate swung upward, and they drove through toward a special, non-designated zone at the back of the building.

A rising doorway set in the block facade rose on the vehicle's approach. Inside, one ramp actually continued into the maintenance department, but another branched downward, to the left, which is the direction Gentry drove them. A heavy steel "BLAST" door rose before them, and they entered a fairly vast, underground cavern.

At the ceiling, a set of steel scaffolding was set amongst the stalactites, with a network of lights glowing down on the project and the surrounding floor.

Set at the center of the smoothly-honed cavern floor was a stacked set of pods connected with tubes, slitted one-way windows looking out onto the canyons beneath the ground, a complex large enough for an hour's tour. A tube ascended from one pod within the complex into the ceiling above.

"All this—down here? Wow," marveled Travers.

"I knew you'd like it. This way."

They proceeded down a walkway to the entrance of the foundation floor of the complex. Gentry passed his same card through an optical reader at the doorway, and the door slid open wide enough for the two of them to enter abreast, carrying their tote bags. Inside, Travers immediately noted the mirrored chromium finish of the walls.

Gentry conducted Travers to the cabin-like room where she would be staying. Although the most homey part of the Complex she had seen so far, it was none too commodious—about on a par with a Motel Six, thought Travers, except that the entire place seemed to lack corners. All the rooms were ovoid in contour. As she strolled about the room and ran her hands over the furnishing surfaces, she realized there were no loose objects. The bed frame was heavy steel and welded to the floor. The dresser was much the same, and she saw that its drawers could not be pulled out all the way.

She glanced upward, wondering how much *terra firma* stood between them and the nuclear power plant above?

Once they had set down Travers's gear, she had a quick tour of the three levels of the complex, concluding at a sizable, well-equipped genetic laboratory set in the ground floor's center pod. Monitors lined the wall, along with chemistry lab accouterments from computer workstations to test tubes, beakers, and funnels; x-ray tunneling microscopes, freezers and refrigerators. The dominant features were at facing walls of the lab, however. One, to the right as one walked in, stood a rather large, clear plexiglass chamber. On the opposite wall there was a short riser with an adjacent large, black one-way window just beyond the platform.

Near the center of the room, a middle aged, pudgy, bald professor wearing round glasses, stood in a morose, arms-akimbo posture. Beside him, a woman of similar age who was clearly under stress.

"Dr. Haas, Dr. Snyder, meet Dr. Travers. I know you never thought you'd hear me say this, but, anything she wants to know about Will—his background, his time with us—you tell her straight out. Understood?"

The two scientists appeared startled at Gentry's request. Snyder slowly shook her head as Haas looked dubiously at Travers. She saw in their faces that Gentry's order ran counter to many years of conditioning.

"So. You're—Will Monday's—*designers*?" asked Travers, trying to be sure she properly understood. If true, this meant they would have had to be solidifying their scientific procedure more than a generation ago, when both were young. Yet, according to the network news, only in the past year had scientists fully mapped the human genome, a labor of decades. Travers instantly grasped that she was in the presence of genius.

"We're the architects of a more than twenty year old project," intoned Dr. Snyder. "With one good result to show for all this time."

"Actually, *not* to show," Dr. Haas sighed. "I suppose, basically, you're here now, because we stepped into an unexpected moral dilemma nearly two decades ago. Now we've evidently reached a reckoning."

"Yes, his appearance—"

"Not just that," corrected Dr. Snyder. "No human clone, before Will, had ever lived so long. Usually, the newborns died in three months or less. But Will has provided us valuable data all his life."

"What kind of data?" Travers inquired.

Dr. Haas took up the reply, "Since 1969, environmental scientists at the Pentagon realized that the earth's climate was undergoing rapid, potentially disastrous change. Some of it was due to the military's own nuclear explosions, and other experiments in the Van Allen radiation belt shortly after it was discovered ten years earlier. Some of it was due to a vast buildup of chlorofluorocarbons in earth's upper atmosphere, dissolving the ozone layer, as I am sure you have heard."

"Yes, I've heard," Travers replied briskly. "Which is why you can't sit on the beach in Chile for more than fifteen minutes anymore without contracting skin cancer."

Haas nodded. "Precisely. The Pentagon team," he went on, "also realized that more weapons of mass destruction, in addition to their nuclear arsenals, would inevitably be developed. These weapons could wreak such havoc that only people whose respiratory, digestive, immune, nervous, limbic, and endocrine systems had great advantages over the current evolution of the species could survive.

"Of course, war preparations proceeded on several fronts. For instance, great stockpiles of biological agents now lie on the threshold of release, due to the gradual decay of their containment vessels. No one has developed a solution to this looming crisis. Congress has not even attempted to budget for it. And there are many such issues of which the public is scarcely aware."

"But General Gentry's mandate with Proteus was to plan for all contingencies," Snyder interjected. Travers noted her clear admiration for the general's vision.

"Fortunately, in our research, we discovered that genetic similarities do not necessarily occur only within a single animal family. We knew we could cull and blend physical traits not just from a cross-section of the human race, but also from across species, phylum, genera—even kingdoms."

"We put our theories into practice," added Dr. Haas, "with the aim of developing the first human beings who might survive the inevitable catastrophes humanity was creating. And the funding for our research was virtually unlimited. For a while."

"So, when was Will brought here?" Travers asked.

The others shared a look among themselves.

"He's always lived here," Gentry replied.

"Right here? His whole life? That's—a little overwhelming," Travers averred.

"We had two choices," said Snyder, nervously, "when we discovered our hybridizing had produced the indigo skin pigment. One choice was to keep him alive where no one could ever see him."

The other option hung, unspoken, in the air among them.

"Anyhow," resumed Gentry, briskly, "now you know 'why' there's a Will Monday. So, I think it's time for you two to meet—again."

Travers and Gentry left the lab and climbed a flight of steps to the middle level of the Project. They reached a door down one of the corridors to the left. Gentry gestured toward it and whispered, "Go on. Knock. I'll be just up the hall."

Travers nodded, nervously, then tapped lightly at the door.

Will Monday swivelled his catlike eyes from the ubiquitous glow of his television screen to the door. He rose and opened it to look once more upon the feminine vision that had haunted his dreams for the past two nights. There she stood, in the door to his cabin.

"Hello again, Will. Time for proper introductions. I'm Pam Travers."

Will gasped, swaying a little before reaching for Travers's extended right hand. "How'd you get here?"

"You have General Gentry to blame for that."

"Really? Well, uh... come in." Will looked to the right and to the left, as if assessing the place. Travers crossed the threshold into his room. It was identical to her own, although lived in, with additional furnishings and accouterments. Posters of pop stars covered the walls, just as they might in the room of a typical teenager. An entertainment center was the largest item in the room, stocked with video and audio equipment. There was also a computer desk, though at a glance Travers saw no telecommunications connections.

Travers turned her gaze back upon Will, displaying a friendly smile as she swallowed her own anxieties. She noted that the black injury marks that had stippled his face a couple of nights previous had diminished until they were hardly noticeable.

"The General's concerned over what happened the other night, Will."

"Yeah." Will glanced down, his face now a mask of guilt. "Guess he is."

"Can you tell me *why* you did it?"

"They made me better than any of you!" snapped Will, suddenly hostile. "I'm *sick of paying for it*!"

"I'm a—counselor, Will," Travers said, soothingly, hoping to placate him. "The General wanted me to talk things over with you. He thinks this experience must have had some very traumatic aspects. I would tend to agree. I was briefed on your life..."

"Right," replied Will, instantly falling glum. "My life. Here it is. In this room. You're looking at my whole past, present, *and future*—except for my stupid romp the other night. I'm *glad* I had that 'traumatic experience.' Broke up this routine I'm stuck with because *they* screwed up. The blue skin thing, you know? So, they always said, I could never 'fit in' out there. Now they want me to think I'm *crazy* for even trying. **Counselor**." He nearly laughed as he said it, then swallowed, nervously.

Travers, nearly as ill at ease as Will himself, began to realize that she was the first young woman he had ever actually met in person. And they both knew the unspoken truth, that several men had died two nights before on the search and rescue mission to retrieve Will. *He* had caused those deaths with his escape from this seclusion—and he had failed to reach freedom.

She had her work cut out for her. She wondered if the General would be satisfied with what she could realistically achieve.

"They do not think you're crazy, Will," Travers said, soothingly. "They only want what's best for you. Let's just take a little talk time—"

"*A little talk time*," Will snarled. He looked up at her from under his brow. Then, he shook his head. "Okay, I'm sorry. What do you wanna talk about?"

Outside in the corridor, Snyder strode up to the General.

"Loitering?" she asked.

"Gina," he grinned, ruefully. "Thanks for coming. It's been too long."

"Don't think I don't realize that you never had time to put this 'doctor' through the clearance process to be here. Are you getting hard up for pretty young things, Morgan?"

"Gina, you wound me. This is an extreme situation. We don't have all those months to wait," Gentry argued. "What's important right now is that she's *not* connected to any branch of the services. Yet, she can do what I need done."

"You're playing with fire."

Gentry gently laid a hand on Snyder's cheek. The professor wavered for a moment, then gently took his hand in hers and pulled it away.

"You realize this is the first time he's ever been near a female who's, uh ..." she began.

"Near his own age? I know." A grin spread across Gentry's face as he remembered days gone by, when they were younger, when they had come to rely on each others' warmth in the cold winter nights of the Northwest.

"He just gave in to *one* big temptation..."

"Desire met opportunity on a silver platter," Gentry replied. "First time in his life that ever happened."

"You think that's the whole story?"

"Well, hell, no," said the General. "Somebody slipped him a remote access controller and a God-damn set of car keys."

Snyder grasped the General's arm and tugged. He followed her lead to the stairs which led down to the base floor. They spoke in low tones, at odd intervals, followed by pauses as they went. Both knew, from long experience, just where the weakest points of the surveillance apparatus which permeated the complex were located.

"But they were the keys to McIntire's Acura," Snyder whispered. "Why?"

"McIntire—gave 'em to him? Maybe he took some weird kind of pity on the kid..."

"Come on, Morgan. If McIntire had planned this, you and your whole NSA would be looking for Will for years. And where was Avery?"

"Sleeping at the monitor? Why not? It's a boring duty. Nothing else has ever happened here. Of course, I'm gonna tear him a new hole over it, but..."

Snyder stopped. Narrowing her eyes, she searched Gentry's expression. "How'd it happen those two nasties were lying for him on the road out there?"

Gentry turned slightly, his back strategically toward the surveillance camera that covered this section of the corridor. He held up his hand, angled horizontally at the wrist, with, two forefingers tightly together. It was his signal not to speak too openly, even in the relatively safe zones. She nodded slightly, understanding.

In a secluded room within the Complex, Major Avery sat watching. A bank of monitors broadcast every corner of the complex before him. He frowned.

9.

"How long do you think I'm gonna live, Dr. Travers?" Will asked.

"A-a long time, I suppose..." Travers stammered.

"However long it is, the simple, obvious truth is that I, 'Blue' Monday, have no reason to live."

"'Blue Monday?' Is that what you call yourself?" Travers asked.

"I've heard Major Avery call me that. It fits, doesn't it?" Will said with a tight-lipped smile.

"But you *do* have a—"

"Save it. Look, I know I was created for a purpose. But now, I don't have a purpose. If it works out the way they think, and the end of the world comes, then I'm the only survivor. That doesn't do the world any good, does it? Oh, I might forage, and feed, and go on in some wasteland that's left out there, but I'll eventually die, and then there'll be no more people of *any* color.

"Or, maybe the world just goes on, and on, and on. Well, that world's not ready to see me, they say. That world is full of people who think some 'God' created them all. I'll tell you something I figured out, 'cause I've had a lot of time to think in here. Those people don't know anything about why they're here, or how. Nobody does—except me. But, they act so sure about all that, 'cause they're scared to think life doesn't have some *big reason* behind it. Well, I had a big reason—once. But the way it's worked out, now I have no reason. So here's the whole scoop. I'm sick to death of everything here, and I've got nothin' else to look forward to—ever."

Will was a bundle of taut nerves and muscles.

"This is good. Let's get all this out," she suggested. "Why not lie back on the couch and relax a little bit. Just keep talking. Anything you want to say."

Will sat down, looking at Travers for a long moment, as if just now realizing someone was actually listening to him, actually encouraging him to say more. He hesitantly lay back. But, he didn't seem very comfortable, craning his neck to keep her in his sight. And he said no more for several long minutes.

"Let's talk about *my* reason for being here, then," Travers at last suggested. "Let's talk about that other night a little bit. The night you bolted out of here. What do you remember about that?"

"Well, I came back from the gym after a workout with Mac, while I changed clothes, I saw some keys and this little remote control thing sitting on top of my chest of drawers. I couldn't believe it. But there they were."

"Really? And you did, what—?" Travers asked, skeptically.

"I—I thought about taking them to Avery. But I had this—*hot buzz* going on in my head. I *knew* what I *should* have done. I should have turned the keys in to Avery. But, the more I thought about handing that lousy, grinning dweeb the keys to my freedom, the more I thought about just taking them, finding a car they'd work in, and—and driving out of here like a bat out of hell ."

Travers noted this down in her little notebook.

"Which you did, obviously. So. They taught you how to drive, down here?"

"Ahhh, I drove a simulator a bunch of times. But I got tired of games, playing by myself—and I wanted to, you know, *just do it*—like they say in the commercials." He arched his eyebrows. No reaction from the psychiatrist.

"Did you feel you were getting away with something?" Travers asked.

"I didn't feel *bad,* if that's what you mean."

"How did you feel, then?"

"Just—excited."

"Maybe you should have felt a little bit bad," Travers suggested. "Didn't you know what you were doing was wrong?"

"Wrong? 'Cause *they* say so?"

"We all have to think about how our actions will affect others," Travers replied evenly.

"I'm not out to hurt anybody, but, Babe, I got nothin' to lose, like I already said."

"But *they* do, Will," Travers ventured. "Don't you feel you owe them anything? And, by the way, I 'm not a 'babe.'"

"All right, sorry. But what do you mean, 'owe them.' For what?" Will demanded.

"For giving you life," Travers stated, simply.

Will sat up. "Not *this* life," he scowled.

"They've done what they could for you, Will," Travers began.

"*Don't lecture me!*" Will sat up suddenly, taking Travers's breath away. His cat eyes fixed her in an eerie stare, making her feel that any moment he would leap on her like a hungry lion and, perhaps, devour her. "You think you're talking to *a human being*? Yeah, somehow, I was born, *Pam*—or, was I *hatched*? Did they ever tell you anything about it? They never told *me*! Did I develop in some woman's womb? Or did they stick a bunch of ribosomes and nucleotides together in some crazy *soup*, and stir it up in a test tube? Whatever. I was a roaring success, except for *one thing*." He leaned forward, jutting his face close to hers. "I'm 'Blue' Monday."

Travers fixed him in a stare of her own.

"What do you *want,* Will? What will make it right?"

Will opened his mouth slightly. He sat back down, looking a little dazed.

A silent moment passed as he pondered the question. He had obviously never had it put to him before.

"Don't know what you want? Or, do you not know what to say?" Travers demanded, gently.

Will shook his head, introspectively.

"Okay. How about this. What did you want when you drove that car out of here?"

"I—don't know. I just felt some kind of wild rush." He hung his head, embarrassed. Then, he stood and paced the room, waving his arms. "I *knew* I was gonna freak people out. They always *said* I would. But right then, I didn't *care*. That remote got me out in the cave, and I just started trying those keys. There were only two cars, so it was easy. I pushed the remote control buttons, and, just once, in my whole life," Will rose, gesturing vehemently with both arms, "that freakin' blast door went up for *me*. I got *out* of this damn place. I felt the *sun* shine down on me and I *saw the blue sky*, and I—I—just *went with it*, okay? I mean, for just a little while, I had—*freedom*."

"Freedom. So, that's what you want? Freedom?"

"Yes!" Will leaped upon her, startling her as he straddled her, holding her shoulder, drawing his face so close to hers they were breathing the same air. "That's what I want! I want—"

Suddenly, Travers's hair rose, as though from static electricity effects. He clothing tugged at the front of her body, pulling inches away from her flesh.

Travers, unnerved, stared wide-eyed at Will, even as they both pulled back from each other, trying to comprehend what was happening. He was obviously afraid himself, breathing heavily, weighing in his mind the choices he had in the next moment.

In a moment, he stood up and backed away. He looked down and mumbled, "Sorry." Travers's hair and clothing gently settled, more or less, back into place.

"Will—?"

Will gave her a frightened look, warning not to go there.

Pam had to wonder if the two of them had just shared some kind of collective delusion. She had never been much given to Yungian interpretations of the psyche, but she was wondering now if she might have to reconsider. Both of them took a deep breath, trying to regain their composure.

"You, um, you obviously have some powerful feelings bottled up inside you, Will," she ventured.

Blue Monday

Will tossed himself over on the divan and lay face down in the pillows.

"I can't help it!" he cried, burying his head in the pillow.

"I'm not trying to accuse you, Will," said Travers, soothingly. "For instance, we all have, uh, natural urges. But my whole point is, that's not how we get along together, just giving in to our selfish urges. That's not what makes a society. What each of us does affects others. Most of us have a lifetime of learning to deal with that fact. We have peers to practice our behavior with. You've been given special gifts, Will. But, in exchange, you've been deprived of peers, friends, family, society. Frankly, I'm impressed that, without any of that in your life, you restrained yourself just now."

"Thank you," Will sobbed, the tears starting to flow despite his manly efforts to stem them.

"The question is, if you're practicing restraint now, why didn't you do the same the other day when you found the car keys lying there on your dresser?"

"Look, I really don't want to feel good for a few minutes if I'm gonna feel bad about it for a long time later," muttered Will. "So, shit. I screwed up. I don't know what else to say about it."

"Okay, you screwed up," Travers gently remonstrated. "But, you gained wisdom. I hear it in your words, right now, okay? You can use that wisdom for the rest of your life. And that may mean more than you think, Will. Because, for all of us, to get what we want depends not only on what we do, but on the way that we do it."

"All of us?" Will asked.

"Yes."

"Us, who?"

"Us. Human beings."

Will looked at her earnestly. "You really see me as a human being?"

"Of course, I do." Travers stood and offered Will her hand.

Will stood, a little uncertainly. With a tentative grin, he extended his hand to clasp hers.

"Very good," Travers declared. "And I've enjoyed getting to know you. Really. We'll pick it up again tomorrow."

Travers stepped to the doorway and opened it, casting a backward glance with what was intended as a reassuring smile. Will's own, confused face indicated he had thoughts on his mind which would take some time to sort out. He nodded and cast a last, fervid look at her.

Outside Will's door, Travers went weak at the knees, clutching at the chromium wall. She caught sight of her disheveled reflection, wiped her brow, smoothed her hair.

She suddenly realized that Gentry was nowhere to be seen. She quickened her pace, trying to contain her feelings of anger and dismay. She could have been in real danger in there!

Behind her, Will's door cracked open. His cat eyes watched this delightful creature who had, ever-so-briefly, visited, to such an intense effect. She was obviously flustered. He saw her pause, look around and stalk off.

Will closed himself in his room again. He leaned back against the door with eyes wide, heart thumping in his chest. He thought of McIntire, the last person to be inducted into Proteus, four years earlier. As mentor and friend, McIntire had helped Will return to a sense that life might be worth living. Lately, he had again begun to wonder what would become of him, to fall back into despair.

Now, his impulsive joy ride in McIntire's car had nearly cost his only friend his life. And, it *had* cost the lives of several men he would never know. His heart sank like lead when he thought about his stupidity in escaping Proteus as he had.

But, that same action had brought Pam Travers into his world.

Will gritted his teeth and breathed the air deeply. He reveled in the lingering scent of her, no longer stifling himself from enjoying it, as he had when she was present.

"Manners," Dr. Snyder had always stressed to him. He was glad she had not witnessed his behavior a few moments before.

Blue Monday

He had felt the rush, the static charge, as Dr. Travers had. Once more, Will wondered with a shiver, *what was he becoming?*

He knew he could only drive himself crazy wondering about this question, with nothing but time on his hands. He needed to think of something else, and quickly. He wanted to get lost in the rhythms of music. The sooner, the better.

He knelt, rummaging through the cabinet of his entertainment center, feeling a wild flutter in his heart unlike anything he had ever felt. The General had locked all his music away as a punishment for his rash action, but had missed his portable CD player and a couple of disks Will had stashed under the bed. He popped a CD into his player, donned the headset, and turned on the machine. In a moment, the throbbing strains of a techno band filled Will's ears. Will translated the rhythms into his moves, into his dance. It was the only way he could totally shed, for a time, all the thoughts of his miserable existence.

Soon, his imagination freely played with the image of Pam Travers, enjoying every wild fantasy he could envision. Will felt ecstatic—almost free.

He opened his eyes, and gasped in surprise.

All of the glass animals given to him by Dr. Snyder through the years, objects that normally lined shelves on his wall, were bobbing in rhythm with his moves—in mid-air. He stopped dancing and staggered back a step.

The glass animals fell. Will dove across the couch, hand outstretched, and barely managed to save the last one Snyder had ever given him—the rearing glass unicorn.

Dr. Snyder had visited the Complex on his tenth birthday, and, as was her custom, had brought along some gifts from the outside world. She had watched as Will unwrapped and opened the box containing this very glass ornament. She told him then that he was like the unicorn, with its nobility and its mystery. He remembered being a little puzzled by the notion that he was a "mystery" to a scientist who had devised his very molecular structure. He knew all his human keepers were impressed with his stamina and physical resiliency, knew he had survived physical trials that would have killed any one of them. But, wasn't that exactly what they had *designed* him to do?

He now blinked at the unicorn in the palm of his hand, and at the broken pieces of glass on his floor that had once been the other glass animals. Along with assorted toys, they were outmoded as Will grew, later replaced by video games, movies on tape, and CDs of his favorite bands from television. Just as they had forced him into daily schooling and dangerous experiments, they had tried to compensate by sharing American popular culture with Will.

Will considered the salvaged relic of his past he held in his palm. Then, his stare circumnavigated a room he knew all too well, but which did not quite seem familiar anymore.

10.

Travers, feeling as though she were in a space ship a million miles from earth, decided to explore, if only to take better psychological possession of her surroundings. If she were going to deal with this Will Monday, she realized she could not afford to lose her own equilibrium. So far, that was shaping up as a challenge. Travers descended the steps, wandered around the "ground floor" a bit, until she reached the pantry. There was a large dining table with chairs enough for a dozen people inside. Beyond that, the bent form of Dr. Snyder was hunched over the kitchen sink, with Morgan Gentry standing by, tugging on his ear.

"Yeah," he was murmuring quietly, "okay, if you check him over yourself. I'll put Haas on the—"

Travers turned to creep back out, hoping she had not been noticed.

"Hold it," Gentry said. Travers froze, then turned.

"Where you going? Sorry about leaving you there on your own. Everything okay?" Travers nodded diffidently, as Gentry took her by the elbow and escorted her back into the corridor. "I've got a slab of folders to lay on you."

Gentry glanced back at Snyder, who half-raised her head, looking at them. Travers glimpsed a drain auger, covered in crud, which Snyder held in one hand, a glass beaker in the other. Then she found herself being hustled up the corridor with Gentry.

They rose to the top tier of Proteus and entered Gentry's rather Spartan office. The "view" outside his office dome was of the deep, dark interior of the cavern. Travers shuffled, uneasily, as Gentry unlocked a cabinet and rifled through some files, selecting various folders until he had a nine-inch stack of folders in his arms. He nodded to her; she opened the door, and they proceeded downstairs to her cabin.

Once there, Gentry plopped the folders onto her bureau, turned, and said, "Look, Missy. I want you to read this stuff, know it—*and then forget it.* It's worth your life to never talk about what you learn here, understand? But you need to know what you're dealing with."

"Missy", indeed. Travers nodded.

"When you came in here, you entered a world different from anything you've ever known. But at the same time, it's exactly the same world you left out there." Travers did not like to think she had really left anything "out there", but she said nothing, pondering Gentry's contradiction in terms. "Everybody trying to pull their weight, trying to win, trying to outsmart the other guy. That's out there. And it's in here. Espionage—which is the world I operate in—multiplies all that by a thousand. It's a mess. And it's dangerous as hell.

"You are *not* to get sucked into any of that, understand?"

Travers nodded, happy to agree, even if she did not understand what Gentry was intimating.

"Don't get mixed up in Haas and Snyder's turf wars, for instance. How they cobbled all the chromosomes together to grow our boy, you don't need to know. I want you focused on the kid and what's in his head. I'm gonna let you read what's in here so you can see how he's lived. You'll need to know about that, because you're gonna figure out how he's gonna live *next*. That's what we're here to do—build his new life."

'His new life?' I don't understand. What's going to change?" asked Travers.

"Everything."

"Why?"

"Because it already has," Gentry snapped. "Just not in any kind of way I'd want it to. You're here because you have a type of expertise I need right now. You can reshape Will's memories of this place, and you will. I am determined to protect this boy, and since he busted out, I can't do it here much longer."

"I'm going to be here a while, aren't I?" Travers said, flatly.

"The sooner you get this job done, the sooner you go back to your old one."

"And what, exactly, is 'this job?' I'm still trying to figure that one out."

Gentry sighed. "Okay. It's like this. You make it so he forgets. He doesn't know our names. He thinks he's had a different life. He gets up in the morning—in a post-hypnotic trance, if need be. He puts on some kind of makeup; I've got Snyder working on a compound. Then he wakes up and 'does his thing,' whatever. You decide. I don't care if he's a forest ranger or a night janitor. Give him an aptitude test or something. But we need to come up with something he can do without a lot of other people around in his day-to-day life."

"Am I hearing all this right?"

"He *can't stay here anymore*, Honey. I've got to hide him out *there*—out there in the haystack," Gentry insisted.

"Now, mum's the word. Read what you can, and come join us for supper at oh-eighteen hundred hours."

"Right," Travers sighed. "Around six." Gentry departed, and Travers shook her head as she looked at the leaning tower of classified folders whose contents she was supposed to absorb. She was beginning to understand that Gentry had placed enormous faith in her ability to do the impossible.

Travers picked up the top folder and sighed. She sat on her divan and began to read. She saw references to an "MK-Delta" project. Proteus had been one component of its secret funding. She realized, reading of the incredible testing he had been subjected to, that Will's designers, creators and nurturers were not adhering to the Nuremberg Accords agreed upon among nations after World War Two. The Accords had set out an international protocol on the terms of conducting human medical trials.

Technically, the creators of Proteus rationalized themselves a loophole to exploit. Will was not quite human, and he did not exist on any official documents. He had no birth certificate, no Social Security number, no legal name, no form of citizenship.

A decade before, Gentry had brought in Eugene Avery, then a Bird Colonel, to tutor Will formally in school lessons up to high school level.

At around the same time, the age of ten, they had proceeded to immerse Will in water for impossibly long times to see if his in-bred swallow reflex, and its accompanying metabolic slowdown, was working reliably. They had burned, frozen, abrased and poisoned, him with sand, frost, ultraviolet rays and toxic gases. They had repeatedly run him through various physical ordeals for a period of four years.

After another four years, Lieutenant McIntire appeared within the walls of Proteus, to mentor Will in high standards of practical self-defense, to discipline his mind and his spirit—and to keep him busy a lot of the rest of the time when he was not in "school" with Avery. Will's subsequent "free" time was spent resting and recovering, watching television or listening to his beloved "tunes" for an hour or so at the end of each day—living "normally," as they said. Those hours were candy breaks in a lifetime of bitter medicines.

Travers ascertained from the files that Will was no invulnerable, superhuman figure exactly. He had been injured to various degrees dozens of times in the tests. But, he was highly resilient. The denizens of Proteus had proven to themselves that he could survive more extreme ambient conditions than any normal human being. Possibly he could even survive a post-nuclear world.

As she learned from studying the available notes, his blue pigmentation had apparently resulted from dual efforts to render his metabolism capable of simultaneously metabolizing atmospheres with higher oxygen levels, and processing sunlight directly for a considerable portion of his nutritional needs. That was ironic, thought Travers, considering he had only once been exposed to even a small amount of natural daylight.

She suspected the Proteus personnel had expected to cut short Will's life dozens of times. But he survived, seeming, as he grew, to become more conditioned by degrees, year by year, so that he could always withstand just a little more physical stress.

How ironic that the leader of this project, illegal in any state of the Union, and in violation of the spirit of the Geneva Convention and the Nuremberg Accords, could threaten her *with the law* over much more minor infractions involving legal prisoners.

The Proteus staff were an odd lot of mixed brutality and sensitivity, Travers surmised as she read on. She supposed some people would see herself and the staff at the state prison in much the same way.

She thought of her own case histories, couched in objective jargon despite her personal opinion of the individual convict or his chances of being rehabilitated. Similarly, Dr. Snyder had made notes about Will's emotional reactions to her little gifts, for instance—then she had gone on in the most callous fashion to document what the sensors detected in the subsequent, brutal ordeals to which they subjected young Will during her and Dr. Haas's research visits.

Travers still had the least idea of Will himself, though, from these records. How had he managed to cooperate with all this? He seemed aware enough of his situation to have formed a kind of informed consent. Yet, what true choice did he have? Surely, there was a festering core of deep resentment inside Will as he inevitably developed the realization that what he suffered in his life, in terms of physical ordeals and bleak social isolation, was by no means the norm for human beings in general.

She realized that, despite his advanced genetic design, in order to still be alive after all his life-threatening trials, he must have had some hope all this time, perhaps a dream that he would one day be released from the confines of Proteus. And now, that dream seemed on the verge of becoming a reality, but only if Will essentially ceased to exist as Will. That seemed to be Gentry's plan. Travers cursed the skills that had brought her to this pass.

Some sort of fulfillment of both Will and Gentry's dovetailing dreams now seemed to depend on her. Yet, she wondered if she would ever be able, as the General desired, to make the marks they had made on him recede into oblivion within his mind. Or, if the hybrid, unique mind of Will Monday would even permit that to happen. Gentry obviously did not realize how difficult his secret plans for Will would be to achieve. Yet, Will's very existence must have also seemed an impossibility at the outset. So, she realized the General must harbor a very different opinion of what was possible than she held.

11.

As mealtime approached, Travers arrived at the mess to find Carl Haas bringing a stack of pre-cooked frozen meals round the counter from a walk-in freezer. An array of dining utensils was already laid out, in paper wrappings, near the microwave.

"Oh, hello," said Haas, flashing a smile intended to charm. "As you can see, the butler has the day off," he added.

"Mm-hm. Any of those say they're 'good when thawed?'" Travers asked.

"Well, let's see—Pam, was it?" Haas laid his bundle out on the counter near the microwave oven. "Here's a beef with rice pilaf and green beans, a chicken with corn, asparagus and cheese sauce..."

Travers looked over the selection, noticing that Haas did not move back to leave her more room. She heard him ask, "So, you work in a prison, I understand? How does our little home away from home compare?"

"There's more of a social life at the pen," she sniffed. "And some daylight gets in."

"We'll have more company soon. The General and the Major went to retrieve the Lieutenant from the medical facilities at Mountain Home Base."

"I nearly met the Lieutenant, at the hospital," remarked Travers. "I'm glad he's well enough to join us." She took a couple of steps to place her meal inside the microwave oven.

"Yes, I'm sure he can provide some insight into your subject," Haas mused, moving alongside her. "What do you think of him, so far?"

Travers shrugged, "His behavior is a lot more 'normal' than I might have expected, although..."

"Yes?" Haas leaned forward, with keen interest.

"Nothing. I mean, it'll take some time before I can separate the real Will Monday from what he's picked up watching TV."

Travers could somehow envision Haas laying Will out on a dissecting table if she mentioned the "static electricity" incident she had experienced with him. But surely, she reasoned, if there were anything extraordinary about Will, these researchers already knew about it. Yet her own discretion might be under scrutiny at all times, especially given the General's stern, though vague warnings to her that afternoon. She decided to shift the balance of the conversation.

"So, I noticed you're a professor at MIT these days," she said. "How often do you come way out here?"

"Less, these days," Haas replied. "It's been about a year, this time. Our work here is basically done, after all," he sighed. "Although I certainly didn't anticipate the opportunity to work with such a charming young lady, for a change."

Travers mustered a terse, "Thank you."

The microwave bell dinged. Travers removed her cooked meal and picked up a bundle of utensils.

Haas picked up his selection and placed it inside the appliance. "The General says you use drugs and hypnosis in your work?"

"Yes, that's right." Travers carried her meal to the table, sat facing across the kitchen, looking at Haas as she unwrapped her knife, fork, and spoon.

"I'm no hypnotist, of course, but I have orders to interpret your normal prescription and render a batch to make it effective on Will," said Haas. "He's resistant to a wide array of substances, you know."

"Which makes you proud, I guess."

"Oh, he *was,* indeed, a source of pride," Haas nodded, taking a big bite of his entree.

"'Was?'"

"Oh, you know how it is with people. We wax, then we wane. We get used to things." He looked around. "Sometimes, though, I feel like I've spent my whole life buried down here," he continued, ruefully. "I wonder if I'll finish my days in one of these shelters."

"'*One* of these—?'" said Travers, surprised. "I thought sure this place was one of a kind."

"Actually, this is one of the smaller ones. Some of them are like compact underground cities." Haas stirred his mixed vegetables with a fork.

"Oh, come on," Travers scoffed. 'Underground cities?' I think I'd have heard about something that big."

"Child," Haas munched a mouthful of food. "Do you know about every highway construction project that goes on? Every mine opening or closing? No? Those things are out in the open, in *public*, and they go unnoticed by the vast majority."

"Really? So, who paid for these 'cities?'"

"Uncle Sugar, of course," Haas replied, grinning through a mouthful of food.

"'And you've got a mountain lion in your hip pocket'," Travers scoffed, "as my daddy used to say."

"How old were you in the savings and loan crisis, in the Eighties?" Haas responded. "Do you remember how much money disappeared from the economy?"

"I—no, not really."

"Half a trillion dollars. That's a lot of money, isn't it?"

"Look," said Travers, firmly, "I'm here only to work with Will Monday until I can get back to my normal life. That's all that I need to know and more than I ever wanted to know." She picked up a forkful of food and stared at it.

"Yes. Will. Isn't it awful? If not for flaws in Dr. Snyder's mutable proteases—" Haas abruptly choked off. Pam glanced to her left, to witness Dr. Snyder entering the room, shooting daggers from her eyes at Dr. Haas.

"Carl, Carl, Carl," she said. "Still in denial, aren't you? I proved, years ago, the indigo pigment was a side-effect of your synthetic messenger RNA. Now you're trying to convince a total stranger that I'm to blame for Will's predicament. Pathetic."

"Please," protested Travers. "I don't understand your field, and I'm not here to lay blame."

"What *are* you here to do, lady?" Snyder challenged, coldly, as she looked over the selection of remaining meals on the counter. "I heard you're here mainly to save yourself from joining your 'patients' on the other side of the prison bars."

Travers turned an equally cold stare on the older woman.

"For some Top Secret, master-spy type, your General sure talks a lot," she cried. "Matter of fact, you all do. Okay? As far as I can see, I'm expected to right a wrong you people did, which nobody knows about, anyway. I'm supposed to bury years of psychological harm, done in the name of some misguided mission to save the world."

"Mm-hm. Just as I thought," sneered Dr. Snyder, folding her arms.

"*What* did you think?" demanded Travers, her nostrils beginning to flare.

"You're out of your depth. You can't do this," Snyder frowned, "so you're ready to judge the whole project 'wrong.' Then, you can feel okay when you can't make it 'right.'"

"An excellent analysis," Travers gasped. "Maybe we should *trade places*, Doctor Snyder."

"I don't think so. I wouldn't be any more *comfortable* brainwashing people in the name of some 'higher good' than you'd be *competent* in micro-biological engineering."

"I do not 'brainwash,'" Travers retorted. "I manipulate the marginal memories of subjects who, at least, had a normal life to begin with. This is the first time I've been expected to work with—" she stopped, sensing another presence in the room.

"Go ahead, you can say it. 'A Top Secret, blue *freak.*' Right?" Will stood in the doorway, gazing over the three mortified people in the room. Then, he breezily stepped over to the counter to glance over the frozen meal selection on the counter top. His presence lowered the temperature in the already frigid room.

Travers cleared her throat. "Will. I was *going* to say, the first time I've had to work with someone permanently deprived of—"

"Sure you were," Will interrupted, pursing his lips as he looked them all over. "But you don't have to think of me as such a *challenge*, Doctor Travers. I want to do everything I *can* to work it out. I mean, if you have to give me a *lobotomy*, that'll be cool. If it'll help me forget this *nightmare* place and these lab *clerks* who gave me the *blue suntan*, then, hey, I'll go for it in a heartbeat."

Travers observed as Haas pursed his lips and uttered a near-silent "harumph." Snyder seemed stricken with genuine pain.

Suddenly, Will's insolent expression turned to grief. All eyes followed his toward the door, where Gentry and Avery entered the room. Between them, Lt. George McIntire hobbled on a crutch.

"Hail, the returning hero," piped Gentry. Dr. Haas rose to his feet and Snyder, after glancing once more at Will, crossed to give the Lieutenant a light hug around the neck and a peck on the cheek.

"So glad you're still with us, George," she said, earnestly.

"Good to be here," McIntire smiled, feebly, obviously still under the effects of painkilling drugs. His fellow officers helped him into a seat. Then, the General himself solicitously took over, preparing the remainder of the meals as everyone else took seats, ceasing their bickering to fuss instead over the wounded soldier in their midst. McIntire raised his good right hand to greet the new initiate, Travers. She greeted him in kind, with a tight little smile. Travers felt a vaguely familiar tug at her heartstrings. It was a feeling she could not quite place.

She observed through the rest of the meal that it was hard for Will to make eye contact with McIntire. His apparent feelings of guilt brought her satisfaction. It was one sign that the strange, blue boy, reared without a society, at least had a conscience.

12.

The White House in Washington, D.C., stood on a sealed-off section of Pennsylvania Avenue, more of a lonely fortress than ever since the advent of President Hollis Ash two years before. Only vehicles with the proper clearance could draw near to discharge passengers who held scheduled appointments with those on the inside. A limousine drew up to the gate on this gusty, partly cloudy spring day to discharge two men who might have been familiar to Bud the bartender and his patrons back in Idaho.

The wiry, bespectacled Jacob Threll drew his lips into a thin line, taking a deep breath as he and his hulking assistant, former special CIA operative, Kent Morris, emerged from the limo.

Once inside the White House foyer, the men were patted down for weapons and ushered into an inner waiting room, where they were served coffee by the staff. A variety of magazines were laid out for the men's leisure time reading, though neither picked one up. Finally, after nearly a half-hour, an attendant appeared at the double doors.

"Mr. Threll?" he asked.

"Yes, please," sighed Threll. Mr. Morris also rose, but the attendant raised his hand.

"Please—wait here," he said, firmly.

Threll looked at Morris and calmly said, "Stay." He nodded, and the huge man resumed sitting, placidly.

The attendant ushered Threll down a corridor and knocked at the door of the Oval Office itself. "Yes," came a voice from within. President Ash nodded at the attendant as he ushered in Threll, and the attendant turned to go.

Ash rose from his desk. He looked at Threll appraisingly as he passed him by, crossing the room to lock the doors to this office of the people's official business.

Upon Ash's return, he and Threll locked gazes, drawing closer and closer until they were less than an arm's length apart. Then, each reached out his right arm and displayed a ruby red ring, emblazoned at the center with a stylized, silver "W". They interlocked their arms at the elbows and began to jointly recite a bizarre oath.

"Under the Grand Architect of the Universe, and in accordance with the Master Plan..." began Ash.

"...shall the Wilderbeeks endeavor to create, and to destroy, the primeval matter..." continued Threll.

"...to undertake the killing of the King..." continued Ash.

"...and to make manifest all things that are hidden," Threll concluded.

The men withdrew their arm link. The president drew back, looking every bit the scowling old schemer he strove not to appear before the public.

"So, it's true?" said Ash, raising his bushy eyebrows.

"Yes," replied Threll. "He's real. He's deep blue all over, and he's..." The wiry man trailed off, looking into the air as if for the words that eluded him.

"He's what?" Ash demanded.

"He's—eerie," Threll shrugged. "There's more to him than meets the eye, somehow."

"Or, less to you and that special agent of yours. How is it that the two of you couldn't bag this whelp, even with Advanced Projects ordnance?" queried Ash, looking darkly from under his brow.

"I was pulling for you, Jacob. But with results like these, how do you expect to change the Council's plans for Project Livingroom?"

"I realize we're a minority on the Governing Council, Mr. President," Threll smiled, tightly. "But I believe we can persuade the others that the only 'Final Cleansing' we need is in the minds of the population. Even a third of them, doing our bidding without question, can eliminate or subdue the rest."

Blue Monday

"That's looking like a long shot," shrugged Ash, returning to his chair behind the desk.

"So did radio, at one time," rejoined Threll. "I'll remind you that I kept my pledge to keep the presence of the Brotherhood of the Wilderbeeks unknown in this affair. I did so, and under rather trying circumstances, I might add."

"Yes," admitted the President. "You evidently avoided surveillance by the NSA, and nobody from the hospital staff 'made' you when you salvaged your 'pet'. That much is to your credit."

Threll grimaced at this characterization of Agent Morris, the man he called "Vee."

"That 'pet', as you call him, is my 'vindicator,'" he retorted. "He's living proof that the mind of one human being can be directed by another. Proof that the behavior of the world's laboring mass can be placed *directly* under our command—"

"Look, Jacob," Ash interrupted, wearily. "It's not that we don't believe your technology works, but you have to see this from the Council's point of view. First, this 'Vee' already lost his position in the CIA due to your work on his brain. He's not behaving like a psychotic anymore—fine. But he can't hold a normal conversation, either."

"But, with more funding—" Threll began.

"Ah! Ah! Let me finish. Your plan to convert a third of the population into people like him—it's too ambitious. That way, with a bunch of implants in the brain? It's too big a job to cover up. For centuries, our best friend has been *secrecy*, Jacob."

"We'll soon have a way to do it *without* the implants," Threll replied. "With just broadcast emissions, on extra low frequencies. I've proven these override frequencies work. All we need to do is refine the way we deliver them into the mind. And I know we can do so on a mass scale."

"But Project Livingroom was already a well-laid plan—" Ash began.

"—when I came along, I know. But I find it unbelievable the Council would rather wipe the world's surface clean and live underground for generations, when we have a viable alternative. One that can reduce the excess population *and* produce a docile servant class into the bargain."

"Look," said Ash, wearily, "I don't make the rules, I just enforce them. And here's where we stand. You have to prove yourself. You must capture this specimen alive, so the tech wing can learn his secrets. They'll either find him suitable for a new breed of hunter-gatherer—or they won't. If they do, they'll make more like him. Hopefully, *white* ones."

"They should expect," said Threll, "to unlock secrets of biochemistry that could be worth billions of 'green ones' in the meantime. Maybe trillions."

"So, the best way you can make your case is simply to deliver what you promised," Ash shrugged. "Your man's a 'vindicator'? Then you can prove it, Jacob, when he vindicates this mission."

"It'll be riskier now. I can have no further contact with the inside," Threll averred. "Gentry's bound to be watching everyone more closely."

"Are you saying you can't do it?"

"I just need a new opening. The Major should be leaving on his supply run in a couple of days. I'll try to coordinate with him, then."

Ash nodded slowly, then watched his fellow member of the powerful secret society to which they belonged depart the Oval Office. The President of the United States felt the weight of its Governing Council upon his shoulders.

13.

The next morning, in the Proteus monitor room, Travers and Gentry sat, reviewing samples of recordings the surveillance system had made over the years. Gentry had shown her several hours of video by this time, reviewing incidents from various stages of Will's childhood to the present.

Travers realized that Will's "social interactions" had largely taken place by means of television, and that Gentry considered himself and his cohorts enlightened to have provided Will this "electronic babysitter." Will also had access to music and a video arcade of his own, in one of the rooms of Proteus. These diversions probably had helped Will retain his sanity, and in a sense, helped educate the lad.

Reviewing the tapes, Travers saw that, pretty much like any normal little boy of the modern era, Will had developed a fantasy world of make-believe where he had interacted with the characters on his TV screen. He had grown from playing cops 'n robbers with imaginary bandits as a child, to lounging around and discussing his angst with the twenty-somethings on evening television series, along the way developing a slang similar to theirs.

Of course, in his quest for an individual identity, he would not want to sound like the scientists and military men who reared him. Consequently, the only one he could converse with him fairly comfortably as a young man was McIntire, who employed the slang of the enlisted man. McIntire had remained single, Travers learned, which may have also contributed to the strength of his and Will's bond. He had less cause than the married Major Avery to resent the long, lonely tours of duty in this isolated region.

Before Dr. Travers and General Gentry, the whole of the Proteus Project was laid bare on monitor screens. The major portion of the first floor was embodied in the gymnasium, the lab, and the utilities. The monitor room stood to the rear of all these, and provided the access point to the cylindrical tube which she had glimpsed on arrival. It ran upward, through the roof of the cavern. Inside the monitor room, its access chamber stood virtually as a sealed vault.

On the second floor were the living quarters and Will's recreation room. On the top tier, the conference room, with its transparent dome, capped off the complex, surrounded by the staff's private offices, some of them vacant.

This morning, Will Monday had, as many times before, climbed the steps to the Proteus top tier, where the conference room served as his classroom. Here he sat, with an open book and notepad before him, in the presence of the dour Avery. As they had countless times, they belabored the pursuit of what was, to Will, mostly useless knowledge, dolefully delivered. Everything about the body language of both men bespoke the unwilling enactment of a hollow ritual.

Travers glanced over at Gentry, who seemed lost in some sort of brooding thought. He reviewed more monitorings, setting cues as Travers monitored the conference room live.

Travers knew certain things from her review of the records. She knew that Major Eugene Avery had served as Will's instructor for ten years, occasionally advancing in rank as he served up a curriculum similar to those offered up to the public school children in the outer world. She knew that Will, though he by and large disdained his schooling, had taken a certain amount of interest in the history and geography lessons, and was most taken with anything he could get his hands on to read, especially stories of travel and adventure.

As Travers had already heard from Will in discussing his relationships within the Complex, one of the closest occasions he had ever shared with Avery was the time they read Robert Louis Stevenson's classic, *Treasure Island* together, six years earlier. Travers had seen some of those moments as recorded on video. Sailing! Adventure! A treasure hunt! The kid that was Will had thrilled to the tale, and even Avery had seemed pleased to read the story with him. As he had related it to Travers, the time they spent exploring that story together was one of the last times Will recalled having seen Avery with a cheerful disposition.

"So," Travers asked Gentry as she observed the screen, "this Major Avery. I suppose it's fair to say he's spent the most time with Will of anyone here?"

Gentry sighed. "Yeah. You've probably already seen them bitching at each other. But Avery does as he's told. I never really had to worry about him."

"Was he a teacher in civilian life?"

"Nope. Into the service straight from an ROTC officership. His daddy's on the board of one of the big contractors. Pulled strings to get him a nice, safe, long-term assignment. That was back in the Desert Storm days, you know? We weren't looking for a hero, just somebody steady—discreet."

Travers watched the screen and realized she owned the only fresh pair of eyes to bear witness to what happened in this strange place. On the monitor, Avery paced about the conference table, as Will stared sullenly at his text book.

"Now, what is the role of Pi in calculating the area of a trapezoid?" a little grey Avery on the screen put the question to Will, who fidgeted in his chair.

"Uh—it is the multiplier of the radius times itself," Will murmured in response.

"Aha!" Avery gloated. "That's for the area of a circle. I'm talking about the area of a trapezoid."

Will sighed, shut his book and pushed it away.

"You got me. Look, I don't feel up to measurin' trapezoids today. In fact, I think I'll take a sick day."

"Oh, so you just *decide* to take a sick day?" demanded Avery.

"Why not? I'm a burn victim."

"Those little burns? You're supposed to be a tough guy."

"I'm sick of being a tough guy."

Avery called after Will as he reached the hall. "Look, *I've* got a *wife* at home with two little *babies*. You think I don't have anything better to do than *this*? Well, I do, buster."

"Now I'm sick with envy," Will called back over his shoulder.

In the monitor room, Gentry suddenly hit the freeze frame button on the monitor he was observing. "Christ *damn*," he exclaimed. Travers grimaced at his blasphemy. That was something her family had not tolerated in her youth, when her parents had been alive.

She glanced over at the screen. It appeared Will was off-balance, and there seemed to be something—confetti—?—flying through the air in his room.

"What is it?" she asked.

"Nothing," Gentry said, obviously shaken. He switched off the screen before she could get a closer look.

"Well, it looks like they just had a real falling out," commented Travers.

"Okay, why don't you go have a talk with Will, then. Go on," he urged.

Travers shrugged and rose from her seat. She felt more overwhelmed by this burden than she had even the day before. She was beginning to worry, in the back of her mind, whether she would ever see home again.

Alone, Gentry immediately began punching buttons on his console. Monitor imagery flickered over various sites within the Proteus Project until he located Dr. Snyder. He then headed out himself, only to encounter Major Avery striding up the corridor.

"Sir, I have to say, the kid is begging for discipline. Do you know he just laid right out of *class*?" Avery fumed.

"Yes. I sent Dr. Travers to talk to him."

"I see," Avery said, lip curled up. "Then, may I report for monitor duty, sir."

"No."

"Beg pardon?" Avery was startled.

"I said 'no.' I'll do the monitoring for the time being, Major. Why don't you head for your quarters and *take a nap*."

"Sir." Avery's cheeks burned red. But, he saluted crisply and turned away.

Will sliced into his cabin and slammed the door. Leaping a couple of feet from the foot of the bed, he punched the air in a roundhouse uppercut. *"That schmuck!"* he snarled. He was surprised when he saw a pillow that had been merely lying there, jump up and develop a deep furrow. But how? That pillow was a good seven feet away.

He had no further time to ponder what he'd seen—or what he *thought* he'd seen—for he heard a light rap at his door. Catching a breath, he opened the door to admit Pam Travers. Sure, he figured, Avery had gone whining to Gentry, and the general had dispatched the "headshrinker" to come straighten him out.

"What do you know," he intoned, flatly, turning back into the room.

"Well. I notice you're not glad to see me."

"Should I be?" Will shrugged. "You're just the General's cop, aren't you?"

So he was already associating her with Gentry. Travers knew that Will's new role, whatever it was to be, would require a "new" cuing system with all the discordant, abnormal motivators excised from his memories. But, in his case, these would be numerous and indelible.

What, looking about the room for clues, would have to fade from Will's life, and what might provide a key to foreground his future? He needed both a positive goal to strive toward, and negative reinforcement against recalling any aspect of this life as it actually had been. Where to begin?

"Will, are you familiar with the notion of, 'reaching a turning point' in your life?"

"Yeah, I guess," Will muttered.

"Do you think." asked Travers, "that you've ever *had* a turning point in your life? A time when things might have gone one way, but you knew they were going another way? And you realized at the time that things would—never be the same again?"

"Look, I don't wanna go over and over what happened the other day—"

"Then let's don't. I mean, at any *other* time in your life, okay? Can you think of one for me?"

Will grew introspective for a few seconds, then said, "Yeah, maybe so."

"What was that?"

"Okay, there was this *one time*, see, when we had *visitors* to this place. Other generals, like the old man. They were all dressed in uniforms with lots of medals and ribbons. And a bunch of guys in black suits were with them, too. They never said much."

"And these people had come—to see you?" Travers asked.

"Figure. Dr. Snyder and General Gentry were all over me before they came. Gave me a big-time haircut, and kept making sure I stood up real straight, and all that. They were real fussy about it, like I figure a real kid's parents act like when they get their high school picture made or something, you know?"

"So, did you interact with them?"

"Like a performing flea. I had to do, like, everything while they were here. Which was about a week, I think."

"Everything? What do you mean?"

"You know—don't you? The whole chamber of horrors," Will grimaced. "I showed 'em my martial arts—and, oh, yeah, my wonderful attitude. Big smiles, that was supposed to be important.

"I fought Mac in the gym for them.—to prove Mac had done a good job with me. I wanted him to look good. So, I made my moves. Took my bows. I could tell they enjoyed that part, anyway."

"The fighting?"

"Yeah. Then, there was the rest—all the stuff in the lab."

"Meaning—?"

"The stuff they *always* did to me. To see how I was coming along. They told you about the kind of things I'm talking about—didn't they? How they tested me and all?"

"They showed me—some files. But, I haven't heard it from you," Travers said. "What was it like for *you*, Will?"

"You've seen the tank in there, right? I spent most of the rest of the week in there. They drowned me, first. As usual, my body took in a gulp of air and I went into, like, a coma. They say my heart rate slows almost to a stop when they do that. I could last about a week like that if I had to, using hardly any oxygen. Then, they went a step further and froze the water."

"They *froze* it?"

"Froze it. They started letting it thaw after that, but it took hours both ways."

"You actually lived through that."

"For three days, end to end. Right after that, they gave me one of their super sunburn jobs with ultraviolet lights. And, I sweated this, like, jelly. I could hear Snyder and Haas speaking to the visitors. They had a microphone stand, uh, what do you call 'em? A—"

"Podium?" Travers suggested.

"A podium, yeah," Will continued. "Anyway, I heard 'em tell all those generals that weird sweat saved my life, that a normal human body can't make that kind of secretion—whatever it was. I know I turned a crusty black the next day. And the day after that, the stuff started flaking off. I had this *pink* skin in patches. It looked so odd on me when I looked in the mirror. I was some black and pink checkerboard color. Then the skin healed and turned normal again. Blue, that is."

Despite Will's matter-of-fact demeanor in discussing these ordeals, Travers felt shaken. She told herself she should have been better prepared to hear about these matters first-hand from Will. The descriptions of the "environmental tests" she had read were depicted in a clinically objective fashion that gave little hint of the tests' true severity. She felt her first pangs of pity for this strange young man.

"What happened after all this—that awful week?" Travers asked.

"Nothing. They went away. Nobody ever brought it up again."

The occasion he was describing, Travers surmised, had most likely been a visit from The Joint Chiefs of Staff of the US Armed Forces. It fit the state of affairs here, she thought. Like Roman emperors of old, they had turned thumbs down on the project. But, why had it not, then, been "executed?" How could it have reached the state in which she found it, a stasis of sorts, limping in bare self-maintenance, deprived of purpose? She had an eerie feeling this secret world she had been drawn into might contain secrets within secrets—that perhaps there was knowledge even more dangerous to be found here than knowing of Will's existence.

"Thank you, Will," she said, quietly.

14.

Gentry ushered Snyder into his office and locked the door behind them. This was the one room where he had taken pains to retain exclusive access and prohibit video cameras or microphones. He always swept the place on each visit to the facility, and was certain now that it was a private haven for the frank conversation he now had to have with his lead scientist.

"Don't tell me I'm here for old time's sake, Morgan?" Snyder said, a bit playfully, folding her arms and leaning back against the locked door.

"These days," Gentry said, without looking at her. "Only in my dreams, darlin'."

Snyder cleared her throat, a bit crestfallen. Old ashes yield no warmth when stirred. Gentry crossed the room and unlocked a filing cabinet.

"What do you have, then?" she asked.

Gentry stroked his chin, grimly. "I reviewed the tapes. I know for sure only Avery and McIntire were in the complex."

"And Will's room?"

"It looked like nobody came or went the whole day, except Will. I still have to check the damn thing for splices."

"Good idea," Snyder agreed.

"And how about that crud you rooted from the sink?" Gentry asked.

"I haven't had the privacy to check it out, the way Carl's been haunting the lab," she replied. "I'm thinking of doing it overnight. I've been working on your 'camouflage.'"

"Good," Gentry agreed. "Everybody working in their own compartment." He tensed his lips, preparing to utter his next words.

"Gina? There's something I never told you about the gene pool we used to cull the raw material for Will."

Snyder tensed. "What?—"

"Will has—a very special gift."

"Something I don't know about?" Snyder asked.

Gentry spread open the folder he had pulled from the filing cabinet. "Eyewitness accounts from the redneck bar say Will burned a couple of guys—on contact with their skin."

"*Burned* them? How?"

"The Agency had genetic material from some people they call VSPs—. Very Special Persons. They wanted it tested along with all the other proteins you and Haas wove together."

"We did this? Without my knowing?"

"'You did your part. Carl did his part. He inserted their DNA strands. He didn't know what they were, either. But then, he'd usually shut up and do as he was told..."

"Whereas I always had to know 'why,' huh?" Snyder said, hands on hips. "So what the hell are you talking about, Morgan? Who are these 'VSPs?'"

Gentry spread out and opened on his desk, dossiers and photographs of three very dissimilar subjects. One face was that of a severe Chinese man, the next, a somber Brahmin girl, and a third, a jolly-looking Slavic woman. Gentry tapped this last photo.

"Burning human flesh on contact was one of Olga's habits," he said.

"You're kidding. Stuff like that, you're talking about old wive's tales, Morgan," Snyder uttered.

"That's probably what the Joint Chiefs thought when they cut us off, 'Gina," Morgan said, sadly. "The blue skin was enough of a blow for 'em, I'm sure. But I know it didn't help when I couldn't show any evidence that he had any paranormal abilities. I mean, they'd scoured the earth for these people. Once they'd identified a few, and cultivated their DNA, they wanted to prove their traits could be inherited."

"You're actually saying these kinds of people truly exist."

"Yep. They're rare as all get-out, but they're out there. And, you know what? One of 'em's *in here*—Will."

"Show me," Snyder challenged.

"That's why I called you in here."

Suddenly, there was an insistent knock at the door. "General Gentry!" Travers's voice could be heard faintly, calling through the thick door.

"Did you call her, too, Morgan?" Snyder quipped.

"Don't be silly," Gentry remonstrated her as he replaced the folder safely in the file cabinet. As the pounding continued, he crossed to open the door.

"Explain yourself, Lady," Gentry scolded Travers as he swung open the door. "What's the ruckus?"

Travers barged in. She took note of Snyder's presence and halted. Then, she continued. "Tell me the truth about this place."

"What do you mean?" Gentry demanded.

"Proteus. It was shut down, wasn't it? Am I right? On the basis of some— bizarre racial prejudice."

Gentry looked at Travers levelly and sighed. "Smart cookie. It's been all over for a couple of years. Officially, at least."

Snyder spoke up. "But let's think just a minute. Just what would it mean to close this project down, sweetie?"

"It would—mean—" Travers stammered.

Gentry exposed his lower teeth. "It would mean Will is 'put down.' For good, Honey."

"'Put down?'" Travers muttered. It made Will sound like an over-the-hill race horse.

"And, I can tell you this," Gentry continued. "It won't be long 'til the human race goes, too. Maybe fifty, sixty years, unless there's some quick changes coming on the horizon that I don't personally predict. Now, I'd rather our descendants be blue than be nothing at all. Wouldn't you?"

"Well—"

Gentry sighed again. "Okay. I've allowed certain people to believe this project had ceased operations. The details, what happened to Will, they don't want to know. They make the assumption they're comfortable with, they assume I've done what *they* would have done, understand? But since Will broke out of here, there's a good chance they're gonna find out different.

"Next year, President Ash stands for re-election. I don't think he's gonna like it if word about this project gets out."

"You mean," Pam interrupted, "that the President of the United States never even knew about this project?"

"He has no *need* to know. Every President wants their plausible deniability about covert ops of all kinds. We give them that."

"The 'mushroom treatment,'" Travers scoffed.

Gentry shrugged. "Now, we might get lucky. Will's little rampage only ran through some out-of-the-way places. We can count on our friends in the big media to keep a lid on. But everybody and their cousin's got a small press now, and everybody's on the Arpanet, I mean, the Internet, all yakkin' their heads off. I can't be sure I can keep 'em all from noticing. Disinfo's a good tactic, but it doesn't always work."

"Okay," said Travers. "It's just—you're asking me to do the impossible."

"I told you she wasn't up to it," Snyder quipped.

"Just tell me this, Missy," Gentry asked of Travers, gently. "You *will* do what you *can*, won't you? You realize what I'm trying to do, here?"

Travers considered their dilemma carefully, then nodded. "I do."

Ron Brassfield

    She turned to go, knowing that it was up to her to help save Will Monday's life. She prayed, within herself, that it was truly the right thing to do.

15.

In the conference room, Gentry sat opposite McIntire, whose left arm and shoulder were bandaged and resting in a sling. The room commanded a view of the cavernous vehicle access area through its transparent dome.

Gentry tossed a photo onto the tabletop. It was a picture of a crumpled, charred Acura resting amidst debris. McIntire winced at the sight of his ruined car.

"Odd, isn't it, Lieutenant, how this happened? In light of our look-down policy on personal possessions—such as car keys," said Gentry.

"Sir. A policy I've always followed," the Lieutenant replied.

"So, how is it Will Monday not only exited this compound, he drove your car, like a maniac, across state lines? How'd your keys end up on his dresser?"

"None of my doing, Sir. I had no motive and no opportunity. I was training with him in the gym at that very same time."

Gentry nodded. "Mm-hm. Of course, you've served your country on more than a few covert ops. For a man with your skills, it might have been possible to place the keys there in advance, through a diversionary tactic."

"I had no motive. The surveillance recordings should show my whereabouts at all times—if you doubt me, Sir."

"No motive? Isn't it possible you took some pity on the kid? Figured you'd cut him a break?"

"I never believed turning him loose on the world would be doing him a favor. I know that as well as you do, Sir. Which is why I led a recovery mission immediately."

"And I wish to God you hadn't had to, Son," the General grumbled, dropping the inquisitor's demeanor to speak man-to-man. "The commander at Mountain Home had to write some very sad letters because of that mission. I want you to know that I'm checking every source as to who those bastards were you ran into that night. And when I find 'em—But, in the meantime, there's a board of inquiry waiting for you at the base."

"Sir?"

"You are to tell them we had a renegade operative who still eludes us, due to the interference of saboteurs whose identities and motives are unknown."

"What if they give me a lie detector test?"

"Your barrister will object. And if they do it anyway, if you flunk, he'll claim it was due to your wounded condition and your grief over the lost men. That'll be kind of hard to refute for the time being. Your record's to your credit, Lieutenant."

"I—understand, Sir," McIntire replied.

"Dismissed."

Gentry felt his age hanging on him like a clammy shroud as McIntire shuffled out of the conference room. For the life he had lived, the project he had overseen for so much of his life, to crumble was nearly too hard for him to bear.

Major Avery, the man whom Gentry had long entrusted to maintain the Project in his absence, issued his usual crisp salute as he entered. He wore his usual pert smile, almost a smirk, as he doffed his cap and sat at his usual seat across from the General.

"Major, care to account for your activities on the date of Will's impromptu egress from the Project?" Gentry asked, fixing Avery in his level gaze.

Avery bowed his head for a moment, then raised it.

"General, I carried out my duties on that day just as I always do, Sir, and always have—"

"Until the shit hit the fan, at which time you were—" the General interrupted, sternly.

"—asleep at my chair in the monitor room, Sir," Avery cut in with his swift confession. "I admit I was remiss in my duties at that point in time, Sir.

Believing Will to be in the competent hands of the Lieutenant, as so many times before, Sir, I allowed myself to fall asleep."

Gentry was a bit surprised that Avery did not even attempt to excuse his slack behavior.

"And how often, in the general course of things, did you allow yourself to indulge in that little luxury, Major?"

"Occasionally, Sir," Avery replied. "Not often."

"So do you have an explanation as to how the car keys made their way to William's room?" the General demanded, squinting a keen eye at Avery.

"I do not, Sir. The lock box must have been opened by someone while I dozed."

"By McIntire? Who else was in the facility?" Gentry queried.

"I saw only Lt. McIntire and Will Monday on the monitors."

"Ah, yes, the monitors. And the only way to verify that now is on the tapes. The tape of Will's room appeared to have been spliced, with the apparent result that a few minutes are missing from the review," Gentry replied.

"My God," Avery swallowed. "Sir, I feel a terrible guilt over what I allowed to happen," he said, remorsefully. "It's true I let myself be lulled by a routine where nothing ever varied. Be that as it may, I realize I have no excuse. My lapse gave someone the opportunity to sabotage all that we've achieved. I must take full responsibility for Will's escape, Sir, no matter how it actually came about."

"You're sick to death of this duty, aren't you, Major?" Gentry said, drily.

"Sir, it is a little harrowing, in its way. The location is beyond remote. The subject is not very respectful, certainly not grateful for his life, or his special endowments. Our efforts to care for him, and to steer him into proper behavior, have been only partially successful. And, truth to tell, Sir, I miss my wife and children more than I've often let on. However, all in all, I'm still grateful—honored—at the chance to serve under your command."

"All right, all right. Dismissed, Major." Gentry rose, returned Avery's salute, and watched grimly as he left.

Now what? Something stank. But Avery had always been a faithful soldier, carrying out his duties as commanded with the utmost dedication over the years. He accepted his guilt without excuses. Nor had Gentry ever had cause to doubt McIntire, so distinguished in the fires of combat and dangerous covert missions.

Yet, almost certainly, one of these two was a liar and a traitor. Which one, though? Avery did not appear to hold any special fondness for Will, true. Had he hoped that Will would meet an untimely end, and release them all from their bondage to this defunded project?

McIntire, on the other hand, was close to Will. Had he succumbed, in a misguided moment of weakness, to an impulse to set Will free from his hated imprisonment in the complex so he could take his chances in the world, and perhaps, against all odds, find acceptance?

And, whatever the truth about the keys appearing on Will's dresser, Gentry felt certain that the two men who had attacked Will on the road had conspired with either McIntire or Avery. Gentry had assigned investigators to determine the identities of those men, based on Will's and McIntire's descriptions.

This whole matter was far too sensitive to deal with in a formal, military sense. The next move was to allow the men the latitude to reveal their true positions within the scheme of things. Neither officer knew it, but NSA case officers had been assigned to follow their every move, report their every contact in the outer world.

The next morning, in the central, chromium mirrored hall of Project Proteus, Avery knelt, bitterly knotting tight a duffel bag. McIntire stood beside him, slinging his own bag over his shoulder.

"I can't believe he's kicking me out with you," Avery muttered bitterly.

McIntire looked down upon Avery as if upon a disgusting insect.

"What? You were in charge whenever he was gone. That's called 'responsibility'. When you blow it, you pay."

"When you blew it, five other men paid, Lieutenant," Avery drew himself up and stepped forward, virtually pushing his rank in McIntire's face.

"Well, maybe that's why I'm headed for a brig while you're off to the Pentagon for reassignment," McIntire said, staring coldly. His good hand no longer held his duffel bag, but was a fist bunched up tightly at his side.

"Wouldn't be that way if you hadn't given the kid your car keys," Avery retorted.

McIntire, despite himself, drew back his fist a notch and spoke quietly.

"You know I didn't give him the keys."

Just then, the feuding officers were interrupted by the arrival of Will, running up the corridor and calling out.

"Mac! Where are you going?"

"I have to face a formal board of inquiry at Mountain Home, Will," McIntire replied, wearily.

"Why? What did you do?"

McIntire shook his head, pained at Will's boundless naivety. "You don't just lose helicopters and men with no questions asked."

Will slumped to his knees in grief.

"Oh, no. This is my fault. Mac. I'm so sorry. I killed those men. I hurt *you*. Mac, you've got to believe, I don't know why I did that. Why did I take off that way just because I had those keys? I don't know what I was thinking!" Tears began to stream down Will's face.

McIntire looked away for a moment, struggling for words. Avery, however, was at no loss.

"Aw, are you sorry? You've got nothing. I stand to lose my commission."

McIntire looked at the major again, with renewed contempt.

"You'll get another homestead, Avery."

"How do *you* know?" Avery demanded.

"I know how the world works," McIntire replied, then turned away to stride up the corridor toward the front portal of the Complex.

Avery looked from McIntire's departing back, then down at Will, and snorted. "See what you've done, you spoiled little shit?" With a sneer, he clomped up the corridor in McIntire's wake.

Will grimaced, clutching his head, needing to speak to his only friend in a worse way than ever before.

Exiting the Proteus Complex, McIntire strode to the van where Gentry waited by the driver's door. Avery trudged into the larger cavern, with Will running from behind, past him to catch up with his mentor. McIntire tossed his tote bag into the van.

"Mac. I wish we could talk. Weird things are happening. I—."

"Will!" Gentry barked. "Stand away."

Will could see by the hard look in the General's eyes that this phase of all their lives was over. The two officers were leaving the Complex forever. And Will was staying behind. His face wadded up again as a fresh stream of tears poured forth.

McIntire looked down a second, shook his head. Then, he laid a paternal arm on Will's shoulder, one last time.

"Stay centered, Will. Remember to bend, so you don't break. You'll make it."

With that, McIntire climbed into the van.

"Get back inside the complex, Will," Gentry ordered. "I'll be back in a few hours." Lowering his voice, he added, "It's gonna be all right."

The hint of kindness in the General's voice surprised Will. Ashamed of what he had done, ashamed of his tears as well, Will turned and ran back toward the Proteus Complex.

Atop the Complex, inside the domed conference room, Dr. Haas gazed balefully down on the scene.

The van departed the complex.

16.

Haas's face, along with that of Dr. Snyder, across the table, was lined with contrasts of white light and shadow as the two scientists took in General Gentry's slide show. The click of his remote control sounded as they reviewed the scenes of carnage that had ensued the evening of Will's escape from Proteus.

They viewed scenes of McIntire's dented, charred Acura amidst scattered debris. The shattered remains of a bawdyhouse and helicopters. The bullet-riddled Lincoln of Will's mysterious pursuers.

"Lot of damage done," Gentry mused, looking from the screen to the scientists' faces.

When Gentry clicked again, they saw a photo of the man called "Vee" in maintenance worker overalls, working on a pipe with a heavy wrench, some sort of heavy industrial interior in the background.

"McIntire ID'd this man from the archives," Gentry said, quietly, still watching the doctors' faces. "According to my people, he was a special agent with the CIA. *They* claim he vanished over two years ago. Turns out, he went to work last year in the nuclear plant. Yet, he got out of there in time to intercept Will."

"The nuclear plant? You mean, the one 'upstairs'?" Snyder exclaimed.

"Are you suggesting the CIA wants to hijack our program, General?" Haas queried.

"We don't know," Gentry replied. "*Yet.* But, based on McIntire's description, we're looking for *this* man..."

Gentry clicked. On screen appeared the face of Jacob Threll.

"Look familiar? Either of you?"

Haas and Snyder shared a look before shaking their heads for the General.

"Should he?" Snyder asked.

"Not likely, but possible. He was a neurosurgeon. Also vanished a couple of years ago. We believe he contracted with the CIA, too. Maybe espionage got into his blood. Anyway, I have people looking for them both, as of today. And we will find them."

Gentry switched off his slide show and turned on the light in the conference room, making the two scientists squint and blink.

He went on, "I've taken the precaution of off-loading all data from this facility to a remote mainframe."

"What?" blurted Haas.

"For now, I think it's safer elsewhere."

"Where could that possibly be?" Haas asked.

"That's for me to know," Gentry replied. "Anyway, I just wanted you two to realize a little of what's been going on. Somebody out there knows what we had here. And they want it for themselves. Now, why don't we get some sack time."

Gentry, Snyder, and Haas exited the Conference Room.

"I'll have your young lady's opiate derivative ready by morning," Haas informed Gentry, looking sidelong at the frowning Snyder. "Good night." He nodded and strode off to his cabin.

"Get some sleep, Carl."

Snyder and Gentry walked the other way, speaking in low tones.

"Morgan, speaking of drugs? I finally got to analyze those food scraps from the kitchen drain. Guess what? They held traces of PCP," whispered Snyder.

"Say what?" Gentry hissed.

"Will had a very special lunch that day, Morgan. I tend to believe him when he says he found McIntire's keys on his dresser. I also think his resistance to impulses was near zero at that moment."

"God damn it, I let a snake eat up the garden."

"Don't beat yourself up too much. We all got lax after all these years."

"Yeah, and now our cupboard's down to a worm in a rotten apple. We've got to move quick." The next day, in the Proteus lab, a spinning centrifuge slowed to a stop. Dr. Haas unclamped a single tube of clear fluid from its grip.

He turned to Pam Travers, displaying the tube between thumb and forefinger.

"I think I've adapted your usual cocktail to work on him. How do you intend to deliver it?" he asked.

"Hm. Does he like sweets?" she pondered.

That afternoon, in Will's cabin, Will munched on his second chocolate brownie.

"Mmm. Y'know, I never had one of these," he said. "They're really good."

"You like it?" Travers asked.

"Oh, yeah," Will said, taking another swig of milk.

Travers knew that his elevated mood was not at all natural, but was an early symptom of the chocolate combined with the drugged cocktail which laced the brownies.

Soon, Travers had will lying back on his sofa, distraught once more even though by now in a deep, hypnotic trance during which she was his guide, just as she had been to so many other prisoners in another setting. Like them, Will was on a memory tour, Travers's way of getting to know his fears and "reaction formations" more thoroughly.

"The light. Can't look at it. Scalding. Sweating like crazy," Will muttered, reliving an incident from nine years before.

On that occasion, a naked, ten-year old Will suffered inside the glass tank in the Proteus lab. Ultraviolet arc lights glared down at him with a merciless intensity. It was the first time he had wished he could die, so as to spare himself the awful duty of living out his unique and thankless life. He huddled into a ball, trying to shield at least his face and hands from the scalding light.

A strange sweat congealed, becoming viscous on Will's flesh. Gradually, he sat up, coated in weird gel, but clearly suffering less.

Across the lab floor, from behind a one-way glass, the General and the scientists who were his progenitors watched, took notes, adjusted the settings of the lights. They were to be always out of sight during these trials they forced Will to endure. Never did the boy have a hint of what their expressions might be as they watched his suffering under their tests, but he always knew they were there, and he always hated them.

"The tank's filling with water," Will said, as the session dragged into its third hour. Travers had heard Will's narration as he relived various ordeals. In his mind, he was now fourteen, panicky, swimming with the surface of the rising water. He caught a deep breath. Then, in his mind, he was submerged. He curled into a fetal ball on the sofa. His breathing seemed to stop.

Travers watched closely for a minute, then two. She moved rapidly to his side, feeling for a pulse, watching her wristwatch. His flesh grew cooler to her touch. She looked at Will in anguish, wondering if she should attempt mouth-to-mouth resuscitation. If Will was merely reliving, under hypnosis, an ordeal which he had once survived in real life, surely he would survive his mind's simulation, wouldn't he? Then, she remembered that no definitive answer to such a question would necessarily apply to a natural human being, and for the first time in her life, she was not even dealing with one.

She was bending, open-mouthed toward Will's face when Regina Snyder burst into the room, startling her.

"Don't do that!" Snyder barked. "Talk him through it."

"What?"

"We were testing a natural reflex we had hoped would kick in. It works in humans in rare cases. We built it into Will."

"The 'swallow reflex?'" Travers guessed, gathering her wits.

"Yes," Snyder replied. "The one that's let some people survive long submersion in icy water."

"So how long was *he* comatose?" Travers demanded.

"Three days."

"And then he rose, huh?" Travers said, shaking her head. Will could not give her any verbal feedback in his current state. Travers had to think what it would have been like, nearly frozen, barely breathing, in a dreamlike state, near death. Snyder stood over her, nervous, impatient. How could she stand there, as though protecting Will during his time of trial, when this time, it was all in his mind? But when it had really happened, she had made it happen to him, mind and body.

And soul?

Travers bent low and began whispering into Will's ears. But she did not speak of where he was then, in the deep, sleeping folds of his mind. She spoke not of the cold ordeal, but of warmth and caring waiting in the here and the now.

"It's Pam, Will. Can you hear me? I'm waiting to see you, Will. I want you to wake up. My arms are warm. I want to hold you. I want to give you comfort. You are not alone, Will. I'm here with you, and I care..."

Snyder's nostrils flared as she strained to hear the words.

17.

A week passed, then two. Travers settled into a numb routine, hearing out Will's hypnotized reminiscences and playing him training tapes on the use of office software. Very routine stuff, very dry. Tapes in mathematics played to Will in his sleep from beneath his pillow. He was to become a cypher, buried deep within the national security apparatus. Skilled, yes, but devoid of strong desires.

That last part was Gentry's demand. It was the one Travers felt least capable of fulfilling. The General planned to find Will a roommate, in other words, a controller who would work with him and control his whereabouts twenty-four hours a day. The plan was to pay Will so little his entire income would be absorbed into the bare necessities of living, so that the bond of dependency would not be broken. The "roommate" would be someone whose very life would be bonded inscrutably to the Agency—Gentry had minions in his agency scouting out the ideal candidate.

Travers could only conjecture as to the mix of rewards and punishments they would use to achieve that end. Meantime, she would apply her expertise from her experience in dealing with the involuntarily confined, to the task of shaping Will's own behavior, and, insofar as possible, his belief system. She had to believe she could accomplish this. It was her way back home.

Despite what Travers knew to be his burning desire for freedom, Will gave them no trouble, none at all. He was spending his days without complaint, manning a computer console, running statistical analysis programs eight hours a day, with only meals and his personality programming sessions to occasionally interrupt the routine.

Travers congratulated herself on the contrast of their smooth sessions with the friction of Will's classes with Avery. Yet beneath it all, she found herself annoyed with herself. She felt the power of Will's ardent sexual attraction. She had caught him staring at her with a star-struck expression on his face—and he had blushed a deeper azure color when she noticed. Neither spoke of the matter. But Travers realized Will was probably so compliant only because he wanted his freedom, and could only achieve it through compliance with her. And she realized that he simply wanted her. And she was exploiting his desire.

She also felt it ironic that, by her mere presence there, working with this semi-human specimen who hoped to find conjugal bliss with her, that she was now reduced to being a prisoner who hoped merely to escape. She put aside such thoughts and concentrated on weaving Will's new mental orientation as much as she could.

It was not easy. General Gentry obviously felt pressured. He passed the feeling along to her in turn.

At length, there was another Proteus gathering in the conference room. Gentry, Haas, and Travers watched as Snyder applied a Caucasian make-up compound to Will's face, then applied a contact lens to one of Will's eyes. They nodded their approval when she stepped back to reveal the "new Will."

Will studied his face in a hand held mirror Snyder handed him, one eye with the cat's pupil, one eye human. When Snyder applied the second contact lens, Will appeared fully human. He blinked, and grinned widely. Gentry, Snyder, Travers, and Haas applauded.

"Looking good, Will, very good," enthused Gentry. "Now, go run your office tutorial awhile."

Will exited, smiling at the nods of approval he got from Gentry and Snyder. Travers avoided making eye contact Will sought as he left the room.

"Dr. Travers. Progress?" Gentry demanded, after Will was gone.

Travers sighed. "Since the Nuremberg Accords, General?"

"Don't go all noble on me now, Doctor," Gentry snarled. "He's not a POW, he's not a disenfranchised citizen, he's—" Gentry stopped himself.

"'Not even human'?" Travers replied. "Or, were you going to say something else?"

"I'm asking you what I can expect. We can make him look the part. How long until he's living and breathing the part? How long until he's believing it?"

Travers took a deep breath. "You want the truth? From what I've seen so far, I doubt I could even discover all his traumas in a year. If you want me to assure you he'll act stable in a new and different environment, well, I can't."

"We don't have a God-damned year, Doctor," Gentry erupted. "There must be some way to expedite the process. Hell, in Korea, the Chinese took red-blooded American boys and had them reciting anti-American propaganda inside of twenty-four hours. These kids had grown up in your Norman Rockwell neighborhoods, some of them had *enlisted*, for God's sakes. Even after they came back home, they kept on talking like Mao's own little parrots. Now, surely you can do something with Will. Hell, he's never had any friends, never known his—" Gentry stopped himself again.

"I'm not Chinese, General," Travers said, levelly. "I didn't work with your CIA in MK-Ultra, either. Yes, I know something about that. The drugs, the hypnosis, the shocks, the lobotomies. But, I never set out to destroy anybody's mind. I'm not a torturer. I want to be a healer."

Once outside the conference room, Will had realized that, with both Avery and McIntire gone, the monitor room would be unoccupied. Curiosity working on his mind, Will decided he would rather listen to what the remainder of the Proteus insiders were saying about him rather than study the workings of some dull office software as Gentry had instructed him to do. So, he trotted down the hall and gained easy access to the room.

Once inside, he realized that not only was there a bank of monitors displaying virtually every room, but a stainless steel vault door with a punch-key set at the rear of the room. He thought about the positioning of the room within the maze, the anterior view of Proteus from the cavern he had glimpsed on occasion, and realized there was a chance this door connected with the elongated cylinder which ran from the rear of Proteus up into the cavern ceiling.

It might be a way out.

Will tried punching the numbers at random and tested the door's heavy, unyielding steel hasp.

Will turned to the bank of screens, found the one displaying the conference room with Gentry, Haas, Travers, and Snyder chatting. He located the audio slider for that monitor and turned it up to audible levels before returning to his safe-cracker task with the vault door. He tried to think of possible code-words as he pressed the alphanumeric buttons on the door's panel.

Blue Monday

At that same moment, an Army personnel carrier truck pulled up to the gatehouse at the entrance to the nuclear plant outside. The driver of the carrier presented papers to the puzzled gatekeeper with papers.

"Orders from the Secretary of Energy?" the guard raised his hat and scratched his head.

"And the secretary of the interior, plus the Attorney General, for good measure," the driver responded with a steely gaze. The guard saw that he and the passenger in the front seat bore the special lightning insignia of Special Forces troops. Something *very* odd was up.

"You gonna raise this gate, or do we have to truck on through?" The driver demanded.

The guard raised the gate and the personnel carrier trucked on through. It drove to the off-limits section at the rear of the gate. The special door rose as it drew near, closed once it had been swallowed in the maw of the forbidden zone. Inside, the special inner blast door rose, the carrier passing through it as well, and down the ramp into the cavern containing Project Proteus.

Inside the monitor room, Will listened in on the conference where his fate was being discussed as he continued trying the door.

Travers was saying, "I'd suggest a false front scenario in a rural setting, maybe an isolated farm in Nebraska or something. Gradually, in five, ten years, he might relocate, if his acceptable behavior has become routine by then."

"*Ten years*?!" Will ran over to the monitor as though to double-check what he had heard. What he saw on adjacent screens stopped him cold.

The monitor which displayed the entrance to the Proteus complex, combat-ready Green Beret soldiers, sporting grenades on their jackets and carrying M-16 rifles crept stealthily within, fanning out in pairs to enter rooms as they covered the mirrored corridors.

As he watched in open-mouthed amazement, two armed Green Berets swivelled into the Conference Room. Wielding their rifles, they covered the nonplused Gentry, Snyder, Haas, and Travers.

"No!" Will cried out. He recognized the smirking face of the figure who swaggered in behind them. The sight immediately snapped this dizzying, unprecedented event into a new perspective.

In the wake of the Green Berets, Eugene Avery strolled triumphantly into the conference room.

"What the hell's going on?" Gentry demanded.

"We're halting a conspiracy," Avery announced, suavely. "Protecting National Security secrets from unauthorized personnel." The obeisant countenance of this officer Gentry had known for years was now replaced by a mien of indisputable authority.

"You mean her?" Gentry demanded, pointing to Travers. "Good Christ, Avery, what the hell are you doing? You men stand down," Gentry commanded the Special Forces operatives. The firm fighting men did not budge. "I said, stand down!"

"Sorry, Sir," one of the men spoke. "We have orders from the top. We take orders only from the Major on this mission."

"How'd you swing this, Avery?" Gentry demanded. I had you watched all the time."

Avery grinned at Travers, leaving no doubt that her had referred to her presence within the Complex as his pretext for leading this invasion. He advanced to the communications control module in the center of the conference table and punched a series of numbers.

"Your men got some other orders, General. From further up the food chain."

The scowling countenance of the publicly self-styled "compassionate" President Ash appeared on the large monitor screen. Avery saluted, then announced to the room, "Ladies and gentlemen, the President of the United States."

"So, that's it," growled Gentry. "You ran straight to Ash." He slapped his own forehead in dismay.

Avery spoke to the monitor screen. "Mr. President. Proteus facility secured."

"Good work, Major," I commend you and Special Forces on your smooth operation."

Ash held up a tabloid newspaper. On the page one photo, Will slept on a hospital cot while a deputy scrubbed his arm. Headline: SHERIFF BAGS BLUE BOY IN BIG BLAST!

Gentry felt his heart sink through the floor.

"Does this—creature—look familiar to you, General?" asked Ash, smoothly.

Stifling his anger, Gentry replied, "That the new model 'Bigfoot,' Sir?"

"Very flip," Ash replied. "You know, I have children of my own, General. And even though you don't have a real family of your own, I understand your desire to protect your young—clone. If he had a soul, I'm sure it'd go to heaven." There was a special twinkle in the President's eye that ran a chill up Gentry's spine.

"Is that what you want, Sir?" he asked tersely.

"I know it's not *your* fault. He couldn't resist calling attention to himself when he had a chance. But this could look awfully bad for the Ash Administration. I can't be pro-life *and* pro-*clone*, can I? You see what I mean, don't you?"

"These personnel maintained air-tight secrecy for many years, Sir," Gentry suggested to the figure on the monitor, with a dark glance at Avery, the obvious exception.

"Now, I know your project began in different times, under a different Administration. Yet, you realize that your Project Proteus suffered a major breach only recently," Ash continued, with his trademark, thick-headed sanctimony. "I understand this led you to violate security protocols, looking for a 'quick fix.' Well, sir, that is unacceptable."

"The treachery clearly came from within Federal government circles, Sir. That was why I reached outside for the skills I needed. And I had to act with dispatch."

"Nevertheless, as the responsible official in this matter, I must request that you resign your commission immediately. But, before I accept your resignation,

I must lay upon you a heavy charge, General—as the Lord placed upon Abraham. 'Behold the fire, and the wood...'"

"'...But where is the lamb for a burnt offering?'"

"Morgan!" Snyder called out. Gentry flinched slightly, but maintained his grim salute to his Commander-in-Chief.

In the monitor room, Will had been punching buttons on the console frantically, with no better luck than before. He turned to look at the screens again. He realized full well who was the lamb to whom they referred.

"I'm glad you're not blind to your duty," Ash was saying. "Carry on."

18.

Will Monday stood, alone and desperate, watching the monitor bank as the Green Beret troops under Avery's command searched the Complex room-by-room. Looking anxiously over the console, Will spotted switches on the monitor complex marked "LOCK". He started flipping them as Green Beret troops entered his own cabin space. The pneumatic doors to the room clicked tightly shut. The same thing happened in rooms up and down the corridors, as pairs of Green Berets cautiously entered rooms, only to find themselves locked within.

Muffled gunfire came from within the rooms, denting steel doors, then quickly subsiding amid the zinging sounds of ricocheting bullets within the cabins. Will saw, from his vantage point, that some soldiers sustained wounds from their own gunfire.

"Sorry, dudes, looks like it's you or me," he muttered. Then, he took off in a run, into the corridor.

In the conference room, the sounds of muffled gunfire from the adjacent rooms visibly rattled Snyder, Gentry, and Travers, who surveyed each other with a fear approaching panic. Dr. Haas slowly shook his head.

Avery remained smug, but feigned sympathy. "Sorry it had to come down to this, General."

"It didn't have to, you smarmy bastard," Gentry burst out. "It was you all along, wasn't it?"

Avery shrugged, his head slightly cocked, admitting nothing and everything.

"Sergeant—the girl," he said, waving a casual hand toward Travers. She shuddered.

The Beret sergeant dispatched by Avery turned Travers toward the conference table, made her lay her palms down, and patted her down with his rough hands.

"She's got nothing, Major," he announced.

"You know what to do," Avery said, cocking his head back toward the door. "She has no family. I checked," Avery went on. "It'll be all right." Travers looked at Avery with horror in her eyes, the meaning of his words sinking in. The beefy hand of the Beret sergeant closed around her bicep.

"No," came a firm, masculine voice from the doorway. Avery turned toward the sound, and paused, startled at the sight of Will standing there—*as a white kid!?*

Will sprang into the room, simultaneously uncoiling a knife hand blow into the other Beret's throat and stomping his instep. The Beret, choked, tried to swing his M-16 upward. Will chopped his forearm, numbing it. The soldier dropped his rifle, and Will's lashing backfist put him down on the cold, steel floor.

"What's going on there, Major? Major?" President Ash demanded. His barking voice quickly became an indistinguishable background noise to the events in the room.

The Beret Sergeant released Travers, and pulled his pistol to fire on Will.

Will dove. A bullet pierced the wall where he stood.

Travers's fist belted the Beret Sergeant in the jaw while his attention was on Will. The Beret Sergeant's elbow backlashed across her face. She collapsed in a heap.

"Major? Major! You kill them all, you hear me?!" Ash's screaming voice rasped across the room.

Avery drew his sidearm, only to cry out as Gentry grabbed and twisted the Major's hand down, painfully, making him drop the pistol. Snyder's face lit up at his bold, manly action. The geneticist, acting quickly, plucked up the pistol from the floor. With trembling hand but iron resolve, she pointed it at Avery. The Major stopped resisting Gentry and simply stood, fuming.

Gentry took the pistol from Snyder and calmly blasted the communications console. The furious, babbling visage of President Ash disappeared from the screen in a shower of sparks and smoke.

Meanwhile, the Beret Sergeant went down, as Will's whipping foot lashed his knee. Will had rapidly rolled across the floor under the conference table. He grabbed the M-16 barrel when the Sergeant fell, thrusting it away from his own body as it pumped bullets into the lower end of the wall. The gunfire sent Haas high-stepping out the door.

Will and the Beret Sergeant grappled with their free hands, Gentry and Snyder watching, unsure how to help.

The Beret Sergeant, stronger than Will, was gaining leverage in their wrestling match. Yet, suddenly, he cried out in pain and dismay. He was finding he could not keep a grip on Will. The boy was blazing hot to the touch. Will grinned. This time he was feeling it, controlling the energies unleashed by his hybrid body under stress.

The sergeant was aghast as Will's true appearance emerged. His makeup melted off, dropping in little cake-like pats from his perspiring face. Steam rose from his body as he snatched the grenade from the nonplused Beret Sergeant's chest.

Make-up running down his face in streaks, the savage-looking Will pulled the pin out with his teeth. "Don't make me let go," Will warned the soldier through gritted teeth.

The Beret sergeant swallowed hard and relented. Will took the M-16 and stood, laying the rifle on the conference table. He re-inserted the pin into the grenade, hooked it onto his jacket pocket.

Gentry and Snyder stood in awe. Gentry's face broke out in a proud grin.

Will knelt beside Travers. He reached out and—almost—stroked her hair. Thinking better of it, he stood up and gingerly tested his own touch against himself, the fingertips of one hand to the backs of the other. Half-satisfied that he was safe to touch, he knelt again and gentry nudged Travers's shoulder.

"You okay?" he said.

Travers stirred, rubbing the bridge of her nose. "I think so. You?"

"Yeah..." He paused, gazing at her adoringly for long seconds.

For Travers, Will stood above her at that moment like a near-divine figure as the room spun around in her dazed senses. He was a terrible mess, and yet... whatever he must be feeling—gratitude?—a crush, perhaps?—she liked the way he was looking at her. It was the first time she had liked anything since entering Proteus.

"Listen, we better get going," he said. As she accepted his hand and stood up, the room slowly stopped spinning.

Inside Will's cabin space, two trapped Berets were taking a calculated gamble on making their escape. They had laid two live hand grenades at the steel door and taken cover behind the immovable, heavy steel chest of drawers and bed. Scrambling, they assumed tightly crouched positions, hands covering their ears.

Two seconds later, the explosion was heard in the conference room, where the floor shuddered beneath the feet of the Proteus crew. Gentry rushed to the door and peered into the corridor.

The steel door to Will's cabin ruptured, bent outward by the force of the explosion. An arm stuck through the opening, then pulled back in. With a loud report, the door trembled under a violent blow from within the room.

The tactic apparently caught on among the other trapped Berets. Another door up the corridor likewise buckled under an explosion. Battering sounds followed, resounding now from two of the Proteus cabins.

Quickly assessing the situation, Gentry hissed at Will. "You've got seconds. Make 'em count, boy."

Will looked in a sudden new light at the military man he had feared and despised over the course of his life.

"You better not," said Avery, with a cock of his head. "I'm telling you, you'll only make it worse for yourself."

"How?" Will shot a look of pure contempt at his former headmaster before turning his attention to his new mentor. "Come on," he implored Travers.

"Maybe they just want information," she said, tremulously. She had regained her senses thoroughly enough for fear to take over.

Will brandished the M-16 he had wrested from the Beret Sergeant.

"Think so? I don't."

Travers hesitated, then ran to the door with Will.

Will paused there take one last look at Gentry, Snyder, and Avery. "Thanks," he muttered to Gentry. He nodded at Snyder, who broke a sob, to his surprise. Embarrassed, he turned his gaze to Avery. "We better never meet again." Then, he pulled Travers along with him into the corridors of the complex.

"Go," Gentry whispered to the empty space they left behind.

Avery also whispered. "See you soon, kid."

At the Proteus entrance, a tense soldier stood guard, on high alert due to the explosive reports from inside. He jerked as he saw Will's head peek around the corner. He fired at the sight, a split-second too late, as the head ducked back behind the entranceway.

A blue hand tossed out a hand grenade which wobbled lazily along the ground outside the entrance. The alarmed Beret desperately kicked the grenade away, even as he caught a glimpse up close and realized the pin was still inserted. He whirled, only to have Will jump-kick the rifle from his hands.

The Beret pulled his knife, ready by the time Will was poised to close on him. But before either combatant could make a move, the soldier stopped cold as he felt the barrel of an M-16 poke him in the back. Will smiled at Travers, who wielded the cold steel. Then, he dispatched the Beret with a hammer fist to the bridge of the nose.

"Good teamwork, *doctor*," chanted Will.

"Watch this," she replied, then proceeded to shoot out a tire on each of the parked cars outside the complex. Will paused a second, impressed, then climbed in the Army truck's driver's seat. He revved up the engine as Travers rounded the truck and climbed in the passenger side. With a lurch, they were off for the rising blast door, and the second time Will would breach the barrier that had always kept him from the outside world.

This time, he reflected, would probably be his last. He glanced at the intrepid young female on the seat beside him, and saw the same recognition of doom on her face.

Ron Brassfield

From behind the nuclear plant, the Army truck sped, smashing at top speed through the exit gate, which had been bound with ropes as a temporary repair. The guard stepped outside his booth, shaking his head in utter confusion.

19.

"Man!" exclaimed Will, at the wheel of the fleeing troop transport truck. "I wish Mac could've seen how I took those guys down."

A tingle of mortal panic ran through Travers' body. She knew Will was only trying to bolster his own morale. Yet, his naive enthusiasm, in the midst of this dire situation, sounded so stupid that she wanted to hit him.

"Sure. Now there'll be thousands of police and FBI agents looking for us. We ought to be fine. Lord, what am I doing here?" She started to open the door, but thought better of it.

"Where's a big highway from here?" frowned Will. "We need to get up some speed."

"What are you talking about? Find a back road—a dirt road, if you can. We don't need to be seen. And we've definitely got to hide this truck."

Will pondered. "You're right." After a moment of intent silence, he asked her, "Do you know how—what do they call it?—how to *hot-wire* a car?"

"Certainly not! Do you? Never mind. We will *not* steal a *car*!" Travers squirmed with discomfort, struggling to master her growing sense of panic. Then, she realized, "Oh, my God. I've got no money, not even a credit card on me."

"We need wheels, you know," Will rolled his eyes at her.

"We need a lot of things. But, I'm not a criminal. Do you know the penalty for grand theft auto?"

"No. But, if it's not the death penalty, we'll come out ahead."

Several miles away, inside a boarded-up ruin of a house with a barn beside it, the front room was jarringly out of place. It was outfitted more like a cross between a combat planning center and a surgical operating room.

"Vee" sat motionless before a monitor screen, eerily lit from beneath by its phosphor glow. He snapped his head to attention when a blip appeared on the radar-like screen. The blip appeared to move along the grooves of a topological map.

The screen was replaced by the livid face of President Ash. "Get me Threll right away!" he snapped. Vee saluted, stood, and mutely stood up, departing into the bowels of the dilapidated house. In seconds, Threll hurried to the console, with Vee trailing close behind.

"Threll here."

"Something went wrong. Avery blew it. You better get on this kid's trail *now*. And I mean, you put him down *stone dead* if you have to. We don't want him getting to any populated areas."

"All right, all right," Threll snapped. "We're on it."

Threll tapped keys on the console and the moving blip reappeared on screen. "He's surfaced, all right. Vee, get the portable tracker tablet. We're about to intercept."

Will and Travers had driven over an hour, at Travers' direction taking any turn that led further from main roads. Now, at the side of a gravelly road, on the edge of an evergreen wood, Will placed a rock on the Army truck's accelerator. Travers watched as Will jumped back from the driver's door, allowing the truck to ditch itself in a shallow ravine, amidst roadside trees and foliage.

"A hundred miles down," sighed Travers, looking around, warily. "Guess they didn't call in the locals. C'mon."

Will, awed by her, by all of it, took his first tentative steps toward raw nature, as he strode behind Travers into the woods.

At the same moment, at Mountain Home Air Base, the silence of the brig's dim interior in the late afternoon was broken by the clacking of boots on the concrete floor. The clink of keys turning in the cell door caused Lt. George McIntire, seated on the cell bunk, to raise his bowed head. Avery nodded to the turnkey and stepped inside the cell.

"So, you took command of the base?" he asked Avery, in mock greeting.

"Watch the lip, funny man" Avery warned the Lieutenant. "It so happens I can get you out of here."

"How's that?" McIntire asked.

"I'm working under a special Executive Order from the President himself. And I've got a *mission* for *you*," Avery said, obviously relishing his power.

"Oh? What's the mission?"

"Apprehend Will Monday."

Avery barked a curt laugh. "Ha! You've gotta be kiddin'. That's what put me *in* here."

"Well, he's loose again," Avery snapped. "So, you have a chance to redeem yourself. Remember, you'll be acting under the President's orders. And under mine."

McIntire suddenly realized what had happened in the days since he had reported in to Mountain Home's command. "You ran to Ash and spilled everything, didn't you?"

"You don't need to know. What's important to you is to play ball. You do as I say, you miss this hearing. Don't—and things might get a lot uglier for you."

"You know you don't need me to find him," shrugged McIntire. "Not with his locator chip. And, unless I miss my guess, you've got some men to boss around already, unless everything you just told me is b.s."

"I'm on the level," Avery said. "You taught the punk all his moves. And you're big buddies, right? You might even talk him into giving up. That'd be a lot better than the alternatives are shaping up. Only thing is, I need your answer right now. 'Cause we're movin' out in five, with you or without you."

McIntire stared at Avery with a face of stone.

"Oh, well. Can't say I didn't try to cut you a break. You *and* the kid. Doubt he'll surrender to me..." Avery turned and signaled the turnkey to unlock the cell.

"All right," snarled McIntire. "I'll do it. I'll go with you."

Avery looked at the Lieutenant again.

"Good," he said.

20.

In the deepening shadows of a forest ravine, Travers plucked berries from a bush, dividing them between Will and herself. Her arms had sprouted goose bumps, and she realized she was woefully underdressed for the chill of the night soon to fall.

"You sure these aren't poison?" Will queried as Travers funneled a handful of berries into her mouth.

"Let's find out," Travers replied sarcastically.

"I take one jump in my life, and everything's ass out," Will muttered glumly, before chewing his own handful of berries.

"Self-pity—very constructive," Travers replied. "Help me gather some sticks." She bent to scour the forest floor for any little bits of wood that might make good kindling.

"You want to build a fire? They'll see it from the air."

"In Scouts they taught us how to not freeze, so unless you have a better idea?" she said, continuing to gather sticks.

"We could, y'know, huddle together for warmth," Will offered.

Travers stood up and glared. "Oh, there's an idea, straight from the goodness of your heart, right? I'll put it on my to-do list, right after, 'jump off a cliff'."

Will, pride stung, bent to search for sticks on the forest floor.

The pair did not realize they were, at that moment, framed in cross-hairs, as seen through two malevolent sets of eyes.

Vee watched from his crouched position behind a thick tree, above them in the ravine. He wore a dark, leathery outfit with weapons strapped and holstered all about his body. His massive form bristled with gear in a utility belt, and in pouches down his pant legs. The cross-hair through which Pam and Will were being observed marked the center of his glassy right eye.

Threll, his own right eye covered by a lens attachment to his headset, saw an identical view. For he, personally, had modified special agent Kent Morris into a near-cyborg with a broadcast camera for an eye.

Threll spoke into he headset mic, "Vee. Start laying the traps."

At the dusky forest edge, Green Berets were spilling from a troop transport. They gathered around the truck Will ditched. McIntire emerged and stepped to the fore. He carried a portable, battery-powered tracking tablet which displayed a pulsating locator blip. Avery stepped up beside him to read the screen.

"Target Blue about 1.8 kilometers southeast of our position," he said. "Take the point, McIntire."

McIntire, with a resentful glance at Avery, motioned for the Berets to proceed. They followed him, stealing into the deepening, dusky woods.

Concealed within the ravine, Vee tapped a thin, metallic bow into a tree trunk at ankle level. Razor wire led from the end of it to similar bows in adjacent trees. Vee pulled back on a lever to tighten the wire, then laid brush over the inconspicuous device. He stole toward the next sturdy tree, unreeling more of the nearly-invisible wire.

Down in the pocket of the ravine, Travers tried, in vain, to get a spark going by rubbing two sticks together over a construction of sticks and stones.

As they drew obviously near the blip on the screen, McIntire waved on the Berets. Vee, having just finished his task, observed them, silent and still as a stone behind a tree slightly above their location. He and Threll saw Avery lag slightly behind McIntire, keeping a close watch on him.

Below them, unaware of the danger, Will, clutching a stick, considered Travers and his surroundings.

"Well, here's everything I wanted. But nothing's like I wanted it. Look—" he told Pam, "I'm stepping off. You're better off without me. Good luck."

Will stalked off a few steps.

"You'll regret it," Travers replied, mildly.

Will stalked back to confront her.

"What?"

"You're a child. You won't last ten minutes, alone, in the real world."

Will clutched the stick he held tightly. Wisps of smoke began to lightly waft from its surface..

"Yes, I will. I can sneak—fight—"

"Stop a bullet," Travers added, laconically.

At that, the stick Will held burst into flame.

"Yeo*owww*!" Will flung the stick from his hand. It landed in a bed of dried pine needles nearby. Will and Pam looked from the flame to one another in stupefied amazement.

Up slope, the Berets turned their heads toward the sound and saw the flicker of flame down in the ravine.

"All right, I'll go first," McIntire began, but was cut off by an urgent command from Avery.

"There's your target. Verify, then terminate. With extreme prejudice."

The Berets charged down hill, toward the dark figures and the growing flame. McIntire whirled to face Avery, only to see the grinning major had his sidearm trained on him.

Will and Travers were alerted by the sound of Berets stampeding down the slope. He grabbed her wrist, prepared to make a desperate run.

Before they took two steps, they witnessed the gruesome spectacle of a charging Beret who seemed to trip, uttering a deathly scream. He had sprung the trap laid by Vee. The Special Forces soldier fell headlong forward.

In the next instant, it was clear that he was instantly severed at the knees.

Will yanked Pam to a sudden stop. A false step could mean sudden death.

It was too late for Avery's charging men, however. One rapid-fire report followed another as hidden hasps unlatched on the slope. Seconds ticked by in slow motion as the rest of the platoon, in rapid succession, suffered agonizing dismemberments. The bounding razor wire laid by Vee caught glints of the fading light as it leapt from the ground and flailed about to and fro, slicing human flesh with a hideous, springlike sound. Bloody bits of soldiers, uniforms, rifles, and helmets flew through the air.

Avery was distracted for just an instant by the screams. That was long enough for McIntire to kick the pistol from his grasp. Avery's smug expression yielded to panic in an instant. McIntire dispatched him shortly with a left jab to the solar plexus and a right cross to the jaw. Then, he faded rapidly to cover, awaiting the appearance of whatever unknown factor had taken out Avery's platoon in such a hideous, treacherous fashion.

McIntire saw Vee emerge from cover. The silent brute stalked among the Green Beret's bodies with a TEC-9, shooting any who still cried out, abruptly ending their misery.

"What's happening?" sobbed Travers, frantic for a place to flee, but too scared to move.

"It's that acid hunk who chased me before."

Will fought his own sense of panic. As he did, he felt the same kind of sensation he had felt in his room. He knew by now he held a secret edge that might save them, if he could only make use of it.

He hustled Travers over near a thick tree. Reaching up, he started pulling as though he were reeling something in on a rope. Travers stared at Will as though he had lost his mind. Then she was doubly aghast, as he bodily left the ground by inches, then drifted down. A tree branch bent down in front of her, as if offering her a hand.

"I don't know, either," Will said to her dismayed expression. "Just grab it, okay? Hold on tight." Will commanded.

Travers complied, dazedly.

"Ahhhhhhhh!" As Will relaxed, the branch rose, taking Travers with it.

Will turned to watch Vee carefully locate, then snip the wire with a pair of cutters from a leg holster.

McIntire, from his crouched position, took aim at Vee's head, his M-16 rifle catching a gleam of light from the spreading fire in the ravine.

However, McIntire in turn was being observed by Threll, himself hidden and flanking the action.

"Vee. Evasive action," Threll whispered into his headset mic.

Vee dove and rolled as McIntire's bullets ripped ground in his wake. The muscled figure returned a barrage of fire up the slope with his TEC-9.

McIntire took another slug in the side, and toppled in agony.

Vee grinned and turned toward Will. Will, wary of the growing flames, edged away, one arm behind his back.

Vee pointed his TEC-9 at Will, and motioned him forward.

Will's reaction was to whip forth his concealed arm and hurl a sizable stone at Vee. It flew straight, with amazing force into the brute's chest, causing even him to double over, gasping for breath.

"Come and get me," taunted Will. He sprinted uphill, slowing to look for the razor wire near the fringe of dead Berets. He eased through the gap in the wire which Vee had cut.

"Will!" cried Travers, dangling on her tree limb. Will looked back to see that the flames spreading across the forest floor had reached the tree in which she was perched. To make matters worse, Vee staggered back to his feet, directly between them. With the slightest hesitation, Will started back downslope, only to pause again as he heard his name called from the direction in which he had been headed.

"Will!" This time, it was the familiar voice of George McIntire.

"Mac?!" he called.

McIntire rose unsteadily clutching his latest wound. "Save yourself. I'll stall him."

"No way!?"

"You're too valuable, Will."

Will ignored McIntire's entreaties and dashed down hill, hoping to feint past Vee and get closer to Travers.

McIntire staggered closer to the break in the wire where Will had stood. Then, it was his turn to be startled by the sound of a voice from behind.

"Peekaboo." McIntire spun around.

Threll, still wearing his headset, thrust a whirling bolo from beneath his flowing overcoat. The bolo cords quickly whirled around McIntire, binding his arms and legs tightly. He fell to the ground.

Threll stood over McIntire and aimed a pistol at his head. "Watch this," he crowed. He lowered his headset mic again and spoke.

"Vee. Let him pass."

Vee stood to one side and demurely gestured for Will to proceed to the burning tree. Will stood beneath Travers on the limb, his hands upraised.

"Let go. I'll catch you," he implored, glancing nervously around. Flames had them hemmed in on two sides now. The fire had definitely grown beyond control. Will repeated his tugging motions, lowering the tree limb. The limb bent, Travers clutching it tenaciously.

"Let me hit the ground," she pleaded, looking at Will with a fear that cut him to the quick.

"No. Trust me," he called back. His face was screwed up in an expression of deep concentration. He was very conscious of his breathing, trying to maintain a fine balance between urgency and deliberation. He felt the tension of the mysterious connection he had established with the tree limb tug at his body, all but lifting him from his feet once more.

Threll watched the drama down the hill and smiled coldly.

"Vee. Fire the gel."

Travers let go, reluctantly, and fell, softly, into Will's upraised arms. He held her but a second, then suddenly cast her aside. She shrieked as she hit the ground.

From a tube-like gun which he had strapped to his leg, Vee fired an expanding, gelatinous blob. Will leaped in an effort to avoid its flight, but the taffy-like goop ensnared his legs in mid-air. He fell to the ground and rolled, but the more he struggled, the less he could move his legs. The gel was rapidly hardening into a kind of plastic cocoon.

"What do you think of our 'non-lethal' ordnance, Lieutenant?" gloated Threll. "Or, do you prefer the 'lethal' kind?" He brandished the gun near McIntire's face.

Just then, regaining consciousness, Avery shook his head and rubbed his sore jaw. Seeing Threll standing over McIntire, he staggered to his feet.

McIntire could not help but grimace, although he remained stoically focused on the action below. It was growing harder to discern what was happening to the figures silhouetted amidst the growing sheets of flame.

Will, bracing himself against the side of the tree that was not yet on fire, had struggled to an upright position. Vee plodded forward and pummeled down his defensive arms, clouting him repeatedly. His ham fists quickly reduced Will to apparent unconsciousness.

Threll grinned at the sight.

"You son of a bitch," came Avery's voice from behind him.

"You? What are you doing here?" Threll asked, innocently.

"Working for the president. We were here to take the kid out. But you wiped out my God-damn platoon."

"The president sent us, too. I thought these soldiers were another search party from Gentry."

"No freakin' way!" Avery snarled.

"It's true. All we knew was that you had apparently lost control of the situation. The Monday specimen was above ground again, on our tracker screen. We went incommunicado once we left the station house."

Avery pondered a moment, then nodded grimly, apparently accepting Threll's explanation. He pondered the gory mass of bodies and flames. The stench was growing unbearable.

"I'll—I'll say the kid did this somehow. We've got him, right?"

Threll gestured at McIntire. "And this bothersome peon, as well." He offered his pistol to Avery. "Care to do the honors?"

Avery considered it. Then, he considered the spreading forest fire.

"Let him burn."

Threll considered the option, and smiled. He holstered his pistol. The two conspirators descended the slope.

Vee slung the semi-conscious Will over his shoulder, the goop encasing Will's legs now hardened to a non-sticky plastic wrap.

Threll gritted his teeth and trod forward, carefully, through the gap in the deadly wire. Avery carefully followed, stepping over chunks of dead soldier meat.

Travers was trying to fend off Vee with a burning branch. Threll approached, aiming his pistol at her now.

"Spunky little girl. Drop the tree, and we can all go home."

"Sure," snarled Travers, scared but still defiant. She expected to die at any moment.

"Then, you can join the Lieutenant, and pay the price for—"

Threll broke off as he glanced toward where McIntire lay, and realized they were all now cut off from him. Not only that, they were completely enclosed in a narrowing circle of flames.

"No!"

Threll lunged at the prostrate Will and slapped his face. Will opened his eyes, grimaced and reflexively grabbed Threll by the throat.

Choking, Threll gurgled, "Fool. You've doomed us."

Will loosened his grip, fearful as he realized their plight. Threll brushed his arm away. "If there's anything you can do, do it now!"

"Are you crazy? What can I do?" Will gibbered.

"You *started* this. We saw it. Spontaneous combustion."

"I was *pissed off*," Will said, desperately. "Now, I'm..." the lad was obviously frightened to the point of confusion.

"Vee. The girl."

Without hesitation, Vee astonished the others by grabbing the burning branch Travers held. Showing no sign of pain, he yanked it from her grasp and tossed it aside into the conflagration. He leaped to Travers, clasped her forearm in his blistered palm and hauled her over to Threll.

"Do something, freak!" Avery screamed at Will.

"You get powerful under stress," added Threll. "I've seen you. Get us out of here, or she burns first."

Vee lifted the panicky Travers above his head, prepared to throw her headlong into the blaze.

"Lift me up," Will snapped.

While Threll covered Travers, Vee hauled Will to a standing position as Avery grew ever more frantic. The smoke was thickening around them, the air thinning.

Will extended his arms, held together, hands cupped in a "v". Inhaling deeply, he slowly raised and spread his arms. The others huddled closer to Will, shrinking from the encroaching flames.

Before them, the flames began to whirl apart along a straight path.

"What does it feel like?" Threll asked, excitedly, fascinated as he saw the expression on Will's face drain away, his countenance become a passive mask.

Will, straining to concentrate, replied, "Like—'feelers'—that reach out—and move like I do."

Will spread his upraised arms. A visible gap now wedged apart the flames before them.

Threll could hardly contain his excitement. Travers and Avery both clutched at Vee's massive arms to keep from swooning at the sight, in the murderous heat.

"Hurry. I can't hold this for long!"

Threll grabbed Travers's arm. They ran through the fire gap. Just beyond the perimeter, he whirled and called to Vee. "Bring him!"

Vee hoisted Will off his feet and ran along with Avery through the fire gap, which closed behind them with every step.

"Ow. Ow. Ow. Ow. Ow. Ow," cried Avery, whose feet were burned as he lagged a step behind Vee, toting their mutual savior.

Up the slope, beyond sight or thought of the others, McIntire had finally, painfully loosened himself from the bolo ropes just as the flames crept within a yard of his prone body. He staggered uphill, barely ahead of the flames. He cast a quick backward glance, to see only flames and smoke approaching.

He bent to snag the tracker tablet he had dropped earlier, before the flames could claim it, then entered a staggering, uphill run for his life. With a sudden thought, he tore his dog tags from his neck, turned, and threw them into the blaze.

21.

Backlit by blazes, Threll and Vee conveyed their captives away in brisk strides. Avery pulled off his flaming boots once they were a hundred yards or so from the forest fire. Threll was exhilarated.

"Incredible," he called to Avery. "What did you feed this kid? He's a blue Moses of the flames!"

"I—don't—know," Avery said, lamely, then returned his attention to beating his boots against the ground to douse the licking flames that clung to them.

Threll whipped a small, pneumatic syringe from under his coat, and swiftly injected Will in the upper arm.

"Hey!" Will protested. He squirmed, but lapsed into unconsciousness within seconds.

Travers gasped. What twist would this living nightmare would take next? McIntire had surely perished, and she had the sinking feeling that General Gentry may have met a similar fate.

Threll's firm grasp on her arm resumed as Avery donned his singed boots and they hurried away from the burning forest, to the secluded spot where they were boarded a waiting Cadillac, which Threll drove. Avery followed, taking the wheel of the troop transport that had ferried the slaughtered Special Operatives.

They drove in silence for about forty minutes, each thinking their own brooding thoughts. Who knew what dreams flitted through the mind of Will, or that of the ever-silent Vee?

Finally, they pulled in to the apparently dilapidated farmhouse whence Threll and Vee had launched their abduction. The doors in the rear of the barn swung opened to admit the Cadillac. The riders all climbed out, Vee carrying Will's limp body, and they skulked quickly across a brief span of lawn to the old, broken-down home.

Inside, the home had been semi-restored. Travers caught glimpses of a functional kitchen and bedroom as she was rushed through the house. The front room, however, was outfitted as a combination command center and surgical operating room.

Vee fastened the unconscious Will down on the operating table which dominated half the space. Avery paced the perimeter, fuming, while Threll moved into a corner and proceeded, in a practiced fashion, to don surgical garb.

"Who are you people?" Travers' cry broke the eerie, near-silence.

"Jacob Threll, at your service, and the service of mankind," said the spindly man, with a half-bow. "My assistant, 'Vee.' Major Avery, I believe you've already met."

Travers and Avery shared a spontaneous sneer of mutual contempt.

"You 'service' mankind through killing?" Travers demanded, trying to keep up her nerve.

"Vee handles the killing—and only when necessary," Threll replied casually. Turning to Avery, he added, "I trust you were going to provide us with *tissue samples* following the kill?"

"I always said, I'd get you at least that. I don't see why you want him alive, anyway."

"I think this way will be better. Don't you agree, now that you've seen his unique power? When we stand before the Inner Council of the Consortium, we can have our culture and Will Monday too—as a *brand new man*."

The words sent chills down Travers' spine. "You mean, lobotomized, like your butler, here?"

"Not lobotomized," Threll replied, taking umbrage at the crude term. "*Entrained*. Vee retains his reflexes, all his knowledge of explosives, stealth, and ordnance. He risks his life for me constantly. His higher reasoning centers never question it."

"I've remade men, myself," Travers responded. "But, they still had a choice afterwards. They weren't slaves."

"Let's not kid ourselves. You never had the means to be as thorough as dear uncle Jacob."

Threll proceeded to scrape tiny samples from Will's skin, and place them in a vial. Then, he affixed a large hypodermic needle to a syringe. He plunged the needle into Will's stomach, drew out blood and tissue into his syringe.

Travers watched closely, hoping, but Will showed scant reaction.

Travers blustered on, "You're a geneticist too, then, I take it."

"In my former life, a neurosurgeon. Like you, I nursed a desire for social reform. *Unlike* you, I found the means to realize my goal."

"So you plan to make the world a better place? One zombie at a time?"

"Society is established to tame the heart, and channel the mind. Too often, it fails at both."

"So you choose to overcompensate for society's failings."

"That's your judgement. But the day is coming when all who will not conform to the right will be converted—or eradicated. I want to save them, all that I can. 'Vee' is my first success story, my 'Vindicator.' There'll be many more to come."

"Really? How many neurosurgeons will that take?"

"There are other ways to direct the workings of the frontal cerebral cortex, the hypocampal formation, the Broca's region..."

"The neurological centers that coordinate decision-making with motor skills. I see. You broadcast your information on their frequencies. Around what, seven Herz, right? With hyper-subliminal messages?"

Threll paused, looking at Travers, highly impressed at her obvious grasp of his techniques. "So, you know a thing or two about the brain."

A knock at the door interrupted their conversation. Threll motioned Vee to open. Once he did, none other than Dr. Haas strode inside.

"So, you have them both," he commented. "Good work." Haas seemed more relaxed that Travers had seen him before, almost jaunty as he stepped into the old wreck of a house.

"Indeed," replied Threll. "And I wonder, why didn't you tell me how much *trouble* your freak would be?"

"What? I told you he was a black belt fighter."

"That he is. But, he also *levitates* things. Causes *spontaneous combustion*. He's a freaking *paranormal*, Doctor. Don't tell me you never knew."

"No. I mean... we always knew he had unusual endocrinal functions... and, there were rumors intelligence had captured some people with ESP and such as that... I never believed it. But, if that were true... if their ribosomes were used in our RNA matrix..."

"Whatever! Once he's made docile, there'll be plenty of time to isolate and study his 'spook factor.' Meanwhile, you're just in time to witness the insertion of the first implant."

"Hm. You mean, the second," Haas corrected him.

"Ah, yes, the second," Threll agreed, leaving Travers to wonder what the two crazed doctors meant.

Threll picked up a thin instrument, which appeared to be a hybrid spreader and injection tube. This was confirmed when he triggered its mechanism a couple of times, testing. He then applied it to pull a tiny microchip from a pad of cotton wadding, sucking it up, into the instrument's grasp.

Travers watched with horrified fascination as Threll knelt beside Will and slowly inserted the device deep inside his ear.

"Let me whisper in your ear." His coo sounded at once affectionate and like the rattle of dead leaves stirring in the breeze.

22.

"You did this for money?" Travers demanded, again hoping for a distraction, if not a miracle.

"Compensation, for a life's work lost, doesn't come along often," Haas chimed in.

"What do you mean, 'lost.' He was everything you designed him to be." Travers replied.

"Oh, he was that. But because he was that, if there were any justice, I should have been famous. *Rich*. I shouldn't have had to labor for twenty-odd years, tied to this project like a fetus to the womb, for paltry sums Gentry called a 'retainer.' No, not for *this* work." Haas bent near to stress his point. "We *isolated stem cells* two decades before anyone else had the technique. Do you realize what that could have meant to the world? Sure, I had the funds, I had the secrets uncovered from the CIA's biological research as my starting point. But, I had to keep the government's secrets even as I projected them deeper into the mysteries of existence. I had to watch, as colleagues who undertook mediocre work landed the most lucrative corporate contracts. I had to maintain the life of a university professor and researcher, keeping state secrets so the world would never know of my contribution."

As Haas justified his betrayals, Threll withdrew his hypodermic from Will's ear. Will began to groan, stirring a little against his restraints.

"When did you drug him?"

Threll checked his watch. "About—ninety minutes ago. You promised me that was a two-hour dose of sedative."

"I was going by the last round of tests. It had been a while," Haas fumed. "Better get another shot ready."

Threll moved to the cabinet table full of medical supplies in the corner. He picked up another hypodermic, along with a half-pint bottle of clear fluid.

"Will! Wake up!" Travers cried. It was a desperate hope, but it was now or never if they stood a chance against their macabre captors.

"Vee. Keep her quiet," snarled Threll.

"Will! I love you, Will! Do you hear me? *I love you.*"

Vee clasped Travers' midsection and cupped a massive hand over her mouth. But it was too late. Will's eyes snapped open. He raised his head, saw Haas and Avery. He strained to turn his head far enough around to catch a glimpse of Travers and Vee.

"You... bastards," he hissed.

Avery, sure of his advantage, displayed his usual courage and grace when holding the upper hand. "Huh. Look who's talkin', We're about to *fix you*, kid."

Will struggled against his straps. Like the ones used to bind him in the hospital room earlier, they began to smolder.

"Good lord," Haas gasped. "Hurry with that serum. Major! Grab him."

Avery now shrank back in fear. "No freakin' way."

Threll topped off the syringe he now wielded with the clear fluid he had drawn from the small bottle. As he did so, the gel binding Will's lower legs bubbled, beginning to soften. Little burn holes appeared in Will's clothing, spreading wider. He seemed to be reaching some kind of critical mass.

Threll rushed Will with the hypodermic, trying to draw a bead on Will's upper arm as the blue lad thrashed in his restraints. Threll jabbed the syringe forward. Just as he did, the strap that bound Will's right arm snapped in two. Will's darting hand caught Threll by the wrist, stopping him an inch away from injection. They trembled, struggling for a few seconds, until Threll suddenly howled in pain. Will's immense body heat seared his flesh. His hand went limp. He dropped the syringe.

"Vee—help me!" he gasped.

Vee threw Travers to the floor, and seized Will's wrist, squeezing, the pressure making Will release his grip on Threll.

Unlike Threll, Vee seemed to feel no pain as Will burned his clutching palm. He forced Will's arm back down, leaning his massive weight into him for good measure. Even as Vee overpowered him, however, more of Will's bonds severed in seconds. He struggled against Vee's weight, trying to get leverage, to get off the table.

Haas, seeing his chance, scrambled to the other side of the operating table. He was peering down at the floor in a frantic search.

"Looking for this?" Travers knelt there on the floor, wielding the hypo, pointing at his midsection like a missile. She instantly jabbed him right in the belly and injected the sedative. Haas screamed and reeled back, taking the syringe with him like an artificial appendage grafted to his stomach.

"Jacob! I need the antidote. Hurry!" he cried before he wilted to the floor, losing consciousness.

Will was losing his battle with Vee, who seemed as strong as several men. And Will was still groggy from poison. No more heat poured from him. His mysterious charge seemed exhausted.

Avery seized Travers and pulled her to her feet. She promptly stomped his instep and pulled free of his grasp as he hopped in pain on one leg. She followed up her advantage by jabbing an elbow sharply into his sternum. He doubled over and fell.

As Travers returned her attention to the desperate struggle on the operating table, Will's legs pulled loose from their semi-severed straps. His heat had softened the polymer encasing his legs. Grasping Vee's arms for leverage, Will jack knifed his legs upward, and swiftly encased Vee's head with them inside the mass of softened, soppy gel.

Like anyone else, Vee needed to breathe. He released Will and clawed at the peculiar substance, trying to pull the gel loose, but the main effect of this action was to entangle his hands within its mass as well. Will drew back both legs, pulling more of the gel like taffy from his legs. Then he piston-kicked Vee in the chest. Reeling back from the blow, Vee pulled most of the gel along with him, freeing Will's legs.

Threll, made desperate by this turn of events, grabbed a scalpel from his surgical tray and turned to wield it. But Will had already gained his feet. His fist smashed Threll full in the face. Threll slammed back into the corner and slumped, insensate, to the floor.

"Team work!" Travers yelled, like a cheerleader. She rushed over to rifle Threll's coat pockets. Triumphantly, she produced a set of keys.

"I thought we weren't stealing any cars?" he grinned.

"I'll make an exception. Come on."

She led Will out the back way of the house, into the night.

23.

Threll's Cadillac veered through the hills and hollows, Travers at the wheel. Her mind raced furiously to devise a plan. Seeking isolation had failed. Could seeking public attention prove any better? She felt they were doomed, yet, being here, alone with the unique, exhausted figure slumping on the seat beside her, also somehow felt like an a rare privilege. Mainly, she wondered at the strength of her own determination that no more wrongs should come to him. She guessed it was the blood of her dear ol' Dad coursing through her veins.

She wondered if this protective feeling she had developed toward Will was a psychological transference. After all, she was single, without a significant other, without children...

"I think I'm dying," Will sighed, without moving even his head.

"You must've burned a million calories. At least you cooled down enough to spare the seat."

"Yeah. Even though I know—"

"You know what?"

"I know now, you..."

"I, what?"

"You feel the same way I do for you," he said, bashfully. He stole the merest glimpse at Travers. She caught the movement from the corner of her eye, without turning her head.

A long moment of silence passed between them.

"That's what I said, isn't it?" she finally replied. "And it worked."

"Worked? It 'worked?!' You mean—you were just yanking my chain? Trying to get me hyped up?"

"Did you expect me to overpower three men by myself?" Travers coolly continued.

"How can you be so—cruel? You—you—bit-" Will spluttered, hurt.

"Don't say anything you'll regret."

"Don't you understand? I never expected to hear anybody tell me they loved me. Now I finally do hear it, and it's a lie. A stinking lie!"

Travers stole a quick glance at Will. In the glow from the dashboard, she glimpsed the motion of a tear running down his cheek. She looked quickly back at the road.

"Will, grow up. You're younger than me—" no, that sounded ridiculous, she thought, and tried again. "We're from different worlds. We happen to be stuck together right now. But once we're past the danger..."

"We'll never be past the danger. Or, at least, I never will be. Like they always told me. Normal people can't accept me. Even *you*."

Travers caught a breath. "I—admire you, Will. You've turned out—at heart, I know you're—you've dealt with your situation better than—"

"Save it. I always ran on hope I'd get out of Proteus someday. You're showing me how it's gonna be now that I have. You're doing me a big favor. Now, stop the car," he demanded.

"No. Will—"

"Stop the car, damn it. Now!" Will grabbed the steering wheel. Travers hit the brake, and grappled with Will with her right hand.

The car twisted to a rubber-burning halt on a dark, deserted stretch of road. Will angrily wrenched himself from the car.

Travers stepped out of the driver's side.

"Have a nice life," muttered Will, over his shoulder, as he strode briskly up the road.

"Will, we're miles from anywhere. You'll be hopeless out here."

Will turned, with a big shrug of the shoulders. "Same as anywhere else," he called back.

Travers was stumped for a reply.

The engine of an approaching vehicle grew louder in the distance. They listened for several seconds. It was the sound of a truck. Then, they saw its lights, and they realized, back down the road, an Army truck headed for them—*fast*.

"It's them!" Will cried. He lost no time in racing back to the car.

"Oh, my God." Travers leaped back into the driver's seat and stomped the gas pedal, roaring into motion with Will barely half-into the seat.

They had not traveled far before the pursuing army truck overtook them. It bumped them from behind, jolting Travers and Will. They were surprised by the sound of a servo-motor whirring softly afterward, behind them.

Will turned in the seat. Looking back he saw the backseat tilt over 90° to become a platform, bristling with exotic weaponry.

"Allll-*riiight*!" Will called, excitedly.

Strapped in place on the platform were manifold knives, small firearms, brass knuckles, nunchaku, throwing stars, gas and explosive grenades, a coil of rope, a grappling hook launcher ... attached to a glove...?

"Guess what?" said Will, excitedly. "You're driving an arsenal."

"Oh, my God," Travers repeated.

The Army truck bashed them again. Travers fought the steering wheel for control. Will lunged for the back seat.

Travers sneaked a quick peek over her shoulder.

"Will, no! You'll blow us up!" she exclaimed.

"Uh-oh," he replied, reacting to something he saw behind them. He flipped frontwise in the seat, grabbed and twisted the steering wheel.

Vee leaned from the passenger side of the Army truck cab, rapid-firing his TEC-9. The swerving Cadillac was sprayed with bullets. Scars appeared in the rear glass and the paint was ripped in thin lines from the body. A taillight was shot out. But the vehicle sped on, essentially unharmed.

Inside the car, Travers twisted the wheel, barely avoiding an oncoming auto. Will released the steering wheel and shrank back, apologetically.

"It's bullet-proof. Sorry."

With a bang, they took another bump from the Army truck. Despite the Cadillac's special fortifications, they knew they were in a death race.

24.

"Damn your fancy gear," Avery jeered at Threll from the steering wheel of the Army truck. "We'll have to run 'em off the road."

Vee pulled back into the Army truck cab. Avery drove aggressively on to ram the Cadillac once more, nearly jostling the car completely out of control. Threll sat, tense and angry, between the Major and Vee.

Haas's face appeared in the screen behind Threll's head. He rode in the back.

"I'm—going to be sick," he groaned.

"I'm sorry I gave you the antidote," grumbled Threll.

In the Cadillac, Will calculated furiously. He strapped the handle of the grappling hook glove to his wrist. He made sure the ends of the long nylon rope were securely tied from the leather thong to the eight-inch expanding tube of the hook. This would be perfect for scaling a wall, or, perhaps...

"Pam. Work your way over here," he commanded. "Next to me. Come on."

Travers hesitated. "What are you doing?"

Will opened his car door slightly and propped it thus with his foot. Travers glanced over at him, aghast. They were jolted violently again, the door swung open and shut violently. Will opened it again and braced it with his foot. He leaned over and slid his arm around Travers' waist.

"Use your left foot on the gas. That's it. Next to me. Closer," he continued to coax her.

She raised her right leg awkwardly over the gearshift, trying to keep driving and keep their speed up on the windy mountain road. The Army truck just missed them on the next curve, wobbling and barely recovering off the guardrail before racing uphill after them again. Inexorably, it closed the gap as Travers maneuvered herself over against Will, straining to keep the gas mashed down with her left foot while half-steering with her left hand.

"Will, we can't just jump out of here!" she cried.

They took another violent jolt. Now they were being pushed along, ground beneath the bumper of the Army truck, as she lost contact with the gas pedal.

"Trust me... okay, now. Hold me tight," called Will.

Will, his arm around Travers, pointed his fingers at the steering wheel. He had a curious, half-vacant stare on his face. The car banked sharply left. Will kicked the door wide open, leaving nothing between them and the hard, rushing blackness inches away.

"No-o-o-oo!" cried Travers. Ahead of them, the guard rail came speeding.

"If we don't make it, I do love you!" cried Will.

They veered at the last moment to miss the railing which would otherwise have prevented their plunge from the road. Near a sloping curve ahead, there was a gap in the rail, and they were now accelerating again, magically, free of the Army truck, straight for that gap.

"What the hell—??" Avery shook his head, stupefied. "They're committing suicide!"

The Army Truck slowed, to avoid plunging from the road. The Cadillac separated from the truck and leaped the incline.

"No-o-oo!" Threll's cry from the Army truck matched that of Travers in the now-plunging Cadillac.

The bodies of Will and Travers were silhouetted against the dark sky as their bodies parted from the plunging car. Will, kicking off with all his strength, had launched them free. Arm extended, he squeezed the hand-trigger mechanism and fired the grappling hook from his wrist into the darkness of the pine trees which lined the steep slope. With a whooshing report, the hook spewed from its barrel. Unseen, its grapples opened out, locked into position, ready to catch onto anything they encountered.

The grappling hook tangled within rustling silhouettes of trees, somewhere in the darkness.

Will and Travers, clinging tightly to one another, felt a jot of tension, then a yielding as they arced widely, swinging behind the tree line at a dizzying speed.

Avery ground the brakes of the Army truck so as not to follow the deadly plunge of the Cadillac. The truck stopped as the Cadillac hit the lower slope and tumbled violently downward, into the ravine.

Avery Threll, and Vee heard, from the back of the truck, the sound of Haas vomiting. Avery and Threll shared a look of disgust before they threw open the doors of the truck and ran to the precipice to peer downward, into the darkness.

The Cadillac hit the ground violently and rolled. They heard the thunderous series of collisions with trees and hard earth as it tumbled, end over end, before bursting into a fiery, cataclysmic explosion which lit the night below.

"Holy shit!" Exclaimed Avery, as he, Threll, and Vee, at the edge of the cliff side, were bathed in the light of the cataclysm.

"No! Idiots!" Threll shook his fist in frustration before turning decisively to Vee. "Get as close as you can. Look for signs of their bodies."

Vee slung his TEC-9 over his shoulder and clambered over the side of the cliff, as always complying with Threll's order without hesitation.

Haas, wiping his mouth with his sleeve, tottered out of the back of the Army truck to join them at the edge of the precipice.

"Oh, my God. I never pictured it all ending like this."

"We have the tissue samples..." Threll mused, already attempting to salvage what he could from the day's vast wasteland of conspiratorial effort.

Nervously, Haas muttered, "Okay. I want the title to my Swiss account. Right away. And—I want as far away from here as possible."

Livid, Avery turned on him. "Oh, yeah? Why? All we've done is butcher a platoon, set a forest on fire, and crash a car! What the hell ya worried about, Haas?" He looked at Threll, whose countenance fairly dared him to launch into similar words directed at him. Avery gritted his teeth, shook his head, and turned, kicking at the roadside.

"What if he turns up alive?" Threll asked of the night, loudly enough for both men to hear. "Names names?"

"Say," remarked Haas, as if struck with a bright idea. "Can't you use your tracker?"

"It was *in the car*," Threll replied. He paused, pondering some new thought of his own.

Threll peered, obsessed, down into the abyss of night. He donned his headset and spoke into his microphone.

"Vee. Listen for someone—probably screaming."

Threll made a slight adjustment to a dial on his earpiece.

Somewhere down the dark ravine, having slammed hard into the branches and trunk of an evergreen tree, Will lay on the ground, bruised, aching, not sure if anything was broken or not. Coming to consciousness, he caught some of the light from the blazing vehicle in the distance. He was surrounded by trees and darkness. He realized he needed to get up, if possible. He needed to find out what had happened to Pam. If he had lived, and she hadn't...

He raised his groggy head, thoroughly stunned. He shook away the cobwebs, looking around the dark forest. His eyes were capable of seeing six times better in the dark than those of a normal human being. At length, he spotted Travers. She lay still, in a heap, resting virtually upside down against the trunk of a nearby tree, one leg hanging over its lowest branches.

As Will sat up, he felt a sharp pain in his arm. Then, one in his back. He slowly realized his wrist was still tied to the hook and rope. He fumbled, weakly, with the strap until, at last, he had removed the device.

Rising painfully, he tottered toward Travers' limp form.

Then, came a new pain altogether.

Will fell to his knees and doubled over, prey to a piercing noise, drilling as if to the center of his head, which threatened to split his skull. Amidst the noise, against all sanity, the loathsome voice of his nemesis sounded clearly in Will's mind.

"Where are you, Will? Talk to me. Call my name. Go ahead. Scream it out. Jacob—Threll."

Will grimaced tightly, clutching his ears in agony. He fell, rolling on the ground in pain, uttering muted little whimpers.

Vee, meantime, had reached the blazing car. He worked carefully around its fiery perimeter, peering into the flames.

At the cliff edge, Threll, through his visor, saw an identical view of the burning wreck. If there were bodies, there were no signs. And, no one could get any closer for a better look. Threll toyed with his dial, turning off the inaudible piercing sound which he had been transmitting. There had been no screams from the night echoing up the ravine's walls. Threll calculated that, even as inured to pain as Will Monday must have become through the years, surely the nerve-shredding waves of his ultrasound broadcasts, beamed at the implanted microchip in Will's inner ear, would have caused such unbearable agony as to produce a loud shriek. But he had heard nothing but licking, crackling flames in the breezes of the night.

Will shuddered from the pain, mingled with Threll's odious voice. Trembling, he propped himself up on his elbows. He could hear only a roaring silence. At last, he crawled, weakly, to Travers. When he reached her, he gazed into her face, then felt her wrist for a pulse.

He placed his other hand on her chest. She was breathing, if erratically—in shock. Will realized it was up to him if they were to survive.

He cast a backward glance to the middle distance, where he spotted Vee from behind, silhouetted against the blazing pyre, rooting around the blaze, turning, looking around in all directions, then scanning the ground for footprints in the earth. There were none to find.

Heroically, Will rose to his feet, with Travers in his trembling arms. Weak from his ordeal, but with a determination burning to match the carnage he left behind, he staggered away, deeper into the woods, bearing his partner.

25.

Avery's face was etched with rage.

In the confined Proteus monitor room, the major watched a screen where a tiny blip moved in minuscule increments across a topological map. Now, into the wee hours of the morning, the men who would seize the living son of the Proteus Project knew...

"He's still alive!" Avery snarled.

Avery's frustration with his former pupil was boundless. Here he stood on the brink of gaining admission to the ranks of the elite circles of world control. Only the capture of this designer mutant standing in the way of his joining the class of men who had, through the generations, used secrecy, wealth, and intrigue to foster Communism and Nazism alike. As few realized, the world dominators intrigued to play nation against nation, plucking up broader and deeper control over the wealth and policies of nations after each conflict. Personally, they moved freely about the globe, above the laws of men, self-styled Olympians aspiring to godhood.

As Avery had learned through whispered tales in the course of his politicking in military circles, such men had developed the British-American intelligence community into an autonomous, world wide system of government agencies and false front companies in the private sector, who served to consolidate and extend the power of the multinational corporations. The intermarried dynasties who owned this power, and to a lesser extent their executives, formed the hidden, inner elite. This vast web's disseminated agents, conscious or unconscious of their true loyalties, penetrated into every profession, every community in the Americas and Europe, with allies in all parts of the earth. They constituted the winners' circle, the path to true and lasting power in a world where political figureheads rose and fell in the course of furthering the covert Agenda.

This all-powerful system, developed over many generations, designed to manage and exploit the world's population, gave orders to presidents and prime ministers, as only through membership in its ranks could one reach such a position in society. It stood ready and able to offer juicy carrots or lashing sticks to anyone who stood in a position to help it further its ends, whether through legislation or assassination.

Unknown were the crimes the ruling cabal had not committed to rise to the apex of the political power pyramid—blackmail; extortion; murder; bribery; thievery; both legally enabled and purely criminal; and terrorism. Unknown were the media of control it did not penetrate and manipulate—the insurance and financial system, police agencies, militaries, the broadcast and print media, lawmaking, corporate policy, and cyberspace.

The system's masters peered into the living rooms and bedrooms of every American, and into places both public and private, around the world, on a constant basis. Yet, they were unknown to all but a fraction of a percent of those whose lives they held in their hands, to promote or to destroy at a whim.

Any who stood in a position to hinder or endanger the hidden empire, any who could not be persuaded or purchased into submission, had been brutally, sometimes quite publicly, eliminated. The message to all others was clear: disbelieve, for your own good. Or, believe if you must, but, at all costs, avoid conflict with the Order of the Wilderbeeks.

Threll, Avery's sponsor in his membership campaign, considered the fingernails of one hand, while stroking his chin with the thumb and forefinger of the other. Vee appeared at the doorway from the Complex corridors, gripping the mortified Snyder by the shoulders.

"Don't worry," said Threll, suavely. "We have his tissue, and all the know-how *to make more*." Threll gestured at another monitor displaying the conference room, where Vee stood, intimidating, over Snyder while Haas sipped a cup of coffee at the table.

"What's that mean?" Avery demanded.

"We can set right to work—without the Consortium's profile being evident in tonight's events." It was the rule not to speak the name of the Wilderbeeks in the presence of outsiders. Threll practiced caution with Dr. Snyder so near.

"So, you're not going to do any more? Your almighty 'Consortium' gets what it wants, and I get to report another disaster to Ash? Great."

"Initiates often pay a price before reaping vast rewards, Major."

"Yeah," said Avery, "but I've still gotta catch the freak—and I'm fresh out of troops, aren't I?"

"You'll get more. The slaughter back there will only heighten Ash's fears. Remember, the lad caused all that carnage himself," Threll winked. "If he is that powerful, he is that much more valuable game." Threll whispered confidentially, "As in *sixty million*. Do we have a deal?"

"Sixty million? In off-shore accounts?"

"All approved by the Governing Council, on my recommendation as *Pro Temperas Emeritus*. Don't mention it, though. It's more than Dr. Haas is in line for."

Fear strove visibly with greed, twitching across Avery's face.

"Look, I am truly sorry about those troops," said Threll, in his best effort at sincerity. "Had we been in communication at the time, it never would have happened. We could have taken him back to Proteus. We could have picked up my equipment from the safe house, and we'd soon have his conversion complete. But that's all spilled milk, now."

"Spilled *blood*," Avery spat. "And Ash is gonna hold me responsible."

Threll laughed his harsh laugh, startling Avery and Snyder.

"The President is a *member*, Major. A Legacy, *Pro Formidibalis Heriditarius*!" Threll declared. "He's in this as deep as you or I!"

Avery's face lit up. "Ash? Really?"

"You thought he was just another cynical politician worried about his image? He'd never be in the White House if we hadn't placed him there. Who do you think spent hundreds of millions waging a PR war on his predecessor, tiring the public with years of trumped-up scandals? They were too weak to resist when our machine placed Ash in the Oval Office. That's what you can do with unfocused minds. What I'm trying to say is, you have a *blank check*, here."

Threll and Avery entered to the laboratory. "She refuses to be of any use," Haas declared. I can't get her to tell us where the off-loaded data is. But I'm sure she knows. She and Gentry were—" he held up two fingers crossed as if for luck.

"But she will tell us," Threll said, suavely.

"Gentry is finished, Doctor," he added, leaning down close to her face, which she turned away. "But that doesn't mean all your years of work with Dr. Haas need be in vain."

"Major, I suggest you muster your troops for one more go. The boy has to be near his last legs. It would mean *a lot*," he winked, "if you brought him in alive."

"What about you and your one-man-army, here?" Avery demanded.

"Under the circumstances, I think it's best we retired back East to begin 'negotiations.'" He waved a hand toward Snyder. "Let's face it, we tripped over each other out there tonight. The President will provide you all the military force you'll need, and more."

Avery pondered, resentful of Threll's control over the situation and his sudden withdrawal from the pursuit. But, he was tantalized by the prospect of a future drenched with power, a life utterly free from responsibility ever after.

"All right. And I will get him, Threll. But I can't promise he'll be in one piece."

"Alive. I have my reasons."

Snyder's heart sank. After Will's escape with Travers, Avery had called for transportation from Mountain Home. With the debarkation of Avery and most of the Green Berets, the hapless Gentry was gone as well, on his way back to Washington. As she now knew, he was being forced to relinquish his position to a Chief Executive who was a monster. Surely, no matter what happened, Gentry would try to reach her, she knew this in her heart. But, with no rank, no position, no access anymore, could such a thing be possible?

Avery studied the frightened scientist, clutched firmly in the meathooks of the powerful Vee. He turned to her colleague, who had so eagerly joined in betraying Proteus into the hands of the Wilderbeeks. Haas tilted his head, encouragingly.

Avery shrugged. "All right. Pipe in some more grunts."

Threll and Haas joined the major, slapping him on the back.

"That's the way," Threll said. "If Lt. McIntire could only hear you now, it'd burn him up—all over again."

They laughed at Threll's grisly joke. Snyder, more horrified now than ever, cringed under a wave of utter nausea. As she blacked out she heard them, as one might hear sounds from a distant shore.

26.

In the pale light of daybreak, across volcanic grounds as hard as steel, Travers, battered and bruised, limped beside Will, one arm draped around his shoulder while the other held a broken branch from the forest to help steady her on the side of her sprained ankle. They were both weak and injured, unsteady on the unforgiving grounds on which they had arrived. The bleak lava field, swollen and pockmarked, was surely an omen of an impending end.

"I—I need to take a minute, Will," Travers sighed, blinking as she raised her head to the grey heavens above.

"We've got to keep moving. It's daylight. We've gotta get out of sight," Will argued.

"Will. My spirit's feeling weak. I need some help right now."

Travers lowered herself onto her knees, bowed her head into folded hands, and sobbed for a few moments before finally becoming quiet.

Will watched curiously, half-inclined to shake her out of her reverie, or even to run on and leave her to her silly ritual. He urgently wanted to find a hiding place before their pursuers closed in again. Yet, although he could not say why, this woman had risked everything to help him, and he had to respect her needs.

He had never seen anyone pray in person before. As with many things from the world beyond, he had seen it done on television. Although the idea was perplexing to him, he understood most people in the day light world held a belief in some kind of conscious, supernatural creator who had made them for a purpose.

He wondered if they knew something he did not? Or if they were simply desperate to believe their lives had such a purpose. Maybe, in truth, they were simply fearful that was not the case. That seemed more likely to Will, for, after all, they had so many different beliefs as to who or what their "God" was, and they constantly fought and killed each other over this idea no one could prove. It was sheer madness. Will did not wish to be involved.

Travers looked up at length, and sighed. She seemed rested and at peace once again. She turned her head, seeing the landscape as if for the first time.

"Oh. I think I know where we are. Daddy brought us around here once, when I was seven or eight. There are caves around here somewhere. Caves, Will. We might find a cave."

"Yeah. Let's do that." *Back underground. Ugh.* But he knew precisely that would be the best thing to do.

They resumed trudging along, keeping a keen eye out for openings in the ground.

"So, your dad brought you here?" Will continued, making conversation. "Let's see, now I say, 'What does he do?'"

"He was a policeman," Travers replied, flatly.

"Was?"

"He was killed in the line of duty."

"Oh. ...That's whack."

"What? 'Whack?' you get this stuff from TV?"

Will grinned, sheepishly.

"What did they tell *you*, Will? About your parentage, I mean?"

"That I'm a—basically—human clone—made up from a cross-selection of genes."

"That's all?"

"Period."

"You still don't even know for sure if you really *have* parents, do you?"

"No."

"Will. If you did—who do you think they would be?"

Will sighed. His reply was spoken briskly, as though he were vaguely annoyed by an unimportant subject Travers was pursuing. "To tell you the truth? I kind of figure I'm an in vitro job. Maybe grown in some kind of incubator. It's no big deal."

"I see. 'No big deal.'"

"I'll tell you what worries me right now," Will responded. "I think maybe I'm *losin' it*."

"Losing it?"

"My mind. I heard Threll—inside my head—on the slope last night. And some horrible noise."

"Will. I didn't tell you. He put something in your ear while you were out of it."

"You mean, you think he *really was* talking inside my head? Oh, man. That's *worse* than going crazy!"

"It may be even worse than that. Haas said it was your 'second implant.'"

"'Second implant?'" Will mused, realizing then, "You think maybe they were—tracking us, then? Like I was maybe, broadcasting some signal from some kind of implanted gizmo?"

"That would make sense. Gentry, the Army. They couldn't risk your getting away. They must have had you implanted for years."

Will stopped, dazed by the notion. He looked at Travers as though, himself, just seeing the world around them for the first time.

It began to rain.

"*Where'd* you say those caves are?"

Once they had searched another three-quarters of an hour or so, they did find the mouth of a cavern. It was a small pock mark in the bucking lava land, hardly big enough to wriggle their battered bodies through, along with trickling streams of rainwater. They had to climb down about seven or eight feet before finding an open, underground air pocket. Inside, in the dim light reflected from puddles here and there, they made out a low, shallow cavern. It rose, not far inside, where they crouched and collapsed against a wall of hardened magma.

Travers shivered, and huddled against Will. Their drenched clothes clung tightly against their bodies. They were out of sight from the air, but hardly better off. Will took a few deep breaths, allowing his consciousness to sink deep, deep within himself.

He needed to find the place that generated his fires, that place of anger and fear that had given him the power to burn his adversaries' flesh, to cause fire to flash in dry wood, to nearly kill them all. He needed to learn how to contact that place, to use what it contained, to learn to control it, to use it at will. Their lives might depend on his ability to do that.

For an hour or more, they huddled in silence. The white noise of the rain fall continued outside. Travers shivered and sobbed occasionally. Then, she began to wonder if she had entered the next phase of dying. Her body, in touch with Will's, was growing warmer. She looked up. She could see the silhouette of his face, a slight gleam of his cat-like pupils gazing back into her eyes.

"Will?"

"Shhhh."

He moved away, then pulled her legs outward, laid them across his own. He ran his hands up her legs, bringing a definite warmth that felt too good to resist. After some minutes of this, he took her by the wrists and pulled her onto his lap, hugging her close. The heat of his body, toasty-warm and magnificent, permeated her torso as he held her and rubbed her. She lolled her head, rubbing her cheeks over his, surrendering to an ecstasy which, she knew from his heavy breathing, he shared. She wrapped her legs tightly around his waist. In time, she loosened her grip and pulled away from Will. She found her clothes were now dry for the most part.

"Thank you, Will," she sighed, resuming her composure. "It's no wonder they're after you," she added. "How in the world did you get this—this power you seem to have?"

"I don't have a clue. It showed up the day I busted out of Proteus."

"You'd probably been developing it for years, but never had such an abnormal stimulus—a highly *emotional* stimulus—like the events of that day to trigger it."

She shivered. He hugged her. Then she felt the contractions of his body, and in a moment she heard him weeping.

"It's okay. Let it out," Travers whispered.

"He's dead, isn't he? They killed Mac. They killed the only guy who ever made me feel like a human being," Will sobbed. "And it's all my fault. Why did I ever take his car keys? Why did I bust out like that? I knew it was wrong. I knew it'd never work. I kept—I kept having fantasies like, I'd tell the world my story... be in the papers, on TV... maybe I'd finally get free and have a chance... I was so stupid..." Travers allowed him to cry for several minutes before she spoke again.

"I know how you looked up to him. Your instincts were right about that Major Avery. And that disgusting Dr. Haas. But, what about your gifts from Dr. Snyder? The glass animals. The posters. The music. Wasn't there another side to Proteus?"

Will sighed. "I figured she and Dr. Haas probably wanted to soothe their conscience if I kicked it while they ran their 'tests.'"

"Is that why you got rid of the glass animals?"

"No. I was—that was an accident. I was—" he seemed embarrassed— "dancing, in my room, and they floated in mid-air. Then fell. That's when I got a clue how freaky I really am. How'd you know about them? Oh. The monitors. You got to watch me on the freakin' monitors."

All the warmth Will had been generating was gone. He crossed his arms over his knees and hung his head.

"Dr. Snyder asked if I'd seen them," Travers explained. "I think she did feel guilty about you, Will. But, I wonder..."

Travers lay back, looking upward thoughtfully.

"Me, too," said Will, at length. "I still don't understand."

"What?"

"Why didn't they ever just shoot me?"

Travers considered that question: when the support was withdrawn, when Gentry had the tacit order to eliminate Will and scrap the Project altogether, why *didn't* they?

27.

Travers raised the branch she had used as a walking stick.

"Will? Do you think you could light this branch? I want to have a look around in here."

"I can see," Will replied. "It's low. Looks like it drops off right over there."

"Please. I want to see it, too. Can you do it, or do you have to be mad at something?"

"I was just pumping out heat for a while and I wasn't mad. I'm trying to get it under control." He took the stick from her hand, clasped his fist around the narrow end. Moments passed. Nothing happened. "I dunno... I'm hungry," Will sounded annoyed.

"You're not the only one," Travers replied. "I'm going to have to go hunt us up something." She grasped the sleeve of her blouse and started to rip the seam loose from the shoulder. Once she had it torn loose, she pulled it off her and used the strip of cloth to wind and bind around her sprained ankle and foot.

"You can't do this. You can hardly walk," Will protested.

"I have to do it, before we both waste away. I've got some idea how to rough it. We're a couple of miles from the edge of forest land, so the earlier I get started, the better chance we have."

Will gritted his teeth, frustrated. "I should go. I came out of the wreck a little better off."

"But you're broadcasting, buddy," Travers reminded him.

Will gave the end of the walking stick one final squeeze, and it burst into flame at last. Travers grinned and took it from Will.

"Look. Over there."

She moved a little deeper inside the space, limping and hunched over due to the low ceiling of their little cavern. She confirmed it did drop off onto a series of shallow ledges she could make out by the faint light of the flickering torch. Will joined her at the first shallow ledge.

"Maybe we should sleep down here. Might be safer if they shine a light in here."

"Yeah, but it'll be cold."

"I'll try to gather some brush while I'm out. Try to soften it up a little."

"Kind of a 'nest', huh? That's a good idea."

"Okay," said Travers as she started back to the constricted mouth of their sanctuary. "And whatever you do, stay here for at least the next few hours. I'll need some time. Meantime, don't you make it any easier for them."

"You sound like Dr. Snyder," Will griped, although he knew she was correct.

Dusk had fallen. Hours of worry had passed by for Will, punctuated by fits of nightmarish half-sleep on the cold, steely hard lava floor, before rustling sounds from the entrance of the cavern woke him from his light slumber.

Travers wriggled down into the cavern, bearing a rabbit bound in vines. She handed the limp, dead mammal to Will, then reached up to pull in her other prize, a similarly-bound collection of sticks and leaves.

"You're great!" Will exclaimed. Travers bowed, then pulled some sharp, flat pieces of flint rock from her pockets.

"We have to skin it," she said.

They did, managing to build a fire which Will was eventually able to light. They roasted the skewered animal over the flame. Voraciously, they used their fading strength to tear apart and devour the cooked carcass, sharing a primitive repast that had them both yearning for the frozen microwave dinners of Proteus.

Soon, having drunk water from the shallow rain puddles, Travers and Will slumbered, entwined, on the "nest" they had laid into place on the first of the low ledges.

At length, Will roused at a new sound. Footfalls and voices on the surface wafted like whispers through the cave mouth. Will gently disengaged himself from Travers.

As he did so, he saw a bayonet thrust through the cavern opening, a scant twenty feet away. He ducked back down as a troop leaned a head and shoulder down inside, shining a light around.

Travers woke. Will clapped a hand over her mouth. She pulled his hand away, gently but firmly. She riveted Will with a steady stare and maintained her calm amidst the fading sounds of the troops outside.

The one who had leaned inside the cavern mouth stood and spoke into his walkie-talkie.

"We're within a few meters of your last reading, Major. Some of that old volcanic ground. It's like a Swiss cheese up here, only lots harder. Over."

"Hard lava. Blocking the signal." Avery's voice crackled in reply. "The mice are underground. Carry on. I'm sending additional ordnance."

While Avery's manhunt continued in Idaho, far across the United States, in the metropolis of New York, inside the living room of a lavish penthouse apartment, Dr. Regina Snyder sat, gagged with duct tape and tied to a wooden chair. She was haggard, hours of struggle having succumbed to exhaustion and despair. She raised her head at the sound of padded footfalls.

Radiant and relaxed, Threll and Vee entered the living room in matching silk robes. Threll checked himself out in a large mirror, and smoothed his short, perfect hair.

"Your burns are healing nicely, Vee. You deserve a reward. Relax."

Vee sat back in a recliner chair. Threll picked up his headset from a nearby table and made an adjustment on the dial and buttons studding its controls, with a flourish, showing off to Dr. Snyder.

"The nerve endings in your flesh might be deadened, but not the pleasure centers in your brain. Show the nice doctor."

In seconds, Vee's face relaxed, then assumed an utterly beatific attitude, as he apparently entered a euphoric trance. His head lolled back, his mind obviously now engaged in some voyage through the sublime.

"There has to be a reward in every system of control," Threll smiled at the doctor. He strolled to Snyder and ripped off her gag, raking a sharp pain across her jaws.

"Doctor," Threll continued. "Will Monday is running for his life. Lt. McIntire's dog tags were sifted from the ashes of a forest fire. General Gentry is out to pasture, replaced by our Judas goat, Avery. In short, you have no hope of rescue. So, if you were harboring any such thoughts, do yourself a favor—abandon them."

"What do you want?" asked Snyder, dismally.

"The other half of your Proteus puzzle," Threll replied, intensely. "I have Dr. Haas's synthetic RNA. Now I want your invention—the mutable protease formulae. Will's life depends on your cooperation."

"But you don't have Will. So, you're bluffing."

"Hah. Not at all. U.S. troops are about to capture the brat. But, even though I do not have him in custody as yet, thanks to satellite technology, I can talk to him right now. Guide him. Wouldn't you prefer it if he came here—alive? We can have our own little Proteus Project, eh?"

"Don't you have a speck of decency?"

Threll appeared wounded, incredulous, even. "Of course I do. Look, the Consortium I represent will reverse-engineer his genetic makeup—and mint several major patents. Now, maybe you misunderstand me. *I'm offering you full participation.* Just speed things up, tell us where your research databank is cached. Then, we share the wealth. That's fair, isn't it?"

"Don't hold your breath. Better still—do."

Exasperated, Threll waved his hands. "Very well, then, Will Monday dies. What a waste, when everyone could go away as happy as—Vee, here."

Vee, spaced-out, euphoric, drooled on himself in the easy chair.

28.

In the dim, pre-dawn light, a slumbering farmyard was visited by two creeping phantoms. They carefully hopped a barnyard fence and crept toward a chicken coop.

Travers's hands silently opened the henhouse door. She stole inside, and in seconds reappeared to deposit eggs into a burlap feed sack Will held open. Then, she sneezed. The hens commenced to raise a ruckus.

Will and Travers scurried across the yard, back toward the edge of the nearby wood.

Inside the kitchen farmhouse, Gladys, the lady of the house, made her way to the window to see what was going on out there.

"Clarence! Come quick!" she called to her husband. "They's chicken thieves runnin' across the farm!"

As Will and Travers ran for it, in the distance behind them, Clarence appeared on the porch with a shotgun. Taking aim, he blasted an ineffectual load of buckshot after them.

The pair of thieves escaped into the woods, but soon Pam had to stop and nurse her still-weak ankle. It seemed to Will as though she had taken another turn for the worse, as she began coughing.

"Pam? What's wrong?"

"Winded. It's so damp—so cold." She coughed some more. "Just—let me catch my breath."

Clarence and Gladys, on their back porch, peering into the distance, were suddenly struck dumb by the sight of a military Jeep, two Trucks, and a Bradley fighting vehicle, tearing across their land at high speed.

Will and Travers heard the engines of the far-off vehicles.

"I *told* you," Travers snapped at Will.

"Yeah, you did," Will said, his brow knitted in anguish. There could be no doubt now that the military was somehow tracking him. It had to be transmissions from his "implants."

Will and Travers took off at a run once more.

At length, they were crossing the vast expanse of lava field, hoping against hope that they could make the haven of their underground cavern once more. It had been the only place where they had found some surcease.

A helicopter flew overhead, then dove, menacingly low. It sprayed machine gun fire before them, causing them to turn and try to run back toward the edge of the woods. But they were too far away, and once more, the splinters of lava spewed through the air before them as the solid magma was chewed up by rapid fire.

The sounds of the other vehicles and troops began to mingle with the roar of the helicopter blades as the chopper settled to the earth. Will and Travers looked into each other's desperate eyes.

"I'm sorry!" Will shouted to her, near tears with grief over the fate he had brought on themselves and others. "Run for it!"

She glanced toward the helicopter and saw four Green Berets running for them from its belly. She nodded in anguish and turned to run, favoring her weak ankle but managing to put distance between herself and Will as the Special Forces Soldiers gained ground.

As they drew nearer, Will took deep breaths and assumed a defensive karate stance. If they shot him, it was all over. If they wanted him alive... if he could draw on the forces inside himself, perhaps he had a chance.

The Berets spread, weapons trained on Will, to his flanks. Cautiously, they began to close in.

"Come on, boy," said one, his head cocked at the strange sight of Will though he had been, no doubt, forewarned about the blue skin. "Don't try anything. We're takin' ya home."

Will circled and waved his hands, staring intently at the rifles leveled in his direction. The nervous Berets had their fingers on the triggers. Suddenly, one of them swung his weapon toward another, who reflexively returned the gesture. Both were stupefied over the feeling of being jerked about like marionettes.

A third Beret instantly charged in, rifle butt ready to strike a blow to Will's skull. With two feet to spare, Will shot a pivoting leg up into the air. As if struck by his solid heel, the rifle sprang loose from the soldier's grasp and flew through the air behind him. The disoriented Beret found himself smashed full in the face by Will's leopard's paw blow.

As the soldier recoiled from that physical impact, Will made a clutching motion with his left hand, and the rifle hesitated in mid-air, then floated into Will's grasp. The other special Ops troops looked at him in a kind of superstitious awe.

Then, they tried to shoot him.

Will karate-chopped the air as he jumped and twisted his body, moving toward the soldiers. Their rifles jerked out of their control, and their bullets flew off the mark. Within a second, Will rifle-butted one of them, then jumped back as another fired, narrowly missing him. That one was dispatched by the butt of the flying rifle Will had directed his way. The rifle, following Will's hand-gestures, pulled back from the reeling soldier, then spun with dizzying speed, end over end, until it smashed into the third of his antagonists.

That effort cost Will, for while he was executing that brilliant maneuver, the fourth Beret lunged headlong at Will, using his rifle as a staff to knock Will off his feet and pin him to the ground.

"Gotcha, freak-boy!" he screamed, pinning Will's legs with his own and pressing the rifle mercilessly tight across Will's throat.

Will had mere seconds to act or lose consciousness, if not his very life. He clawed the air, clutching desperately for the face of his attacker. At last, he grabbed hold of the man's jaw. He could feel the energy flow along his arm, and the scream of pain was something he had come to expect when he decided—yes, now he was deciding—to burn his enemy. It was easy when he was in such a panic, the adrenalin flowed and activated his strange electro-chemistry.

The Beret, in an effort to finish the battle, pulled back, blisters already beginning to well up on the side of his face. Enraged, he raised the rifle above his head, ready to smash the butt down on Will's skull.

Will coiled his torso upward, plowing a knife-hand blow into the man's abdomen and evading the rifle butt as it smashed into hard lava. Then, another body piled onto theirs. It was the first adversary, momentarily stunned but now back in the fray.

Yet, not for long. As the two Green Berets together rose, hoisting Will to his feet between them, one felt the explosive blow of a rocketing uppercut while the other suffered the intense pain of a fierce stomp to his instep. In the next moment, a backhand fist finished the job of disabling his final attacker.

Four specially-trained fighters were on the ground, and their would-be captive stood free for another moment.

A bullet whizzed by Will's ear. As he dropped for safety, Will caught a glimpse of the pilot, still near the 'copter, firing at him. Behind him, an armored troop transport rolled into view.

Will scrambled over his downed attackers, plucking grenades from about their bodies. He stuffed the handles of four grenades into the tattered openings of his shirt, then pulled the pin on one and tossed it toward his remaining pursuers. They were too distant for the grenade to kill anyone, but he hoped to keep them away. If his booty of grenades could raise enough smoke in his wake, he might be able to rejoin Travers in their little rabbit hole. Then, they could see how far into the earth they might follow that hollow pocket.

Will rose and took off like a broken field runner, pausing to pull out a pin, whirl, and toss one grenade after him before darting in a different direction. One bullet after another ricocheted off the ground around him. He caught a glimpse of the smoke he had raised behind him. It would not last long, and he figured some of them could still make him out. Any second could be his last... but, there was the little hole they had slithered into before. Will spun, tossing one last grenade, before he scrambled for the small opening and slithered down into their erstwhile sanctuary once again.

"Pam?" he whispered fiercely, nearly out of breath.

"Down here!" came her reply.

Will hustled in a crouching run to the ledge, and stepped quickly down to join the trembling young woman who awaited him.

"I never thought you'd make it," she whispered.

"Neither did I," he whispered back, breathlessly.

The thumping of running soldiers' feet grew distinct near the cavern entrance. "Ground's full o' holes up in this part," they heard someone growl. "Which way did they go?"

"Don't matter," they heard an authoritative reply. "We're gonna fill them holes, boys."

Will snuck a glance toward the entrance to their little cavern, then swiftly ducked back down as he saw a hand appear with a flashlight. He ducked beneath the ledge again just before the head and shoulder of a soldier could follow, peeking inside. White light played over the ledge for a few seconds, then all was quiet, for just a few seconds more.

Then, a loud explosion shook Will and Pam to the core. A sheet of flame rushed by, inches above them as they clung to one another in terror. The Berets had tossed an incendiary bomb into the cavern. Within seconds, loud reports from other nearby caverns echoed through the ground, as the tactic was repeated in the various nooks and crannies of the lava land.

The sounds of soldiers and bombings gradually trailed off in the distance. It seemed they had either moved on, or were now awaiting silently for signs of life. The two lay huddled together, silent and as still as they could be, breathing together.

After a long time, Travers sat up. She was straddling Will's midsection, breathing deeply. Their eyes met. Neither of them moved, for a long moment. Then, as one, they joined, in a hot, tongue-lashing embrace. They clung and rolled in total abandon, hands grasping and pulling at ragged clothes, grabbing at each others' bodies, sharing all that they had in the nearness of death.

29.

Will and Travers neared the cavern entrance. All had been quiet for hours. The special forces troops had seemingly left the area. The couple even allowed themselves a short nap. A dim light revealed their features to one another. Travers tossed her hair, now with a seemingly liberated air about her. Will, however, hung his head, lost in thought as they took seats against opposite walls of the cavern.

"Will?" Travers said.

He shook his head. "I shouldn't have done that. I'm sorry."

"You weren't sorry at the time, as I remember," Travers teased him. "And you didn't do it. *We* did it." She shrugged.

Will gave her a grateful smile of relief. Then, in only a few seconds' time, he lapsed back into a morose state. "How much damage am I gonna do, though? I didn't mean to get those soldiers killed. I didn't mean to burn that forest. And I do know how babies are made—normally. I'm the last person who ought to be taking that chance."

"Don't think about that," Travers urged. "We have other problems." She stood up and shuffled toward the cave entrance. "You stay here, and we'll probably be okay, at least for a while," she said. "There's no doubt they're tracking you somehow. We're safer if I sneak around alone."

Travers squeezed through the little entrance into their cave and pushed herself back out into the surface world to go foraging.

Will dozed off again, with nothing to do, and no idea in the world how they were going to ultimately escape their dire situation.

After a time, Travers squeezed back inside the cavern with a freshly-killed chicken and some kindling. Will roused himself, astonished and delighted at the sight.

Will, refreshed from his nap, built a fire with the kindling sticks. Travers plucked the chicken, which was soon skewered and bound to a tripod of sticks bound with feed sack twine they had cadged from the farm.

Travers reached up through the opening and pulled in her final booty—a heavy blanket.

"Holy—!" said Will, now more amazed than ever. "What did you do, go in the old people's house?"

"Father forgive me, yes. I sneaked in while they were out."

"I'm not your father," griped Will. "Or do you think there's somebody else in here?"

"I didn't mean to annoy you. I'm speaking to Our Heavenly Fa—"

"I know, I did get that from TV. The big old man upstairs that created everything."

"Don't blaspheme, Will. I may be breaking the Commandments, but I expect to pay a price as it is."

"Whatever. I know my creators personally. They're no Gods."

"My dad always said there was a higher purpose for all things, in the sight of the Lord. He said that He would guide us with the Holy Spirit in times of doubt. And, Will, I felt that way when I saw those soldiers coming for you. I got the feeling that Major Avery is an evil man, acting for selfish reasons. He acted like some of the convicts I've known—manipulative, deceitful. He betrayed the General's trust. Something deep inside me made me—made me want to help you.

"I know you don't think much of General Gentry or Doctor Snyder, but... and I've had a hard time accepting that they could do the things they've done to you. I didn't want to work for them, Will. But, can't you see they did care for you? And I was raised to believe that our Heavenly Father cares so much more for all of us than any person ever could."

"Spare me," Will muttered. "No one cares for me. If your God is up there, ask him if he gave me a soul. Because if *he* cared for me—if he *made* me—why did he make it so I didn't stand a chance?"

Travers just shook her head. He seemed hopelessly cynical. She quietly tended to the rabbit she had caught and was cooking for them. At present, they began to tear it apart, not looking at one another as they worked at taking this sustenance into their bodies.

The pair had scarcely finished their meal when Travers sneezed. Will, ashamed of the rancor he had exhibited before, unfurled the blanket and gently wrapped her in it. She submitted, lying back, exhausted. It occurred to Will that she lacked his level of resistance, and was suffering from exposure to the elements. He knew this present arrangement could not ensure their survival for much longer.

As Travers rested silently, Will decided to try honing his new-found powers. He wanted to see what he could do with a little concentration, in a situation that was less spur-of-the-moment than the ones in which they had manifested up to now. He took a burning twig from the fire and shuffled about the cavern floor, picking up pieces of shrapnel from the exploded incendiary bomb. He gathered them into a small pile on the cavern floor.

He looked at them, breathing deeply, meditating, trying to find the emotional space within himself like the ones in which he had moved objects.

He considered that it had first occurred when he was euphoric, having an inkling of freedom to come from his confinement inside Proteus. His incendiary power, on the other hand, had manifested at times when he was frightened and angry.

Then, he realized that in the course of his repeated battles for life and liberty, he had already gained more control over his emotional state and his powers at the same time. Earlier that day, fighting the Special Forces in the open, he had experienced an elevated feeling indistinguishable from the fear and panic that had driven him at Wild Bill's or in the forest he had set ablaze. But it was also an adrenaline rush similar to the way he had felt when he had floated the glass animals. He decided to try to make himself feel that same elevated sensation now, as he worked to raise the metallic bomb shards from the cavern floor.

Little by little, the pieces twitched, then lifted themselves up and rose into the air. They hovered there, trembling in the half-light.

"Good." Travers had been watching. "Now, try to bring the pieces together," she urged.

Will did so, moving his cupped hands closer together. Mimicking his movement, the shrapnel gathered itself together into a rough little ball.

"It helps if I focus the vibe through my hands. It's like air-sculpting," Will commented.

"The 'vibe'? What does it feel like?" Travers asked.

"Kind of a tingling. It's almost like electric current, but it doesn't hurt. It's almost—solid, like a rope, but stiffer... I don't know how to describe it."

"Now, take some of the pieces out."

"Hard to move just the ones I want," Will reported, trying to follow her suggestion. Slowly, a couple of the shrapnel fragments moved away from the clump, but within seconds, all the shards fell to the ground.

"I don't know," Will said. "You should have seen me whipping a rifle around in mid-air while ago. I was, like, a wizard."

"So, it's easier with one object," Travers commented.

"I can't concentrate on too many things at one time. It weakens the field, or whatever you want to call it."

"But it's like some kind of vibration?"

"Yeah. I heard once, everything's really a field of vibrations. Guess I cast some pretty strong vibes," he quipped.

"Somehow, you connect with these objects—their molecules? Hm. How much weight can you lift this way?" Travers asked. "Have you ever tested it?"

"No." Will turned his attention to a smallish boulder nearby. With a two-handed pantomime, he lifted it from the ground. "I can feel this, tugging on me," he grunted. "I feel the weight. I'd say I can only move about what I could normally lift this way."

"I've heard stories about people with powers like this," Travers suggested. "Maybe they're true. Maybe you 'inherited' them from that 'gene pool' of yours. From what I saw in the folders, the chromosomes of thousands of people were experimented on when they put your DNA together."

"Maybe," Will acknowledged. "Like I needed something else to make me a little weirder. "All I've figured out for sure, is, like, if I'm mad, before I know it—something might catch fire. If I'm happy, I channel the energy some other way—maybe something floats. If I catch what's happening, I can damp it down."

"That's it. You have to be in tune with your body, aware of your moods—all the time. You have to be able to switch your emotional wavelength at any time, Will. There's a price for you, if you're going to control this ability you have."

"Yeah. I think you're right about that. It won't be easy. But it might be worth it. This 'power,' or whatever you call it, has save my life more than once."

"Maybe it'll help us get to safety somehow."

"'Safety?' Where would that be?" Will asked.

"I don't know. Maybe Canada. If we could get across the border, get your story out, maybe we could find some kind of asylum," Travers offered, just before sneezing again. "Like Gentry said, you're not a citizen. But, you were, 'Made in the USA.' If enough people knew your story, there's bound to be plenty who would take up for you, as a victim. It might give you some protection. People like Avery and Haas won't do in the light of day what they think they can get away with under cover of darkness. Maybe they'd back off."

"Maybe," Will said, unconvinced. But he had to listen to Travers, his one and only ally in this new, fugitive life. He knew of no better options.

30.

Travers smiled wanly, in what was meant to be an expression of encouragement. Then she suffered a sudden coughing fit. She lay back down, curling up in her blanket. Will knelt beside her and gently stroked her hair.

"I can't thank you enough for coming on this crazy ride with me," he said.

"It looked to me like we were both in the same danger," Travers replied. "But, crazy as it may be, I believe I did the right thing."

Will watched over her, admiringly. He knew that her exposure to him would likely prove lethal in the end. But, if they did manage to survive together, he would do anything for this precious woman.

At length, she slept. He picked her up and carried her back to their crude "nest". He spooned his body with hers and drifted into sleep as well.

Will woke to the sound of Travers' teeth chattering. He felt her forehead. It was distinctly warm. Not a good sign. He wrapped his arms around her, and gently, ever so gently and slowly, mustered all the panicky thoughts he could think of, trying to simulate enough of the kind of fear and panic that would generate his heated molecules, if that's what they were. He felt the psychic engine come into play, as he then moderated his thoughts, his feelings, just enough to radiate warmth into her body.

After a while, Travers roused from her sleep.

"Daddy?" she whimpered. "Daddy, I'm cold."

"This can't go on," Will whispered. "We've gotta get you to a doctor."

"Will?" She seemed to be waking further. "No. Too dangerous," she protested.

"They've told me that all my life," he shrugged.

And so it was that another dawn found the two intruders once again crossing the farmyard they had pilfered before for paltry supplies to sustain their lives. Will carried Travers in his arms, wrapped in the blanket as he staggered toward the farmhouse. As luck would have it, more rain had fallen throughout the long, weary trek. He had had to set her down several times, to rest his arms before continuing. He fought the horrible mental specter of helicopters, tanks, and jeeps of troops appearing to blast them both into oblivion before they could reach any haven.

As they crossed the barnyard, Travers murmured incoherently into Will's chest. Her free arm hung limply, dangling from her body. Her own danger was immediate and desperate.

Will staggered toward the goal line he had selected in his desperation, taking the steps up to the front porch of the farmhouse, only to be greeted at the front door by a shotgun muzzle in the face.

Immediately he pleaded with the farmer, who looked at them in terrified bewilderment. "This girl? She's real sick. She really needs a doctor."

"You stole from us," said the farmer.

"Yes, I admit, we stole. We were lost, and starving. We took some eggs, and some twine—and this blanket. But I brought your blanket back—sorry it's so wet."

"How 'bout you? How come you're all blue like that?"

"It's a—bad side effect—of an experiment."

"You volunteered for some weird experiment?" he asked.

"Uh—not exactly." Will said, looking around for signs of attack. It had to be well over an hour since they had left the relative safety of the lava pockets.

"D'you hurt that girl?"

"Look, I don't want to cause you any problems. I just want to save this girl. She's innocent, and I think she may be dying. Please, Mister. A doctor?" Travers's teeth chattered, poignantly. The farmer hesitated. "Do you have a phone?"

The farmer shifted on his feet, wielding the gun a bit nervously. Suddenly, his wife sidled up and gently pushed its barrel aside.

"Gladys? What the hell you doin'?" said the farmer.

"Being a Christian," she said. "Can't you see this gal's sick? You youngsters come inside," she said to Will.

Will stepped into the foyer. It was his first look at an old-fashioned country home. There were heavy oak furnishings, a coal burning stove, and a cuckoo clock on the wall that may well have been a hundred years old.

"I can't stay. Can we just call for help? Please?"

"That's right," Clarence agreed. "I don't want them Armies tearin' up the yard again."

"Call a doctor—please?" Will begged.

Gladys nodded Clarence toward the kitchen and pantomimed a phone with her hand. She winked. Clarence, catching her meaning, nodded, and made his way toward the kitchen.

"Why, she's just a sweet, innocent child, just look at her..." Gladys cooed over the prostrate form of Travers, now lying on the parlor floor.

In the kitchen, Clarence spoke softly into the wall phone.

"Yeah. Clarence. Yeah, Sheriff. I think I met that same blue kid they took a picture of last month... in the papers. They had him in a hospital, you know, caught by that sheriff down in Nevada. Right here—*now*. Yep. *In our home,* I'm tellin' ya. Okay? We will. Bye."

Back in the living room, Gladys offered, "Let's get her out of these wet things, don't you think? I'll go get some towels and a nice, dry blanket."

Will shrugged, and unwrapped the wet blanket. He barely resisted sobbing as he began to unbutton her blouse, in a situation so different from the only other time he had done so.

"Pam," he whispered to her, not knowing if she could hear. "They're calling you some help. Sorry I couldn't do more. I—I have to go," he choked.

Ron Brassfield

Travers opened her eyes and nodded. She was semi-comatose.

Gladys re-entered the room laden with towels, a robe and a quilt.

The front door stood open. Will was gone, run away into the downpour.

In moments, the blue lights of the law flashed in the house windows. A searchlight beam played over the lawn as the sheriff looked about. Clarence stood alert on his front porch.

Within seconds, a helicopter zoomed by overhead, causing their clothes to flap about their bodies as their gaze rose to the sky.

Will ran alongside a slowly moving train, and caught an open boxcar door. He hoisted himself up into the car, and rode the train into the distance, picking up speed.

An Army helicopter appeared overhead, and kept pace with the rolling train.

31.

Dusk.

The train rolled to a stop at a huge industrial depot. From time to time as the train rumbled along, Will had heard the sounds of the helicopter overhead, shadowing its progress. He prepared to make a stand, possibly his last. At least no one else would be around to get hurt this time.

Will poked his head out the boxcar door. He caught a glimpse of shadowy figures. Troops scattered along the length of the train, assuming positions.

A Green Beret, followed by a second, stole aboard the motionless car. The door slammed behind them. They turned, only to be battered from behind by flying hay bales. Will leapt from the car and sprinted away before they could regain their feet.

A Beret leapt from between cars to block him. Will whipped knife hands through the air. The soldier shuddered, unstruck by Will's hands, yet telekinetically suffering the force of their karate blows.

Will wrested the rifle from his grip and leapt onto the couplings which had been the soldier's perch. Leaning out, he saw some Special Ops troops searching the other cars. They took notice and cried out.

Will leapt out onto the gravel bank and swiftly pivoted in a circle, holding the gun barrel in his hands, then he stopped and released the rifle. It flew toward the men, twirling like a flying discus, propelled by Will's muscles, augmented by his eerie psionic force. The two transfixed soldiers recovered their reflexes and ate gravel, barely in time to evade its impossible flight.

Will ran for the building. Soldiers ran in hot pursuit. One blew a whistle. Bullets tore up the train cars and gravel bank in his wake.

Will reversed direction and hurdled the car couplings yet again, back to the other side. Troops climbed across the train after him, as those on this side spotted his motion and fired shots in his direction.

Another whistle blew, a train whistle this time. Will dashed across another set tracks in time for a train running the opposite way to cut off the troops. His energy beginning to flag, Will tried one last, desperate gambit. He reached out and willed himself a connection to the ladder on the side of one car, a few feet beyond his actual grasp. His power allowed him to take hold of it and hoist himself into the air. He pulled himself close enough to gain an actual grip on the rungs with aching muscles.

He had gained a few minutes or more. So far, they had been unwilling to actually fire on a moving freight train in order to get him. Or perhaps it had taken them a while to move their forces to his location. At any rate, having come so close, they would not be long in catching up to him again, and as he continued to elude them, he could not be sure they would not pull out more stops in their efforts to capture or kill him.

Will climbed to the top of the train car and ran along the length of the train, hopping the span from one car to the next until he finally gained access to his next temporary rolling sanctum.

It was approaching midnight in New York City at that moment. And, within a penthouse sanctum apartment, a closet door whipped open to reveal the bound and gagged Regina Snyder. Rough hands seized her. Vee hauled the haggard scientist into the luxury apartment. The incandescent light, though none too brilliant, was brighter than her eyes could yet bear. She tumbled to the floor as Vee released her, her legs too numb and weak for support. She writhed and trembled, humiliated, having soiled herself in the interminable hours she had spent standing in the cramped closet space.

Vee grabbed her by the hair and pulled her though the apartment, past opulent furnishings. She whimpered inchoate sounds. Vee slammed her bodily onto a water mattress filled with icy liquid.

In a moment, the dark form of Threll loomed above her. He bent and opened a black, hard shell case. Snyder turned her head to view its revealed contents, an array of gleaming surgical instruments. She struggled against her bonds.

"Isn't this relaxing, after all that standing up? Feeling chatty, perchance?"

Threll lightly dangled a scalpel above Snyder's eye. Snyder clamped her eyes closed and shuddered. Threll picked carefully at the edge of her duct tape gag with the sharp scalpel. He gained an edge, then roughly ripped off the tape.

"Ahhhh! You're insane!" Snyder gasped.

Threll frowned, then promptly duct-taped Snyder's mouth shut again. He picked through his case for another torture instrument, then displayed a pair of sharpened tongs. He moved in closer, speaking intimately.

"Wrong answer."

Before Threll could make another move, his telephone rang and he paused to answer it. "Yes."

At the other end of the conversation, Eugene Avery had news. "He slipped by a platoon while ago. It's like he's prepared for us, the son of a bitch. I want to give the shoot to kill order."

"That would cost you a lot, but, it's your call, Major," said Threll, his lip curling up.

A moment of silence followed before Avery continued. "Well, there's something I thought you should know. Gentry never showed up to resign."

"What? Where is he?"

"Vanished from the face of the earth. We had a team watching for him... he was scheduled for a terminal event. He never showed up in Washington. Never went home. I never thought that straight arrow would go underground."

"Yet, he did, didn't he? However, my own identity, as he knows it, is untraceable. I certainly doubt he has any means of getting at you, either, though I'd keep my eyes peeled. And he certainly couldn't know Will Monday's whereabouts, in transit as he is. So, I doubt he's any threat. Thanks for the advisory, just the same."

"It's a definite concern," Avery warned. "He's been in intelligence a long time."

"Perhaps. I would guess he might have surmised your intentions. But, he probably skipped the country, in that case."

More than halfway across the USA, Will sat on the cold steel floor of a train car and struggled to come up with a plan. He abruptly realized, to his horror, that he was not truly alone.

"Good news, Will. You're heading our way. East, across Wyoming. Come join us. Talk over old times."

The voice was purely in his head. The loathsome voice of Jacob Threll—followed by another voice, one he had known since his infancy. Now, it was exhausted, trembling.

"We're somewhere in New York City, Will. I—want you to know, I won't betray you. And, I want to say, I'm sorry—for everything."

"No, no, no...!" Sparks flew up from the floor as Will pounded his fists on steel. Suddenly, in the wave of Will's miserable frustration, the sound of Travers' voice, from his memory, also lingered in his inner ear, saying *"They cared..."* He had been a tragic misfortune to all who had ever known him. He was more powerful than any human being, yet... so powerless.

McIntire spoke to him from memories that were only days old, yet, it seemed centuries ago. *"Know your opponent's mind and you'll know how to defeat him..."* Will took slow, deep breaths to try to calm down—to try to think, to come up with some way to defeat his enemies. Yet, how could he use this advice? How could he understand such people, how they could be so cruel, so relentless? They had everything. Why must they pursue him, too? Why would they kill and lay waste to anything that stood in the way of possessing him, Will Monday? Why? He stiffened, every muscle growing taut, teeth gritted. Suddenly, sparks flew off the walls of the train car. Will realized that if anything flammable had been in the car with him, in his rage he could have ignited another conflagration.

That was when he startled to hear Threll's disembodied voice break up in static.

"Damn. He's bli*kin* ou* again. No. There he is... How human are you, Will? Can you care for another person? Let J*cob be your g*ide..."

Threll's voice cut out entirely. Will relaxed. The voice resumed.

"—*ead due east. The Green Berets are going to kill you, Will. I offer you a safe haven. Come *n—"

Will exerted his power once more. Threll's voice crackled and cut off again. Will nodded grimly, finding confirmation in these occurrences. When he exerted his psionic power, the transmissions from Threll were jammed. He took deep breaths, relaxed, and listened calmly as the voice reappeared.

"I will keep you posted, Will. Listen to me, and I'll tell you how to evade the soldiers. Come to me, and you'll be safe. Once you're here, you can do as you please with this 'doctor' who caused you so much misery all these years. A new day is dawning for you, Will. All you have to do, is do as I say."

A series of small, mystifying incidents were reported over the next few days, in small, out of the way places across the United States. Rumors and fleeting eyewitness accounts of a mysterious phantom in blue who appeared and disappeared in a twinkling.

For example, in a small community in Nebraska, the weather was brisk but pleasant as a certain young family pulled into the local McDonald's for a meal. Three young children romped about while their parents unloaded bags of fast food onto an outdoor table.

As the father turned to calm the kids, one meal carton floated away, rounding a nearby shrub. The mother saw, and caught a nervous breath. She shook her head in disbelief. Addled, she picked up the Happy Meals she had unloaded, and calmly replaced them in the bags.

Behind the shrub, Will wolfed the hamburger and french fries down as the mother walked unsteadily back toward the restaurant, the bewildered father and kids following, calling and waving after her.

32.

At a loading dock, a workman with a clipboard watched as a second, driving a fork lift, deposited a palette of freight in the rear of a truck trailer. They walked inside together.

Will scrambled across the pavement and leaped up onto the dock. He scrambled to find cover inside the truck trailer.

A driver emerged from the rig, and closed the doors to the trailer. The truck proceeded to roll hundreds of miles across superhighways, the trailer finally settling to rest against the loading dock of discount department store.

A dock worker watched as the driver clipped the seal, and opened the door. Then, Will leaped out. No longer blue, but still startling to behold. He now wore new, youth-style clothing, and a thick application of pancake make-up.

The driver and dock worker shrank back a step. Will leaped from the platform and sprinted away. Inside the trailer, ragged shrink-wrap torn from freight palettes, broken cosmetic cartons, and strewn men's clothing marked the activities he had engaged in as a stowaway.

Not long after, Will, huddled under a tarp in the back of someone's pickup truck, stuck his head up to sneak a peek at the road. A green airport sign flashed by. In moments, a strange figure made a daring leap from the truck bed onto the roadside, going limp and rolling so as to minimize the impact.

Back in Idaho, Travers lay on a gurney among sick, uninsured unfortunates, in the emergency room of a county hospital. She could not remember having ever felt so miserable, though personnel had given her an icy immersion bath to break her fever, just on the threshold of permanent brain damage.

Now, she wondered what lay in store for her. She had carried no identification and had refused to identify herself to hospital personnel. But, she realized, that in itself would soon have local authorities looking into her situation, and very likely they would have been asked by Federal authorities by now to be on the lookout for her.

But, she could not have anticipated the appearance of the man who did appear at her side. McIntire, left arm in a cast, stole up beside the gurney. He held his finger to his lips and set a plastic bag of clothing on the gurney.

Whispering, he said, "Figured someone besides me might end up in here. I was signing out when I caught a glimpse of them wheeling you in here. Could you travel?"

"I'm weak—but—willing," Travers smiled.

McIntire checked her wrist band. "You didn't tell 'em your name?"

"No way. You?"

"One of 'em," he grinned. "Had one lying around I hadn't used lately. And I paid by money order. Hey. You made the news." He pulled a tabloid newspaper from beneath his cast. Its headline read, "BLUE TERRORIST SURRENDERS FEMALE CAPTIVE TO RURAL COUPLE."

"'Terrorist,' huh? Oh, great."

"Will always thought he could be like Michael Jackson if he had the chance. Weird, but famous," McIntire chuckled.

"Well, now he's both," Travers replied.

McIntire shoved the bag of clothing at Travers. "I went shopping for ya. Let's see if we can't slip out of here. Try these things on."

In the hospital parking lot, McIntire escorted Travers to a Monte Carlo.

"Impressive wheels. Where'd you get 'em?"

"Rental. Under my nom du guerre. You're not gonna catch this boy without some mattress money."

"Apparently."

As they drove from the hospital, McIntire said, "Reach under the seat."

Travers did so, surprised to pull forth the tracker tablet McIntire had used in the woods.

"Watch the blip," he said.

"So this is how you did it. It's moving ... East."

"Did Will say anything about going East?"

"No. But—you know, judging from what Will told me before, by now, *he* may be 'talking' to him. Maybe that's why he's going East."

"Who are you talking about?"

"The enemy. Jacob Threll."

33.

McIntire drove with his good right hand while Travers watched the tracker tablet.

"He called it gradual entrainment," she explained, as McIntire listened intently to her account. "It's a beam broadcast on extra-low frequencies into a tiny microchip—implanted inside a victim's head."

"You're sure Will's implanted?" McIntire asked.

"Yes, but I'd need a CAT scan to prove it."

"How about the muscle man? 'Vee?'"

"Brain surgery. Lots of implants. Threll shoots massive nerve interference to his frontal lobes and their partners in the brain."

McIntire thought about it a moment, then shuddered slightly. "Any way to disrupt this 'entrainment?'"

"Maybe—some counter frequency? Or, if we can just pull out the chips—wait a minute. Here's his blip again. And he's moving *'way* faster."

Will stole across the tarmac of the airport, pacing a baggage cart, hunched low so as not to be noticed by its driver or any other observers. He read the tags on a suitcase, only to have the voice of the "guide' who had helped him get this far, resound once more in his head.

"*Aurora Airport. Congratulations. Now you need Flight 38 to Chicago. Stay concealed there and wait. The next leg of your journey will bring you to the Big Apple itself.*"

Baggage handlers loaded luggage onto a conveyer belt running into the plane's belly. Suddenly, they started at the sight of suitcases jumping off the other side of the car. One Baggage Handler wet a finger and raised it to the wind, pulling down the corners of his mouth as he looked wide-eyed at the other.

The second man shrugged, and joined his companion in walking around to retrieve the cases that had jumped off the cart.

Will crept from behind the conveyer and jumped on, riding up into the cargo hold while the men were distracted.

Once the full load of baggage was on board, and the engines were sufficiently revved, the jet left the tarmac, climbing into space.

By early evening, Washington Square Park in downtown Manhattan found an incongruous trio sitting on a park bench while skateboarders and frisbee throwers, hustlers, tourists, and children plied and played at the stump-ends of another raucous New York day. On a bench sat Jacob Threll, glancing at a laptop computer. The morose Regina Snyder sat beside him. From her left, with his arm around her, Vee rested his hand heavily on her shoulder.

"Remarkable. He made it. All the way across the country. Of course, those signal dropouts hindered the Major's progress, just as they made me lose contact. The boy's unique energies in operation, I'd guess." Threll raised an eyebrow toward Snyder. She had nothing to say about the "unique energies."

"He might be coming *for* you, not *to* you," she stated, flatly.

"Yes, why exactly is he coming?" asked Threll, rhetorically, stoking his chin. "My offer of asylum? To kill me? Or you? I have to admit, I find him fascinating. I mean, normally, I wave money—people fall all over themselves to serve me. But money means nothing to him. I sic Vee on him—I mean, *look* at him, he's *invincible*—and your son of a test tube actually *fights back*. He's from an altogether different context, like no one I've ever known. Ahhh. And he's very close now." Threll's anticipation seemed palpable—even, Snyder thought, *personal*.

Threll snapped his notebook shut and stood up for a look around.

Will strolled, hands in pockets, into the park, his stubbled face terribly swarthy from his crude layer of make-up. Despite his intense curiosity about people, Will had carefully avoided eye contact with any of the thousands of pedestrians he had passed. If any noticed the feline cast to his eyes—well, he had no way of knowing how they might react. He had walked many miles, resting occasionally and cadging food along the way from restaurant dumpsters like the other vagabonds of the city. Now, as he entered the park, still awed by the city's majestic sights, he gawked like a tourist from the outback even as he cast quick, furtive glances about in search of his tormentor.

He flinched as Threll's voice resounded in his head, yet again.

"You take directions very well. Now, there's a bench at the south end of the park. Go say 'hello,' won't you?"

At the same moment, unseen by any of these, McIntire and Travers, edgy and haggard from their marathon road trip, strode rapidly from another direction. They had managed, in the fits and starts of Will's delays while hiding and sneaking about airport baggage compartments, and his trek from LaGuardia across town to lower Manhattan, to close the gap in time to converge on the blip which they, like Threll and Avery, had been tracking cross-country.

At the park's edge, amid the random activities of the park visitors, a raffish young thug with a yo-yo spied Threll's nod of his head. The thug whistled loudly, a signal for others to mobilize in turn.

A second thug, fifty yards away, rapidly walked up to the couple of policemen strolling on foot patrol, and discreetly handed off a small, brown paper bag. The cops put their backs to the world and took a peek. Exchanging grins over what they saw, they turned together and strolled from the scene.

Will approached Vee and Snyder on the park bench. With his pancake makeup, face-to-face with the burned Vee and the frightened Snyder, the trio resembled an open-air meeting of some kind of bizarre support group.

"Ta-da. Here's your co-creator and long-time tormenter—alive," crowed Threll, in his ghoulishly cheerful fashion. "Come with us and you, too, can live on. Torment her in return, if you like." He strolled closer to Will, his voice growing more ominous, more emphatic. "Otherwise, the government who created you, is coming to destroy you. It's, as you say, a 'no brainer.'"

As Threll spoke, a van with dark windows rounded the corner opposite the park. Two more thugs approached from the interior of the park, converging with the previous pair. Vee pulled Snyder to her feet, and headed with her toward the van. As they moved away, Will started in their direction, until he suddenly found himself cut off and surrounded by the four thugs who had just sauntered up.

Snyder's haggard face reeked of desperation, even as she shook her head at Will. "Get away. He's a maniac," she called, over her shoulder.

"Coming, Will?" Threll turned to follow in the wake of the others. "As you can see, I've provided you with escorts."

Will shuffled, a tight bundle of conflicting emotions.

Vee handed Snyder off to a pair of the thugs by the van's sliding side panel door, and walked around to the front of the van. As they pulled the side door open, Snyder, her fear getting the best of her, started trying to pull free.

Will sprinted forth, but Threll's four thugs seized him. Will engaged them in hand-to-hand combat.

McIntire stopped short as he and Travers roamed the park, on alert.

"There! Damn, they've got Snyder. Stay back. Call the cops."

McIntire, his training coming into play, sidled up beside the van, covering the thugs with a Walther P-99 he drew from inside his jacket.

"Let her go," he commanded, boldly.

"McIntire. Oh, thank God," Snyder's relief was nearly hysterical.

By this time, Will's martial arts skills had put down two of this attackers. While struggling with the other two, he spotted McIntire, and the danger approaching him from behind.

"Mac?!—Look out!"

A karate chop to the back of the neck took McIntire down. The massive form of Vee stood over his fallen body.

Thugs pulled Snyder back toward the van's open side door. Vee turned, only to take Will's leaping kick in the chest. He went down! A thug turned on Will with a knife. Will grabbed his wrist, twisted it under, and belted him an uppercut to the chin before he knew what had hit him. Two thugs caught up to Will and grabbed his arms.

"Check this, shitheads." Will knew what he could do now, and was prepared to do his worst. The air around him shimmered. The thugs drew back, but it was too late as their clothes actually caught on fire. They screamed wildly, and broke off their attack in a panicky effort to save themselves. In the few seconds which had elapsed, the other two had dragged the wildly struggling Snyder into the van.

"Will!" she screamed.

Vee's foot kicked Will's head, knocked him rolling across the curb. Holding his skull, Will tried manfully to recover. Just as he had raised himself up on an elbow, Vee planted himself between Will and the van. Will pivoted his body, throwing a kick in the air, all his telekinetic power behind it. Vee, caught unawares, hurtled back against the side of the van. As usual, however, he seemed scarcely to feel any pain.

"Are you—my mother?" Will called to Snyder as the van's sliding door started to close.

"Yes!" she called back, before the sliding door sealed her inside.

34.

"Your 'mother?' I wonder just what that means, don't you? Well, if you'd like to know more, put yourself in Vee's hands. Right now." Threll spoke into his headset again as he guardedly made his way toward the driver's seat of the van.

Will rose, fiercely determined not to submit as Vee confronted him once more. Yet, even with Will's telekinetic powers to augment his fighting skills, the mighty, insensate giant stood as a daunting obstacle.

Vee stiffened for a second, as though listening to something. Will realized they shared the voice of Threll inside their skulls, but the wicked manipulator must have been broadcasting to the two of them on separate channels. Vee suddenly grinned and dashed off toward a nearby subway entrance. As he did, Threll's van took off, with a screech, in the opposite direction.

Will chose to sprint after the van. Taking a desperate leap, he tried to catch onto the back door ladder. He fell short by a couple of feet, but hung in midair behind the van, as though he actually held a rung. It was the same trick he had used to catch a train, and now he was going to catch his tormentor instead.

The van, "towing" Will through the air, drove by Travers.

"Will!"

A siren grew audible. The policemen in the park, who had turned away before, heard Travers' cries and turned up from somewhere in the park.

"All right, lady, calm down. What's up?"

"The van! It's a kidnapping!"

They followed her pointing finger to see Threll's now-distant van rounding a corner, Will "flying" close behind.

One Policeman shrugged to the other, who shook his head, not quite sure what they had just seen. He pulled out his notepad and asked, "Did you get the license number?"

In the next block, now out of sight of the park, Will "swam," hand over hand, closer to the van until he had a hand grip on the ladder. He pulled his feet up onto the rails.

Inside the van, one of the thugs called to Threll from the back seat, "Hey, Mister Bankwad. You got a hitchhiker back here!"

Threll glanced at his rear view mirrors. "Perfect."

Threll fumbled in a bag beside him and pulled out his headset.

Will, climbing to the top of the van, heard a sharp, sudden squealing in his ears for a few seconds. The pain made him grimace.

"Testing. Testing," he heard Threll's taunting voice. Will tried for a solid grip on the van's roof.

"Don't be mad at me, Will, I'm your only chance. I want you alive, understand? I'll save you, but you must submit to me."

"No way!" Will screamed, at the top of his lungs.

At the wheel, Threll twisted a dial on the earpiece of his headset. The piercing sound he had heard in the canyon out West screeched anew in Will's head. He had forgotten the intensity of the pain. He clutched at his head with one hand, barely managing to hold onto the ladder with the other. To unsettle his hold, Threll sped up suddenly, skidding the van around a corner into an alley. There, he slammed on the brakes and came to a dead stop.

Will tumbled to the pavement, holding his head with both hands.

Threll got out and strolled to the back of the van. For the first time, he spoke in sincerely hurt, grave tones.

"You'd resist me to the death, wouldn't you?"

For Will, the words were lost as the world reeled and squealed from his prone position on the ground. He sensed Threll towering above him. With a supreme effort, he managed to lumber to his feet and throw a punch. Threll easily sidestepped the blow. Then, he adjusted his headset, intensifying the sound which was ripping Will's soul.

Will keeled over again. The sound of a siren grew louder. One of Threll's two young, urban accomplices rounded the corner of the van as the other remained inside, keeping custody of Regina Snyder.

"Quickly! Haul him inside!" Threll barked.

"Uh-uh, I don't think so," said the thug, looking warily at the writhing Will. "He ain't human, man."

"Oh, he can't hurt you now."

The thug cocked his head. Raising his eyebrows, he put his palms up and stood there.

Exasperated, Threll rolled his eyes, then pulled out his wallet. He whipped out some bills and slapped the cash into the young thug's palm. The hoodlum slipped the money into his pocket and bent toward Will. But he stopped abruptly, caught in flashing blue lights as the police car whose siren they had been hearing stopped at the end of the alley. Two police patrolmen stepped out of the vehicle and, resting their hands on their pistol butts, walked slowly toward the scene.

"Get back inside and keep the woman quiet," Threll whispered. His hireling obeyed. Threll glanced down and saw Will, wincing but eyes open, gritting his teeth and shaking his head.

Threll hesitated only a second, calculating his move, before throwing out his arms in a gesture of delighted welcome for the men in blue.

"Officers! So glad to see you! This maniac attacked us. Hounded us right out of the park. He was wild! Savage! We tried to get away, but he clung to my van like a leech," Threll went on in effusive, faux relief over their arrival.

"Looks like he's sick," one policeman observed.

"Looks like he's *weird*," the other one noted.

By the time they had taken Threll's statement, a crowd of onlookers had gathered at the end of the alley, and by the time an ambulance arrived for Will, a news crew had arrived as well, capturing the event on video as many tongues wagged, speculating on what was the meaning of this young blue man collapsed in the alleyway.

35.

Threll's van drove the downtown streets, its driver seething.

"Thanks for nothing," he snapped at the thugs who rode in back. If you'd simply lifted him into the van, we could have been on our way."

"I's thinkin' I was gonna get burned, mister."

"That bonus money I paid you—"

"Hey, man, don't gimme grief. I was gonna pick him up. *You* froze when the fuzz showed up. Told me to get back in, man. Hadn' been for that—"

"All right. Shut up," Threll snarled. His mind seemed to wander off to other matters as he drove.

In the back, Snyder fought the latest panic attack, wondering what came next. She feared Threll would take his frustrations out on her once more, as soon as they were off the streets.

The van soon pulled into a nondescript off-street garage—actually, she observed once they were inside, a chop shop. The door was open only long enough to admit the van. At the other door, facing outward, sat a black Mercedes Benz with tinted windows.

Threll, Snyder, and his two hirelings emerged from the van, to be greeted by a beefy, unsavory man in a white undershirt and jeans, sporting a Colt .45 pistol in a shoulder holster. He was surrounded by several other lowlife characters.

"Well? Have a nice turn on the town?" he asked Threll.

"That's about all," Threll replied evenly, casting a bitter glance at the two thugs who had ridden with him. "But thanks for the parking privileges."

"Hey, we did our—" one of the hired thugs began. Threll held up his hand.

"Think nothing of it," he said, through gritted teeth. "The muscle, the van, and the parking ... as we agreed." Threll counted out still more cash into the outstretched paw of the garage proprietor.

"Don't do anything with it I wouldn't do," Threll said, matching the man's cold smile.

"Pleasure doin' business," said the man. "Call any time."

"Sure. See you around." Threll clutched Snyder's arm and pushed her toward the Mercedes, depositing her into the back seat. He circled to enter the driver's side.

The garage man grinned and waved him off.

The door opened fleetingly, and Threll drove out onto the cracked and buckling New York side street. He cruised at a moderate speed down the block. Snyder looked back, trying to make out their whereabouts. Just as they were turning the corner, the ground beneath them palpitated. A blazing yellow and orange blast erupted from the garage they had just left behind, blowing the steel slatted garage doors in pieces across the street. Snyder screamed in horror, then turned to look at Threll through the glass panel which partitioned the front seat from the back.

Threll turned his head, his eyes wide in mock horror. "Looks like we left in the nick of time, eh, Doctor?" The knowledge to be seen in his glittering eyes only increased her horror.

A blotchy, broken ceiling of plastered concrete swam into focus before Will's eyes as he awoke. He found himself lying on a jail cot, blinking himself awake. He sat up, wearily, looking around. His wide eyes met those of a prisoner in the cell across the aisle.

"You. Your eyes. They're like a cat. You're from the government—aren't you?. They're experimenting with new breeds, aren't they? I *knew* it!"

"Who—who told you?" Will looked up, amazed. This seemed to be a person who had somehow learned the truth.

"Oh, I know. They're gonna exterminate the working classes, worldwide. All they had to do was catalog all the genes. I know."

"But how do you—?" Will stammered.

"That's what those cattle mutilations are all about," the prisoner continued. "Yes, and you know about it, too, don't you?"

"Well, I'm not—exactly sure what you're..." Will began, wondering where this conversation was going. He hadn't heard about "the cattle mutilations."

"When they're through, they're gonna set off anthrax bombs everywhere. The rich will be safe in their underground cities built by FEMA. They cut a deal with the aliens. Right?"

"Right. That's right." nodded Will.

The prisoner started shaking his head, slowly. He drilled a hole through Will with his staring eyes, filled with horror. Slowly, he backed up against his bunk and sat down, finally casting down his eyes upon the floor.

Anything's possible—isn't it? Will thought. This crazed bunker might be locked up precisely because he held secret knowledge of a plot menacing mankind. Just as he, himself, was locked up for *being* something very real and strangely menacing, to these people. It looked as though it was going to be as bad as General Gentry had always said it would be if Will got into the general population.

In time, a couple of cops came along and opened Will's cell. They clamped his hands and feet in manacles and chains. Then, they escorted him, walking in humiliating baby-steps, to an interrogation room, where a fat, dumpy, and cynical-looking police captain named Chastain awaited him. In a few silent, lingering minutes, they were joined by a cigarette-smoking man whom the cops addressed only as "Detective."

Both police men leveled surly, accusing stares at Will for another long time. No one spoke. Will felt they were trying to cover their fear of him with their hostile glares. They were annoying, accusing him with their eyes like that. He had done nothing wrong, he felt, yet he was already, in their eyes, a criminal.

Will kept his hands below the table. He was hungry. He felt the vibration within him, his power stirring a little. The unseen feelers he extended were now probing, probing along the links of the chains. Will sat motionless as a stone.

Finally, Chastain picked up a clipboard and flipped a page. "Let's see what we've been up to today. Disturbing the peace, disorderly conduct, assault..." he arched an eyebrow, "...*suspicion of arson*..."

"Oh, great," muttered Will.

"We see you paint yourself up like this, you attack pedestrians—we see a cry for help, here. Well, here we are. You got our attention."

The sound of clinking chains rustled in the room. Will raised unshackled hands above the table. The detective nearly swallowed his cigarette. He and Chastain shared a "do you see that?" look.

"Guess I did," Will said.

Elsewhere in the city, McIntire and Travers sat, glumly, at a bar. The local evening news played on the TV overhead, the anchor announcing, "The President arrived in New York this morning for a roundtable discussion with business leaders..."

McIntire held an ice pack to his neck. Travers scanned the New York Yellow Pages, searching for something.

"WBNT crew took this exclusive video near the scene of the incident in Washington Square Park this afternoon," said the news anchor. Travers and McIntire riveted their attention to the set.

On screen, police and ambulance medics retrieved Will's unconscious form, as Threll hastily climbed into his van in the background.

"The police got him," Pam gasped.

"Even Threll didn't want to start slaughtering cops in the middle of the city," McIntire observed.

"What do we do?'

"Snatch him before Threll can. Get to the neighborhood precinct where they're holding him," McIntire replied. "I can bust him out if I have to, but..."

"Then let's go!" Travers charged out of the restaurant.

"Wait!—" McIntire called. "What the hell."

He stood up and trundled out after her, his head still throbbing. Still, he had heard her horror stories and had to admire her spunk. For some reason, she seemed as deeply devoted to helping Will as he was himself.

Back in the precinct interrogation room, Chastain marched the length of the table, toward Will.

"Get those shackles back on."

Will gestured with his forefinger. Chastain's tie flew up, and the shocked Captain found himself dragged by the tie, right into Will's grasp.

Gagging, Chastain grabbed for his shoulder holster. Will whipped double-knuckles into the back of his hand, rendering it useless. The detective drew his gun, but the hapless Chastain blocked his shot at Will.

"I don't care if this is my last minute alive, you hear me?" Will whispered fiercely. "You're gonna unlock my feet, right now."

Will looked past Chastain, at the detective.

"Then you're gonna shoot me when he bends down, right?"

Will grimaced, and with a grunt, he threw up his arm. The table flew upward on its end, swatting the detective like a fly. Unconscious, he dropped to the floor. The table floated back into its normal position.

"Oh, God, wh-what the hell are you?" blubbered Chastain.

"Innocent. Did you ever think of that? Drop your charges," Will demanded. "The man I was with when your people picked me up—that man is holding a hostage. I have to get to her. He's capable of anything. I've seen him slaughter a whole platoon of soldiers. Instead of holding me for nothing, you could be catching a murderer."

Chastain's face was etched with uncomprehending fear, but he swallowed and said, "Okay, okay. I didn't realize. Where do we start?"

"Like I said, we start by unlocking my ankles."

Will gripped the man's shoulder in a nerve pinch and forced him to his knees. Keys and chains clattered as Chastain unlocked the leg shackles. Then, Will pulled him back up by the necktie.

A cop, alerted by the noise from the table, peeked inside the door. His face registered alarm as he took in the scene in the room. Chastain, red-faced, looked at him, gurgling.

The cop rushed inside, drawing his gun. It flew from his hand the instant he raised it—right into Will's outstretched hand.

"Don't make me have to hurt you," he told the policeman.

"He's—magnetic 'r somethin,'" Chastain gasped.

The Cop drew his nightstick, only to have it whip up into his face and knock him cold. Will pivoted over toward the door. Stretching out his right hand to grasp the cop's shirt, he yanked him inside and dropped Chastain to quietly shut the door with his left hand.

In a moment, Will slipped through the door and began strolling through the booking room. Cops at desks gradually started to take notice and ignore the perps they were booking. A wave of eyes grew fixed upon Will as he moved through the area. The notice was not lost on Will, who turned and looked at the spectators for a second.

Chastain staggered out after him, croaking, "Stop that freak."

That was Will's cue to sprint toward the front doors of the precinct house, hearing the shouts and pandemonium in his wake.

Will tore out the front doors, into the night, only to face a phalanx of press photographers who sprang to life, frenetically clicking off shots of the mysterious blue man who had been glimpsed on the evening news broadcast. Excited cries erupted from their midst in various voices. "It's him! He's real! Page one! He made bail? I think he's escaping!"

36.

Will was plowing through the midst of the assembled press before the first rank of pursuing policemen emerged into the night to pursue him.

Just down the block from the precinct house, a cabbie peeked over his shoulder at Travers and McIntire in the back seat. He warily slowed the vehicle to a stop. "Excitement up ahead, folks," he said, laconically.

McIntire slipped the cabbie a bill as he and Travers debarked from the taxi for a better look. They caught glimpses of Will as he shoved his way through the photographers, who were still vying for more pictures.

"Get out of the way!" snarled a policeman, shoving through the crowd after Will, his Glock pointed toward the sky as he shoved reporters and photographers from his weaving path.

Will spotted a manhole cover, and saw a chance. He put his hands before him, level, palms up. He crouched, then made a lifting motion, straining greatly. The cover rose and slid off the manhole.

As the cops broke through the press, Will leaped down into the darkness. Cops rushed over to the hole within a second behind him, shooting down into the hole. The sound of a splash mingled with resounding echoes of their gunshots, but they could see nothing in the blackness.

"Somebody get some lights!" called Chastain, struggling to reach the site. "We'll catch 'im. He sure can't see down there."

Travers and McIntire shared a horrified glance, realizing they were too late. McIntire hardly missed a beat. He strolled toward the scene as the cops turned their attention to dispersing the crowd. Casually, McIntire sidled up near the manhole, taking a sidelong peek to assess the fall. Then, he dropped neatly inside, himself.

"Mac!" called Travers. She put her fist over her mouth. He knew what he was doing. She had to hope so.

Angry and confused cries erupted from the cops as they noticed, too late, that a man with his arm in a cast had dared to do what none of them would. "Hey! God damn it, what now? ... All right, get outta heah. ... Hurry up with those lights, will yez? ... Ropes! ... We need a harness here!"

In the sewer, McIntire picked himself up from his paratrooper landing and took a few staggering steps into the darkness before calling out, "Will!". Echoes rang hollow in the dank tunnel.

"Will! It's me—Mac. I've got Pam with me. We want to help. Will!"

A hand clasped McIntire's wrist, in the darkness. The warriors and friends stood reunited at last.

"Didn't get a chance to tell you how glad I was to see you today," Will said.

"Yeah, I left my dogtags in Idaho. Hoped they'd think I was dead. The bastards left too many barbequed soldier parts for anyone to tell for sure."

"How'd you find me?"

"Same way they did, I guess. I held on to one of their tracker tablets."

"You did? Tell me something. Did it—cut out on you a lot?"

"Yeah. How'd you know?"

"Just a hunch. Listen, you're the greatest, Mac. But, please, back out of this. Look at you. I don't want you getting hurt any more. For me, it's just a matter of time..."

"Don't talk that way. You can beat 'em."

"Mac, you know how you told me I had to get in my opponent's head? Well, *Threll's* in *my* head. He wants to—*own* me, I guess. I just want to put him out of my misery, before..." Will choked up.

McIntire fished in his pocket, handed Will a folded scrap of paper.

"Look, I gave Pam a cell phone. That's her number," he said, emphatically. "She found a place in the phone book where they can locate your implants. Get *rid* of 'em. Understand? Threll'll be out of your head. Avery won't be able to track you."

"Really? That's fantastic! Where is this place? Can we go now?" Will asked.

"No. It's a medical clinic, it's closed. We'll have to get their technicians to run the machines. If you can make it till morning..."

Faint echoes of the police voices reached them. Lights shone down into the tunnel, back at the manhole. They were nearly in range of the waving beams.

"How 'bout you? Can you make it out of here?"

"I'll play the cops," McIntire replied. "Buy you a minute. Go!"

Will nodded, turned, and ran into the darkness.

On the dark street outside the precinct house, the crowd's excitement was still at a high pitch. Travers watched as the cops labored, hauling McIntire up on a sling which they had lowered into the sewer. She heaved a huge sigh of relief.

"Thank, guys," McIntire said, laconically. "That was scary."

The captain seemed about to burst a blood vessel. "Why the hell'd ya jump down there?" he demanded.

"*Jump?* I was *blinded* by all those *flashbulbs*. I *fell* in."

"Watch your step, Mister. You coulda got killed. Take care of him, huh, Lady?" he added, as Travers, nodding gratefully, made her way forward to take his arm.

The cops focused on the manhole, preparing to lower some of their own number into the sewer. McIntire limped away with Travers.

"Thank God," she whispered. "Did you—"

McIntire nodded. "Yeah. He's okay. I told him our plan. Told him to make it 'til morning."

"Then what?" Travers asked. "If we can save him, what kind of future does he have?"

McIntire sighed. "I don't know. Still underground, I guess."

"Will he accept that?"

McIntire sighed. "He sounded half-resigned they're gonna kill him. Not that I blame him. But, there's hope."

"Is that why we're—trying to help him?" Travers asked, plaintively.

McIntire paused, and swallowed a lump in his throat. "For the sake of hope? I guess. I only know he's innocent. And those bastards chasing him are the worst sort of scum. Guess I've seen their kind win one too many times. And I owe 'em something personal, too." He held out his cast.

Elsewhere, in a shabby motel room, the nightly news played to a man seated in a recliner. A pistol lay on the table beside his elbow. The on-screen announcer was saying, "The mysterious, 'blue' arson suspect continues to elude authorities tonight. At this point, no one has an explanation for what we're witnessing here."

Before the eyes of startled nightly news viewers across the nation, there stood a nameless blue youth, raising his hands in a lifting motion, a manhole cover rising from its place in the street and sliding to one side.

"The strange young man was reportedly without identification," the announcer continued. "Captain Bradley Chastain was questioned about the incident."

The overweight police captain was visibly shaken, sweating as he rasped into a phalanx of microphones, "We have no comment at this time."

The man stood up, his entire body clenched with resolve. Former General Morgan Gentry picked up the pistol and strode to the closet. A calm, ice-cold resolve was written in his face as he pulled forth a suitcase, donned a shoulder holster, and strapped in the pistol. He pulled on a jacket and carried his bag out into the night.

37.

Another grueling night had passed for Regina Snyder. Once more, she had spent the night standing, gagged and hog tied, in a closet with no room to move more than a light shift of her weight. An alarm she faintly heard woke Vee once every hour through the night, and he in turn woke Snyder by pounding upon the door, shaking her very body with the blows of his massive fist against the oak panel. The giant would then catch another catnap on his comfortable sofa before awakening to bang the door again. Some time after dawn, the scent of bacon and eggs wafted into the closet. The aroma was excruciating; Snyder was famished.

Once Threll had finished his breakfast, the closet door was thrown open. In sheer gratitude, Regina turned and fell onto her side, on the floor.

"Good morning, Doctor," came Threll's cheery voice. "Today, you're in for a treat. *Lifestyles of the rich and famous,* dearie! You'll love it."

Snyder squinted, feeling somewhat disoriented. The hunger in her guts and the agony in her muscles seemed nearly all her brain could process in an orderly fashion. Random memories from the happier periods in her life, childhood, adolescence, the launch of Proteus, her time with Morgan Gentry, collided and grew confused within her sleep-deprived mind.

To her surprise, Vee untied her, and Threll proceeded to lead her to the bathroom, where scented soaps, plush towels and a robe were laid out for her. "Pull yourself together, Doctor. It's a big day."

The men allowed her privacy. A quick search of the bathroom turned up no razorblades, nothing sharp or heavy enough to conceivably used as a weapon. Snyder stretched and bent to try to pull her body back into shape after her ordeal, then she took a leisurely shower, relishing the tingle brought on by the warm spray as it rejuvenated her tortured flesh.

After Snyder donned her robe, Threll spent an attentive hour performing a manicure, facial, and makeup session with her. Vee stood over them as Threll had her bare her legs. His touch was delicate, almost effeminate, as he shaved her legs and proceeded to dutifully wash and trim her facial features.

Despite the threatening gestures he had made at times during her captivity, Snyder realized Threll had actually been careful not inflict scars on her face. The scars he had inflicted were all on parts of her body that would not show unless she were, say, sunbathing at the beach. He seemed to want to demonstrate that he could walk her around in public if he so chose, and that, with Vee along, his massive hand resting on the nape of her neck like that of an attentive fiancé, she would still be in his complete power.

It was just so that they descended through Threll's high-rise building to the parking garage, entered his limousine, and exited after perhaps twenty minutes. The men guided her inside a posh modern structure of steel and glass, with occasional symbols such as golden pyramids or globes with laurel wreaths, adorning marble walls and pedestals in hallways along the way. At one point, they passed a beveled eye within the span of a compass. It was a strange logo, but it seemed as though she had seen something like it before.

All the hallways were at once nondescript, yet they had their own succinct, understated sense of identity. The place emanated a corporate aura, but there was nothing Snyder could glimpse to give her an idea of just what corporation might be the tenant within these walls. Occasionally, they passed a smartly-dressed young man or woman carrying a valise or a clipboard, and each time they did, Snyder felt the grip of Vee's hand tighten a bit on the back of her neck.

At length, Threll and Vee pressed her through a door and past a reception area where the desk clerk merely nodded pleasantly as they passed. "Good day, Doctor Threll," she said. Threll returned her smile, pleasantly enough.

And then, they were inside the ceremonial chamber adorned with trappings similar to a church. Among the first items that caught Snyder's eye, down at the lower level, were an altar and an ornately-trimmed electronic organ. Then she turned her gaze to the steps as they descended a terraced aisle. They proceeded past rows of embroidered, tasseled velvet seat cushions on either side, enough of them to host a sizable gathering. When they reached the dias area, Snyder saw, behind the altar, a canopy of draperies embroidered with rich gold tapestry which adorned the flanks of an elevated, ornate golden throne.

Above the throne was a huge plaque bearing an arcane combination of globe, eye and compass. Before the altar lay a jade sarcophagus. Snyder realized, to her horror, that it was probably just about the right size for her own body. Could this exotic coffin, she wondered, actually have been custom made for this occasion?

"Do you believe in the Resurrection, my dear Dr. Snyder?" asked Threll, coyly.

"I'm—a skeptic."

"Don't be. You must have faith, Doctor. Now, don't go away." Threll strode to a portal at a side corner of the chapel and exited, leaving Snyder in the cold space, alone with Vee.

The huge man watched her like a hawk as she took tiny steps about on the dias area, running her hand across the lip of the coffin, walking to the throne and inspecting it. She turned from the throne, and without warning, broke into a run for the terraced steps, hoping desperately to make the exit.

Vee was on her in two bounds. His steely hands grasped her shoulders and stopped her cold. In a calculated move, she spun around and punched him square in the solar plexus with the digging palm of her hand. Such a blow to a normal man would cause excruciating pain, but Vee barely exhaled, sagging forward only about an inch. He swiftly caught both her wrist and his own breath.

"No! No! Please, you've got to let me go! Please let me *go!*" Vee's only reaction to her desperate entreaties was to roughly haul her back to the spot where they had been standing. He grabbed her shoulders and gave her a more than friendly squeeze, pumping the air out of her. As she recovered, she had occasion to notice the ornate wood carvings adorning the curvature of the velvet throne. At its apex, peacock figures lit into a strand of vegetation from two sides in a feeding frenzy.

A robed figure entered from one of the side portals into the chapel. With a smile and nod, he seated himself at the organ. As he commenced to produce pompous, circumstantial chords from the amplified instrument, a procession of men draped in ornate gowns with silken sleeves solemnly entered to take seats on the velvet cushions. The first man inside, his head obscured by a mammoth hood, was dressed most resplendently of them all. He stepped forth, carrying a smoking chalice which he placed on the altar.

Turning, the man announced to the assembling congregation, "Brethren, Officers, take your respective stations and places." They sat.

"Are all present Master Members?"

"We are," they chimed in unison.

"Let the initiation begin," the leader / priest intoned. "Brother Junior Deacon. Brother Senior Warden."

"Worshipful Master,"responded two who were near the head of the stage."

"Brother Senior Warden, all present are Master Members," announced the voice of the Priest.

"Worshipful Master," demurred the "Senior Warden," as well.

"Brother Senior Warden," replied the Priest.

The music still swelled once more. Then, entering from the room's rear portals, Vee and Threll, now robed like the others, escorted the similarly resplendent Carl Haas, who beamed as he paced their stately procession. A startling sort of inchoate joy bathed his implacable features. Snyder wondered for a moment if he even realized she was there. He wore his proud smile all the way to the platform, when he turned his head and looked at Snyder. Here, it appeared, was his reward, or some part of it anyway, for betraying the Proteus Project.

"I will ascertain through the proper officer and report," intoned the Priest.

An elaborate rite ensued. As the proceedings warmed up, Snyder turned, revulsed at the sight of Haas' pretentious initiation into this coven of fanatics. The cryptic words of the ceremonial participants drifted from the forefront of her mind, settling into a neutral drone. She began to study the features of the congregants instead. She passed over many faces, noticing features... wait. That one. He was a senator. And, she recalled, he'd long ago been counsel to a government investigative body, accused by some of intimidating witnesses. And then she recognized a third, who used to be a Federal prosecutor she'd see interviewed on a late night news magazine. And... aha, another resembled a corporate broadcasting magnate who owned the biggest of the non- "Big Three" networks.

This vivid but useless lucidity of mind was like a fresh torment to Snyder, contributing a bolt of despair into the burning embers of her heart. "The password is right and duly received in the East," murmured one of the robed figures. It was all so strange, so discordant.

And the Priest responded, "How are we tyled?"

And the Junior Deacon responded, "By a Brother Master Member without, armed with the proper implement of his office."

"His duty there?" asked the Priest.

"To observe the approach of cowans and eavesdroppers," replied the Junior Deacon, "and suffer none to pass or re-pass except such as are duly qualified and have permission from the Worshipful Master."

"Brother Senior Warden," intoned the Priest.

In the disconnect between the here and now and anything that might make sense to her, Snyder had only her memories. In her mind, she wondered if they shouldn't have known, if she and Gentry shouldn't have provided the other old-timers a convenient exit before their ennui and antipathy had finally led them to betray everything they had all worked so hard to achieve. But the general had thought it better to keep them involved, and thereby keep closer tabs on them, as well. She realized now how much they had resented him for it. As for how they had hooked up to this gaggle of weirdos, she could not imagine. But the fact that Vee and Threll were apparently members in high standing surely bode her nothing but ill.

But she had no time to pursue that, or any other thought further, for she was now being bodily grasped, shoulder and hip, and lifted off her feet by the immensely powerful hamhock hands of Vee. "No! No!" she screamed. Vee held her high above his head. She gasped and grew silent, poised above the beatific congregation. There was an unusual, eerie gleam in their eyes now, a joy approaching Haas' own at his apparent elevation within the clan.

"And from the West, what do you bring to the congregation, brother Haas?"

"I bring this one," boasted Haas, gesturing toward Snyder's helpless body, "and, beside my sponsors, I pledge the capture of one who is even now, making manifest among the unwashed, the things that are hidden."

Snyder thought of Avery, and she craned her line of sight over the assembly to see if he, too, might be among those hearing these words. Threll had used him badly in secretly handicapping his cross-country pursuit of Will, although she felt that might be the sole reason Will had managed to make it all the way to New York. She could not understand the ubiquitous duplicity which seemed to ooze from the pores of Threll's being.

"In accordance with the divine Statutes, let the ceremony of Final Immersion commence." The Priest raised his head as he intoned the words. And Snyder, catching her first look beneath the hood, now recognized, him, too. It was the face of President Ash!

There was no time to pursue that thought, either. Within seconds, she was lowered inside the coffin! She kicked and flailed in vain before being swiftly entombed within embroidered casks she could feel but not see—in total darkness.

38.

In the morning, newspaper headlines across New York spread the sensational news that a painted blue "terrorist" was on the loose, wanted by police. "NYPD BLUE SEEK BLUE FUGITIVE" was the mildest of the copy that greeted morning commuters. Tabloid papers had a field day with a range of speculative banners. "BLUE PRANKSTER - CROSS-COUNTRY FIRESTARTER?" "NYC'S BLUE BOY - AREA 51 MUTANT ON THE LOOSE?" "BLUE KID'S MAGIC TRICKS CONFOUND COPS." The stories pulled together interview material from phone calls which had poured in from eyewitnesses across the country who had caught a fleeting glimpse of Will here and there on his long trek.

The colors were just bleeding from the dawning sky as a business-suited Major Avery, face straining, near breaking, strode into the main terminal corridors at JFK International Airport. He paced a dozen similarly-dressed, grim men toting gear along on rolling carts. Avery snatched up a copy of the *New York News* as his entourage passed a newsstand.

Morgan Gentry, who had arrived on a different flight, had just boarded a taxi seconds before. It was only pulling from the curb as Avery and his men started loading gear into a van that pulled up to meet them.

The curb cop, ticket book at the ready, recoiled from their identification badges, shaking his finger at them and saying they'd better be quick about it anyway. Avery stood, reading his newspaper and grinding his teeth as his men loaded the gear on board.

At the same moment, on a city street, Will himself stole from behind the corner of a building and approached a soft drink vending machine. He knelt in front of it, pointing a finger at its lock and concentrating deeply. He sought to apply his newly-developed lock-probing trick.

"Come on, little feeler," he whispered, concentrating like a safe cracker listening for tumblers to fall.

He moved his finger, probing, probing. Gradually, the lock slit turned gently to the right. Will swung open the machine door and scooped up some quarters from its collection box.

"Nitro."

McIntire's rented Monte Carlo was parked on the street just a few blocks from Will. McIntire and Travers slept lightly in the reclining seats. Travers' cell phone rang, rousing them. She stirred, groggy, but lost no time in grasping the tiny, portable phone and flipping it open. "Hello?—Will?!"

Will stood at a public telephone, looking around uncomfortably as he spoke. There were already passersby giving him a wide berth as they saw him. One man who stopped to check the newspaper, stopped to check out Will again before hurrying on at a brisk clip.

"Gotta hurry, I'm wide open here. I spent the night scouting. Did you know there are street signs in the sewer?"

"No. Where are you?" Travers asked.

"Near some 'Bleecker St.'" Will replied.

"Really? Then you're close. The clinic's downtown. Duane Street." McIntire quickly traced Will's route for her on a street map as Travers described to Will how to proceed to the clinic she had selected from the phone directory.

"Okay. How long does the thing take?" Will asked, anxiously.

"A half-hour, maybe," said Travers.

"See you there," said Will, and he was off, running from the view of numerous startled pedestrians.

Within minutes, Travers stood before the front doors of the clinic. She was fretting when Will came walking up from across the street, with a crushed milk carton floating in front of him.

"What in the world are you doing?!"

"I think if I'm beaming my 'frequency' it screws up their signal somehow," he explained. "And this is a light object. It doesn't wear me out."

"Oh, well. They're gonna need smelling salts in here," worried Travers as they pulled open the clinic door, grabbing Will's arm with the other hand.

At the desk, a startled receptionist looked up, smiled her professional smile for a half-second, then dropped her pen, the smile considerably rounder at the corners of her mouth.

"I'm Dr., uh, Dr. Threll," said Travers, improvising. "We're here for an emergency MRI?"

The receptionist tried to carry on as normal, eyes darting among the items on her desk, back up to the floating milk carton and the strange duo in quick succession. "I... don't see you on the list...Y- you'll n-need to make an appointment. If you want to fill out this form..."

"Oh, I'm sorry, but this is critical. Can't you see his color?"

The Receptionist blinked, looking down.

"I'm certain there's an organic cause. I'll just fill out the forms back here, okay?"

Travers snatched the clipboard and turned to hurry Will on back, just as a mother and her young daughter walked into the clinic. Seeing Will, the mother did a double-take before emitting a little, mouse-like sound and covering her young daughter's eyes.

"Mommy, mommy," protested the little girl. "Was that a blue man? Is he a magic man?"

The mother had her mouth open, as if to speak, but she stood rooted to the spot, remaining silent.

Travers spoke brightly to the receptionist, "Mass hysteria." Shaking her head lightly, she hustled Will toward the inner section of the clinic.

Left alone in the reception room, the worried mother hustled her daughter back outside. The receptionist started to punch phone buttons. Will ran back from around the corner, leaping over to the desk, where he reached in and grasped the phone cord, yanking it out of its receptacle. As he did so, he lost his mental hold over the milk carton, which dropped to the floor. The receptionist nearly swooned when she saw him point to it and it floated back up to his chest level.

"Take out the rest of the phones," Will told Travers, who had followed him back to the desk.

"Of course," she said, sheepishly.

"Chill," Will told the receptionist. "We'll be outta here in a few minutes." The poor lady nodded nervously.

Travers and Will strode rapidly up a hallway, where they encountered a young, female M.R.I. technician standing by the machine with a clipboard. The technician looked up, saying, "Hello—oh!"

Briskly, Travers demanded, "We need a CAT scan of his head."

"Yeah. Right. Am I seeing—what it looks like I'm seeing?" The technician asked, looking wide-eyed from the floating milk carton to Will. She looked beyond Travers and Will, to the worried receptionist who had followed, still nodding, a tense expression on her face.

"Uh. O-o-oh-kay," sighed the technician. She efficiently produced a metal bowl. "Least we're not headed to Cuba, right?"

Wow. This lady was kind of cool, Will thought. Maybe not all the regular people were totally fan-on, after all.

"All right," the technician continued, "any change, jewelry, charge cards with magnetic strips, metallic objects of any kind, leave 'em in the tray."

"Why?" asked Will, scooping his recently-acquired change into the tray.

"You'll be inside a strong magnetic field," explained the technician. "And that kind of thing'll mess up the results. Uh. Do you have to be, uh, doing the magic tricks?" she asked, pointing to the carton dangling in mid-air.

To Travers, Will said, "A strong magnetic field? Think that might throw him off, too?"

"I don't know. We've got to do it."

Will shrugged his agreement and allowed the carton to clatter on the floor, then he lay down on the MRI platform.

39.

"Lie still as you can. You'll hear some loud clacking sounds," explained the technician. "Don't worry about them. We can hear you talk to us over an intercom if you have to. Got it, Sport?"

Will gave her a thumbs-up and a grin. She pressed a button and Will glided into the machine.

At the police precinct house where he had been held the previous day, news of the anonymous call had spread rapidly. A Glock handgun slid into a shoulder holster worn by Captain Chastain as a police scanner chattered urgently in the background. Police were mobilizing to move on the tip in massive numbers. Beefy hands loaded bullets into clips. SWAT gear was being donned; shotguns, gas grenades and tasers checked out of ordnance.

"We're gonna bag this whatsis, boys," declared Chastain, with relish. "This time we're gettin' to the bottom of—whatever's goin' on."

"No. *We'll* bag the 'whatsis,' Captain," declared a voice from behind Chastain, who turned to have a look at the source of this insolence.

"Who th' hell're you?" Chastain demanded.

Avery, standing with his dozen secret agents, showed his NSA credentials. "We're the big boys, Captain."

"Christ, what next?" Chastain threw up his hands.

"The bogey you're chasing is a fugitive from our jurisdiction. Got any more SWAT uniforms? We're gonna need to blend in with your operation."

At the same time, Vee and Threll sat in a Limousine in midtown. Like McIntire and Travers, they were on stakeout, awaiting the inevitable news and strategically poised to reach any part of Manhattan in minutes. A police scanner played while Threll studied his laptop map. Vee munched on a bagel and swigged orange juice in the passenger seat.

Threll's cell phone rang.

"Yes. Ah. You don't say. Bids are rolling in already? Fantastic. Yes. Yes, I did plan for it to hit the news. Of course. 'Make manifest all that is hidden', don't you know? Um-hm, if you can get some news crews downtown, we've been picking up traces of him... I understand my cohort is even now co-opting the recovery effort. No, I don't doubt we'll take possession today, not at all. Yes, I'll keep you informed. I'm certain he *will* be making news again in just a bit. Right. Should generate lots more interest from the various parties. We'll win either way. Yes. Goodbye."

Turning to Vee, Threll declared, "Well, his eluding me yesterday was all to the good, actually. We got a lot better press than we could have with just that fracas in the park."

Suddenly, Threll's sight dropped back to the laptop screen, where a stationary blip blinked into view.

"Signal. He's nearby!" he exclaimed.

As Threll snapped alert, McIntire slipped into the Duane Street clinic building. Just as the receptionist tiptoed back into the anteroom, looking back over her shoulder, McIntire was bumping a couch with his hip, nudging it toward the front doors.

Noticing the startled woman, he casually remarked, "You may want to stay back there a while. I figure New York's finest trouble shooters may happen along any minute. If ya know what I mean." He pulled his pistol from beneath his cast. The receptionist, really frightened now, started backing up the way she came. "But first, whoa! How 'bout giving me the keys to this place?" McIntire added.

The receptionist dithered around in her desk and produced a set of keys for him. McIntire locked both sets of glass front doors, then body-slammed the couch toward the inner ones.

Just as McIntire had predicted, within moments, a motorcycle cop pulled up to the clinic. He tried the door, and, finding it locked, spoke into his radio.

"*Ten-sixty-six, one-four-six Duane Street, Tribeca. Area units, ten-ten,*" crackled Threll's police scanner. He consulted a police codebook for the translation.

"Ah. 'Investigate an 'unusual incident.'" He punched keys on his laptop with the global positioning system display. "One-four-six Duane. Hmmm. It's a medical clinic." Threll's face darkened with the implications.

When Threll and Vee rolled up Duane Street in their Limousine, there was already a cordon being laid in place. Three police cruisers and an armored van had reached the scene. Police in riot gear poured from the back.

"Yes. He's in or near that building. And, is that—?"

He produced a pair of binoculars, and focused on figures emerging from the armored van. There was the police captain, and beside him, the familiar, unctuous face of Major Avery. Threll double-parked the limo a discreet distance from the scene. Looking over at his strongman, Threll asked, "Think I should have another chat with the lad, now that the channel's open?"

Vee returned Threll's grin, and nodded.

Inside the clinic, as Travers and the MRI Technician studied a monitor bank intently, the muffled sounds of Chastain's megaphonic voice filtered faintly into the room, reciting a timeless mantra of officialdom. "This is the police. You are surrounded. Escape is impossible. Come out with your hands up."

"Well, there they are," Travers sighed tensely to McIntire. He nodded, checking his pistol clip.

"And there's what you were lookin' for, I guess," quipped the technician, pointing to the resonance image on screen. There, deep within a nasal skull cavity, was one strange-looking electronic chipset. Another, the one added by Jacob Threll, lay within Will's inner ear.

Will, oblivious to developments outside, glided out of the tube and sat up.

"All right. How'd we do?"

"Looks like two devices in your skull, all right. Look here."

Will looked at the screens, nodding grimly. "I must have had that one for years," he said of the sinus implant.

"And this one's in your tympanic cavity. Perfect for hearing 'voices in your head,'" observed Travers.

"If we had time, we could get them out with minor surgery," observed the technician.

"What? How long would it take? Let's do it," Will enthused.

A mighty crash at the front door blew a shock wave through the room. The five people gathered around the MRI scanner were jolted by the sound of the first set of front doors exploding into glass shards.

Will flinched a second time, just as the others tried to recover their poise. *"They're all over the clinic, Will. Avery's men, and the police. If you can get out, I'll try, one last time, to save you."*

"It's *him*!" exclaimed Will. "It's *Threll!* He says Avery's here with the police. He says he wants to 'save' me."

"Don't buy it," warned McIntire.

"Maybe I should let 'em have me, Mac. You know they've got Dr. Snyder. Maybe they'll let her go. What chance do I have, anyway?"

"We didn't come all this way to hear that kind of shit," admonished McIntire. "Don't let him confuse you."

On the street, an additional four squad cars were now stationed around the block. Police had taken to the fire escapes of surrounding buildings, taking positions on rooftops. A paddy wagon rolled up toward the clinic. The riot squad, in their protective gear, leapt out as it came to a stop.

"Fan out. Cover all the exits," Chastain boomed through his megaphone.

40.

"We're out of time," Will pounded his fist into his palm.

The second set of glass doors was being battered with a ram. The police would be upon them within seconds.

"We were so close!" he spat.

"Next time, pal," said McIntire, trying to sound casual as he re-entered the room from the rear. "Look, there's a ladder to the roof back here. Head a block south, look for me."

Seconds later, on the roof, a hatch opened. Will climbed through the opening onto the roof. Travers peeked her head up behind him, hissing, "A block South, okay? Do you know which way is South?" Will quickly scanned the sky and then nodded back at her. "Good luck!" she called, then closed the door against his desperate gaze. She saw him take off as she nearly had returned it to its closed position. She tried the keys in the hatch lock until one fit.

A huge and final crash sounded down in the building. At the front, riot police, shields up, used a steel ram to batter their way through the doors and the furniture barricade McIntire had wedged into place.

Will reached the next higher roof and took it in a jump. The next building was about twelve feet taller. A little too high to jump.

He had a sudden inspiration. He held his arms up, half-closing his hands. Above him, the metal carapace fringing the next rooftop dented a little.

Will, his outstretched hands nearly six feet beneath the rim, felt a tingling in his fingers. It was as though he felt the edge of the rooftop in his grasp. Will jumped up and found he could scale the wall by pulling himself up, hand over hand, as if climbing with an invisible rope. He was pleased with the techniques he kept discovering to use his power.

Cops swarmed through the clinic Will had left a couple of buildings behind. Some reached the service ladder in the rear, just as Travers reached the floor level again.

"He got out—that way," she said, pointing up the chute that led roofward. She slipped away as cops started to shove up the ladder. Soon, they were shouting, "Damn thing's locked! ... Somebody go get a freakin' key!"

Travers, still carrying the keys in her pocket, slipped out a fire exit door, setting off the alarm. A motorcycle-style cop halted her outside.

"The blue man! In there! Quick!" she shouted, writhing hysterically as if frightened out of her wits.

The policeman took the bait and rushed inside, to her immense relief.

"South," Travers said to herself as she ran into the street, into the path of an oncoming auto. The driver slammed on the brakes, screeching to a halt, inches from Travers. Its driver stepped out, shaking a fist. "Hey! What's a mattah witch you?!" he demanded.

"Sorry, Mister, it's an emergency." As she spoke, she edged closer and shot both thumbs into the pressure points under the man's jawlines.

"Ow! What da hell?!" he yelled.

"Sorry, Mister. I really hope you're insured."

She backed him up a pace, then shoved him. He reeled, stunned with disbelief before leaping at her, screaming curses. But she just managed to slip into his Toyota and lock the door against his pounding fists. She revved up the auto, gunning it around the corner within seconds.

Too late, she saw oncoming traffic and realized she was going the wrong way on a one-way street. An oncoming car stopped, but not before smashing front fenders with her.

Down the block and up on the rooftops, Will leaped down from one rooftop to the next. Ahead of him, some riot cops topped the roof's edge ahead of him, climbing from the fire escape. Four of them, carrying shields, reached the top and confronted him. Slapping nightsticks into gloved hands, they advanced.

Will looked around, and spotted a roll of roof sheeting standing upright near a section of roof that was to be patched later. He ran toward it, reached it, bent and managed to heft the heavy bolt upright. The riot cops spread a little farther apart, but they did not seem terribly worried about this gesture.

Down on the street, Travers backed up, leaving the driver she collided with gesturing and hollering at her. She tried to straighten out and go up the street she came, but it likewise turned out to be a "wrong way," too. The driver of her hijacked vehicle ran toward her, with the cop she had duped earlier at his elbow.

She backed up again, the rear of the Toyota striking another car that was trying to swerve around her wild maneuvers.

Will peeled back a length of the roof sheeting. The riot cops exchanged quizzical glances.

Will, grimacing with effort, threw his whole body into casting the spool of sheeting, while holding onto the end with both hands. The sheeting trailed a loop through the air, completing an impossibly wide arc around the cops in seconds. They struggled, but their all by then was too little, too late. The spool circled swiftly around until they were bound tightly within.

Will felt a wonderful exhilaration again. He had been able to boost the tarpaper's thrust by boosting the momentum his throw generated with his telekinetic capabilities. And to steer its flight path, too!

Will ran forward and body-slammed the tight knot of riot cops. They toppled as a screaming, cursing unit.

He ran to the far edge of the roof, where he could look down and see the next street South. On the street below, round the corner came the stolen Toyota driven by Travers. In pursuit, a police car, siren blaring, lights flashing, in hot pursuit.

At the intersection ahead of Travers, at the opposite end of the block, another Police Car appeared—backup, apparently, pulling across her line of flight, stopping dead center of the crossing.

"Damn!" Travers slapped her palm on the steering wheel.

She swerved desperately, tires screeching as she took to the sidewalk, clearing pedestrians and barely missing the second black and white. She charged on through the intersection, halting alarmed, horn-honking drivers.

The two police cars got it together and followed in her wake. McIntire's Monte Carlo swiftly rounded a corner behind the both of them. The lieutenant was still in action, too, still trying to assist Will.

Will dropped to the pavement from the fire escape as Travers skidded around the corner. Will dashed out into the street, boarding the Toyota once she brought it to a sliding halt.

They raced down a wide avenue, only a few feet now ahead of the cops. Ahead, traffic was stopped at a red light.

"Hang onto your chromosomes!" Travers called, as she careened the Toyota along a sharp turn. Their car whipped around into incoming traffic, and with a couple of quick games of chicken, passed a whisker between two autos in the cross-traffic.

Will clutched the dashboard, terrified.

Travers yelled, "I'm going down with you, Will! You could at least say, 'Attagirl!'"

"Attagirl," laughed Will, letting go. She was right, they had only the moment, and nothing to lose now. He couldn't believe that she was actually here with him, in this situation, in New York City. These were to be their last few, frantic moments together. They both knew it in their hearts.

They rocketed up the block. Travers had the accelerator floored. Ahead of them, traffic was stopped at the next traffic light, as well.

"You're going to way too much trouble," called Will.

"Comedian!"

Travers started to cut around traffic again, but four police cruisers lurched into the intersection, cutting her off. The Toyota screamed to a sidewise halt, barely avoiding a catastrophic collision with the police.

"In here!" Travers screamed, and she gunned the gas again, wrenching the steering wheel wildly.

"Sure!" shouted Will, though he felt anything but sure.

The car gunned up, jumped the curb, and scattered alarmed pedestrians as it bucked a bumpy ride down the steps to the World Trade Center's lower shopping concourse entrance.

41.

Travers and Will flung themselves from the Toyota and made a dash across the open plaza. Down the steps they ran, before astonished passers-by, to burst through framed glass doors and into a branch of the WTC shopping concourse.

Travers pulled Will by the hand into one of the first shops in the branch, Benjamin Books.

"Go. Find a back door—hit it," she hissed, before turning to the astonished desk clerk.

"Keep a secret for one minute?" she asked, talking to keep the sales lady off balance. Meantime, she managed to breeze around the checkout.

Through the window, Travers sighted the eight police officers run inside, followed by Avery, looking intently around. Travers ducked behind the checkout counter.

A pair of male and female police officers entered the bookstore, bringing a chatter of police radios in with them.

"Miss, you seen any strange parties just come by here, in a hurry?" the woman asked the clerk.

The hapless clerk cast her eyes down behind the counter.

Will, by now at the back of the store, realized too late that she intended to be a decoy for him, to delay them for him. Suddenly, he couldn't take the plunge through that stockroom door before him.

He peeked around a bookshelf and saw the Female Cop handcuffing Travers at the front counter.

"Don't give us any guff, Miss!" the man was sweating her. "You were wasting my men's time back at that clinic, too, weren't ya? You and that 'patient' in the cast you had in there with you."

Blue Monday

"Guess what," the female cop was saying, "I think your little caper's brought you a little white heat from the Feds, Sugar."

Will started to march up the aisle, when suddenly, through the shop window, he spotted Avery showing his almighty credentials to a Cop. His blood ran cold at the sight. He decided that was *it*. He strode boldly, deliberately forward—mad as hell.

In his wake, books twitched and jumped on the shelves as he proceeded up the aisle.

The female cop arresting Travers drew her gun on Will.

"Hold it there, Mister."

Will stopped, incongruously looking very much at peace.

Outside the complex, Threll's limousine stopped by another entrance and discharged Vee, who swiftly proceeded inside the building.

Above the scene, a transport helicopter with NYPD markings whipped high above the city, descending toward the twin towers of the Trade Center. *"Roger, Unit One. Operation Special Guest en route to WTC to intercept. Over."* its radio crackled.

Just inside the other entrance to the concourse, still a good distance from any shops, a policeman halted Vee's ingress.

"Hold it, Sir. We have an incident in the mall. I'll have to ask you to please step back outside."

Vee peered past the cop. At the distant juncture of corridors, some police set up a barricade at the doors they had just entered by, as others hustled shoppers out of the side branch where Will and Travers were now fugitive. Vee feinted for a second as if to leave, but doubled back and karate-chopped the startled Cop in the neck, dropping him. Vee turned and proceeded to the elevators. He entered the next to open, going up.

In Benjamin Books, Will saw several more cops pile in the doorway as the excited voice of Avery began to cry, "There he is!" Arrayed against Will in greater numbers, in tight quarters, these cops were drawing their Glock sidearms.

"Hands high, pal! These triggers have a feather touch!"

But the cops looked to Avery to take their cue—drop the kid where he stood, or—?

Will saw the struggle written on Avery's face. He sensed part of him simply wanted Will dead. But another part was fighting that impulse for some reason.

Will took advantage of the precious second to raise his hands, and, as he did so, to also turn his back on the police. Calmly, but intently, he looked over the book-filled room. The Cops shared puzzled and annoyed looks. "Turn around here, Mr. Blue." growled a cop in front.

Will turned, yelling, "Pam—duck!"

He whipped his arms forward in a wide arc. Travers dropped to the floor as a hurricane of books flew off the shelves of the bookstore. The incredulous cops froze at the sight. Within two seconds, they were buffeted by a maelstrom of flying volumes, some of which burst into flames in mid-air.

Suddenly, the police were more intent upon dousing their flaming uniforms and reeling from the book barrage, than making an arrest. The store front was shattered by flying volumes, setting off an alarm as Avery and his men hugged the floor amid the hail of flying glass shards.

Will's palm slashed an uppercut to the chin of Travers's arresting officer, who dropped her snub-nose revolver. Will scooped it up.

"Quicker this way!" he shouted. Will pulled her arms back and shot through Travers's handcuff link. He took her hand, and they leapt out into the Concourse. The cops who had hit the deck began to raise their heads—and, once more, their pistols—as they gained their feet again, now knowers and believers in the power of Will Monday.

Display windows of "The Limited" clothing store shattered from the gunfire the police left in the wake of their dashing prey.

Directly in the path of the fleeing pair, a gang of SWAT-garbed men, in reality Avery's "assault team" of covert agents, descended the escalators, aiming their weapons.

As the vanguard prepared to fire, Will swiftly body-blocked Travers into the doorway of the Warner Brothers Store. Automatic weapons fire shattered the storefront, blowing plastic figures of Tasmanian Devil, Daffy Duck, and Road Runner to bits.

On the rooftop of the World Trade Center, South, a police helicopter sat, blades spinning in idle mode. Its pilot spoke with another cop standing beside the open door. Neither spied Vee crawling underneath the chopper.

"Don't it cheese ya off to play taxi to these guys?" groused the cop to the pilot.

"Yeah, in a way. But, y'know, if there's something real heavy going down there, I'd rather it fall on the Feds than on our guys."

"Yeah, like they don't already have us framed for whatever goes wrong."

The pilot just smiled noncommittally, shaking his head slightly, though whether at the Feds or at this police officer was not entirely clear.

"Yaaaahhh!" was his only comment after that, as he practically vanished, bodily striking the ground and then disappearing beneath the helicopter chassis. The pilot leaned down to see Vee, who had grabbed the man's ankles, was just rendering him insensate with a sharp punch to the face.

The policeman, scared as hell, instinctively tried to climb into the copter, looking for a quick way out of the situation. He worked frantically at the controls for three seconds, then gave the matter no more thought after Vee's fist grasped his shirt and pulled. Vee lashed a beefy backhand across the man's face, swiftly and without mercy.

Many floors below, Will and Travers lay among shattered glass and debris in the doorway to the Warner Brothers Store.

"You look tired," Travers observed.

"Yep. But, I know now, I don't have to make it far." Travers' face turned quizzical, but she did not have time for another whispered remark.

"Come out with your hands up. You have no chance of escape." a megaphonic voice echoed through the concourse.

Will steeled himself to launch back into the fray. Travers laid her hand across his chest. She dared to lean over on her elbow, and give Will a kiss, which he returned with ardor.

"For luck," she said when they broke apart. Will gazed at her with tender appreciation. Then, abruptly, he snapped his attention elsewhere, listening.

"Tell the police—you were my hostage, okay? It might work. Avery can't afford to tell the truth." Will turned over, carefully amidst the glass, onto his belly. He concentrated on the debris around them, waving his wrist, slowly gathering the shards into a growing debris tornado.

He sprang up and ran into the Concourse, pulling the whirlwind of particles with him.

"Will!" Travers screamed.

42.

Like a baseball batter, Will slammed his tornado at the escalators area. The collection of debris scattered like shrapnel from a bomb as it blew at Avery's men with a gale force. Despite their protective garb, the flying shrapnel staggered back the SWAT crew, inflicting some slight injuries.

Will was not done with them. He already had lined up his next move. Across the corridor, store windows of Cutlery World exploded in a deadly rain of shards which caught the foremost of Avery's "SWAT" soldiers in mid-rush toward Will. Their quarry, losing no time, windmilled his arm like a manic traffic cop. Just as the battered "cops" were regaining their bearing toward him yet again, Will was directing a flight of a thousand steel knives from within the store—right at the assault team! *"Use the environment!"* Mac had drilled him a thousand times. He was doing his best. Neither had ever thought, during one of those sessions, such tactical instructions would ever lead to results such as these.

Avery's assault team members screamed, moaned, and fell backward as some few among the thicket of knives made their marks through chinks in the men's armor. Will took off in a full-blown run, diagonally across the SWAT line of fire. The agents were rather stunned at the turn of events, so Will was hoping he could now get at the man whose voice had been tormenting his mind for the last few minutes while his situation had worsened in the WTC.

At the far end, across some devastation and near the doors, Will heard Avery shout, "Do not fire!" He dared glance back, over his shoulder, at the real cops, who had their guns raised. From their point of view, Avery's men were arrayed behind Will. Avery didn't want any more of his own killed, apparently, especially not in New York, in broad daylight. Then, he saw that Travers was also running, almost right on his heels. "What are you doing?!"

"Don't trust 'em!" Travers panted. The NYC cops engaged in pursuit across the concourse, closing on them. They were both near exhaustion. Now, here was more hard slogging. They heard a shot fired into the air. Travers and Will dashed left toward the main concourse nexus, the joint of the mall facing out toward the elevators. In seconds, they were there.

"Stay back," Will warned her earnestly, as he tapped the "Up" button. The elevator doors opened to reveal Jacob Threll, wearing headset and wielding a Taser pistol.

"Good boy. You came, on my call."

"Sure did."

Will shoved Travers back and lunged into the elevator. He hit the door button. The elevator doors closed, leaving Travers dumbfounded. The police caught up within seconds, seizing the dazed young woman by the arms.

Gentry rushed through the door, eyes darting. No sign of Avery, Threll, or Vee. He stepped into the knot of cops, flashing his NSA credentials.

"Hold it! The girl's one of ours. I'm with the major."

One cop took his badge, showed it to another. "Whattaya think?"

The second one scratched his head. "I saw one of these once. Looks real to me."

"It's real, and if you gentlemen will kindly notice, I outrank the major. "Now, let's release the young lady to my custody, and I think we can get out of you gentlemen's and the City's hair."

"You heard the Captain. It's *their* show." said the second policeman, who respectfully handed Gentry back his badge. The other cop shook his head in disgust, but only slightly. They released Travers, and pushed the elevator button to pursue Will.

"Morgan?" Travers whispered.

"Shhhh!" He hustled her out of the building. McIntire pulled up in seconds. They swiftly climbed in his rental and took off.

"Look who I found wandering around!" McIntire exclaimed.

"Yeah, good thing I clung to that badge and kept an eye out for news of the kid. We got lucky, too. I guess Avery hung back a few seconds to rally his men."

"Will really let 'em have it. My God, I can't believe we're all alive, after all this. General?"

"Once I saw what was happening, I wasn't about to pack it in, Missy. Now, you tell me why the hell Will jumped in that elevator. We were a cat hair of gettin' his ass out of there."

Travers' face blanched. "I think he decided to give up."

"Holy Christ," Gentry muttered. "Are you saying..."

"Threll was in the elevator. And Will got in with him on purpose. That's all I'm sure about."

Gentry addressed the lieutenant. "What about it, George? What's the kid doin'? Is he suicidal?"

McIntire grimly shook his head, pondering the question.

In the rising elevator, Threll kept the taser trained on Will all the while.

"You really do want to save me, don't you? You could have killed me before, but you went to all this trouble..." Will stammered.

Threll's eye gleamed as he caressed Will's cheek with the backs of his fingers.

"I know this was a painful decision for you," he whispered. "But I can erase all your pain. The pain in your body—and the pain in your soul."

At the roof, Threll marched Will, under the gun, to the helicopter where Vee sat waiting at the controls. Once they were near, Will offered his hands, and Vee locked on a pair of handcuffs made of some barely malleable plasticene material. Threll suddenly threw a black hood over Will's head from behind, and pulled tight around his throat with a drawstring. Now that they had him secured, the pair stowed Will into the helicopter. Threll then took the controls.

Will, within the black hood, heard Threll's taunt. "Feel free to set the bag on fire, pretty boy."

Will did not strain, or push against this abduction. He relaxed into a peaceful repose. Vee looked at Threll, who merely shrugged.

"He chooses to live." Vee nodded, understanding.

The helicopter wound off across the city skies at top speed.

Avery joined Chastain and a gaggle of police tending to their felled 'copter pair on the WTC roof. The operation looked like a fiasco—and who the hell was riding off in their helicopter? Avery strode forth and demanded of the police, "What happened? Your men have him in custody somewhere?"

Chastain, disgusted, waved his thumb in the direction of the fallen pilots. "Nope," was all he said.

On a hunch, Avery recoiled from them and strode across the rooftop, whipping out his cell phone, punching buttons once he was ten paces from the others.

In the stolen police helicopter, Threll pulled out his own, beeping communicator and flipped it open. "Yes," he said. "Ah. Indeed. We do." Threll was genuinely cheerfully. "Thanks for sending him our way. Oh, no, no, no, don't worry. We'll work out something... We're a team, aren't we? Tell you what, let's get together—yes, right *now*. How about the airport?"

"You better believe the airport," snarled Avery, on the WTC roof. "Jesus Christ, did you jerk me around. You could have let me know what you were up to, you scared the shit out of me. We're gonna blow out of here quick as we can. Go to JFK, got it? I'll see you at the helipad."

Avery snapped his communicator shut. He got another beep. "Yeah? ... Psyops? It was a *success*," Avery affirmed. "No details, but we can't deny anything. I'd say we're stronger if we actually don't, but...look, later someone shows up in the paper with something to do with today's "vandalism" stamped all over 'em, that's all. Right now we're apprehending him, later the public sees his picture with the makeup 'washed off,' understand? I can live with it. The NYPD? They oughtta love it. For once, they brought in somebody alive. No, just any loser we can find. Somebody no one'll miss, you know the drill. "The psyops people were preparing the media cover story to cover the day's chaos. Details, details...

Avery departed the roof, leaving the police who were tending their own.

43.

That night, after nine PM, near the Lost River Sinks in Idaho, a dark, shiny van pulled up to the nuclear plant gate, Avery at the wheel, Threll a passenger. Avery showed the posted guard their clearance to access the hidden, auxiliary sector of the plant.

Once the vehicle had accessed the cavern, they were in pitch blackness, except what the headlights illuminated ahead of them. The place seemed shut down.

Vee exited the van, bearing flashlight. He pulled Will out and shoved him forward. Will's hands were bound behind him. A bag covered his head, bound by a rope about his neck. Threll and Avery assisted Dr. Snyder out. Her head was also covered with a black bag tied at the throat.

Inside the Proteus Complex, lights switched on in the mirrored corridors. In near silence, the abductors goaded their victims along. Threll checked himself out once more in the mirrored walls of Proteus. *Still looking good*, he thought. And, at last, he had plenty to feel good about, as well. With this exploit, he was bound to gain influence in the Council and steer them his way, a way that would nullify Operation Livingroom and promote his brand of mass-biomedical telemetry to the top of the societal agenda.

The pneumatic doors slid open, admitting Threll and Will to the lighted lab. Threll, prodding Will with his pistol, forced him to sit in a chair near a large table. Across from them, only a few feet away, stood the thick glass chamber where Will had endured the majority of his environmental testing ordeals.

There, Vee hustled Snyder into the chamber through the rear hatch, and pushed her down, onto her knees. He yanked the bag from her head, and the gag from her mouth leaving her bound and wide-eyed in the chamber. She looked at Threll, then at Will, so helpless-looking, and finally at the darkened observation window across the lab. As if to reassure her that her fears were justified, Carl Haas appeared at the doorway and waved at her momentarily, before enclosing himself in the opaque observation booth again.

Vee reentered the lab and Threll removed the bag from Will's head, revealing him and Snyder to one another. He nodded gravely upon seeing Snyder. Threll ripped Will's gag off and swiftly moved behind him.

Will started to turn his head, but Vee promptly pointed the barrel of a pistol into the back of his neck.

"Forgive me if I doubt your sudden conversion," he whispered to Will. "A great man once said, 'Trust, but verify.' Besides, this little reunion between you two, even from opposite sides of this glass... or maybe because of that, will likely be kind of—emotional."

"Look, you saved my life," he began...

"Then you owe me a favor, don't you? Why don't you be a good boy and ask your mother, there, to give us access to the data on your nucleotide sequences. That's really all I'm asking. Dr. Haas has already been able to supply a lot, but, well—we want it all."

"You're—my real, true mother?" Will asked of Snyder.

"Yes. I bore you to term in my womb. It was my choice. Originally, we had plans that—didn't work out. We didn't plan on having to hide you."

Will felt himself overwhelmed with a strange set of emotions, the bitter and sweet striving within him over knowing he was born like other people, and finally understanding that right here was his mother, the woman who actually gave him birth, like a real human being.

"In other words, they put you through a torture regime for years," declared Threll, "just because you turned out the wrong color. Now—say goodbye." Threll turned to look and nod at the dark glass of the observation deck.

In the environmental tank, jets of refrigerated gas shot from the ceiling. Snyder looked bleakly at Will as she grappled with the silent panic welling inside her.

Outside, at the guard post, a delivery van pulled up to the gate. Pam Travers, wearing a cap and coveralls, drove. McIntire's tracker tablet rested on the passenger seat beside her. The guard, openly suspicious, took a card from Travers and disappeared inside his booth. Momentarily, he reappeared.

He opened the door and said, "Your code number's revoked. Please step out of the vehicle."

Travers complied, meeting the guard at the front of the van.

"I don't understand," she lamented. "I get a service call this late, I expect to at least be let inside."

The guard, hand resting on his sidearm, turned Travers around.

"Hands on the vehicle, please. Legs apart," he said. Then, under his breath, "Huh. Service call."

Travers complied, and the guard patted her down. He found nothing.

"I'll have to ask you to open your vehicle for inspection."

"Nice hands. Does this mean we're friends?" Travers raised a hand toward his face. He brushed it off.

"Hey," he snapped. Don't get fresh, lady, it won't work. Around back of the van." He followed, prodding her there.

"Open the door."

Travers did. The Guard peeked in, only to find himself staring down the gun barrel of a pistol held by Gentry, now dressed in black Commando gear.

"Get in, or eat a bullet, Bub," Gentry drawled.

The nonplused guard complied. Travers shut the door on them and trotted to the guard booth. She rifled the drawer inside and came up with a blank pass badge. She located and threw the gate switch; it rose to admit them.

Travers rejoined Gentry, now waiting in the van's front seat. Travers held up the badge. "Got another one," she said. "Great," said Gentry. I think with a little trimwork on our wallet photos, we'll be pretty good to go in a few seconds. Find someplace to park."

Travers parked the van and strode to the back. She opened the door and McIntire stepped out. "How is he?" Travers asked.

"Sleeping. He'll be sleeping for a couple more hours," McIntire said. "Listen, I should be—"

"No way," came Gentry's stage whisper as he rounded the corner of the van. "Look at you, you're all patched up."

"I made that jump into the sewer in the dark," McIntire offered. "Not a scratch."

"This is a much higher fall. And we need you to guard the prisoner. You're also to keep the van ready for a high-speed run, if need be."

McIntire barely restrained himself. "Look. There's no way you'll get in there with us and just walk around like *that*," Gentry went on, meaning McIntire's cast. "Let alone climb down. Now, you've done plenty already. Let the old man take a simple operation. If this works and we even get to step two, we'll be right where we can threaten to cut off their air—and mean it. So, okay, these might help us reach step one." He showed Travers their new "photo ID" badges. "We may make it if nobody looks too close. Ready?"

"As I'll ever be," Travers vowed.

Down in the lab, Snyder, in the glass chamber, disappeared in white gases.

44.

"The tables always turn in time, Will. Enjoy the show, eh?"

Will was fascinated. As he realized that he was mentally preparing himself to watch Snyder die, he knew that Threll was right, that some part of him did want to see her suffer. Although he was built with enhanced survival mechanisms, he felt as much pain from sharp impact, heat or cold as they, the normal humans, did. And she had inflicted a lot of agony on him over the years. Yet, he heard himself shouting out the words, "Stop! Don't kill her!"

Threll pursed his lips and raised his brows, registering surprise. Was it, this time, genuine? Who could say what he truly felt? With an ugly smile, Threll shook his head at the observation window and swiftly darted out of Will's line of sight. The jets of gas in the glass chamber stopped their flow of cryogenic gas.

The black hood flew back over Will's head. He felt Threll's bony fingers re-tying the binding string.

"And now that we've heeded your heartfelt plea, we'll see if your mother feels as much for *you*."

This statement, too, had the desired effect. Will wondered if he had not just committed a horrible blunder. Would Regina Snyder's courage hold out now that her own life had been in such imminent danger, and might be again? She must have been through a lot already in her time with Threll. When would she break? What would be the last straw?

Snyder, shivering inside the tank, had been cognizant before the frost ran up too high on the glass for her to see out. She now waited by the hatch for Vee, whom she expected and hoped would arrive soon. Clearly, Threll was out to divide them, play them off against not only one another, but their own fear of death as well, until they gave him total surrender.

The hatch opened. Vee reached in and took her by the waist, lifting the shuddering, coughing Snyder out into a block-walled access hallway. Lined with pipelines, it passed an elevator tube and went to a door beside a steel stairwell fixed to the wall.

Vee tromped back the same way, this time, manhandling Will along. He dragged Will inside the chamber, and tossed him tumbling along the floor. Afterward, he closed the hatch, turning the wheel clockwise until it clicked, with Will locked inside.

At that moment, Gentry and Travers, in their coveralls and dangling badges, were near the main work entrance to the nuclear plant on the lava-encrusted surface. They were stalking along the shadows on the wall, headed toward the door, when they were startled by the abrupt appearance of a security guard. They flattened against the building, realizing in seconds that he appeared unaware of their presence.

The Security Guard looked around furtively, then broke out a pack of cigarettes. He bowed his head to light one up. Gentry stepped from the shadows, toward the guard.

"Hey, you too, huh?"

His voice startled the guard. "Oh, shit," he sized up Gentry as a plant worker in the dim light. "Can't seem to kick the habit."

"We just finished one ourselves," he reached back his arm, and Travers stepped into the half-light, acting kind of bashful.

"Hey, don't sweat it. Remember when we didn't have to sneak outside for smoke breaks?" the guard says.

"I know. Hell, they're treatin' us all like criminals now. Every once in a while, ya just gotta," Gentry proclaimed. "Well, guess we'll be headin' back to the grind."

"Yeah. See ya inside."

Gentry and Travers entered the plant. They did not dawdle. "Back this way," Gentry said. "We're headin' for that back left corner."

Travers peered across the expanse of the plant interior. The spot Gentry indicated appeared to be across a couple of football field lengths of steel scaffolding and live plant operations. It was a very eerie feeling, being in a nuclear plant for the first time, but they had to remain nonchalant. Step one now accomplished, they had to succeed with step two, in the process placing themselves in mortal danger.

Snyder, still shivering, now sat in a chair, unfettered in the lab. The hatch on the steel riser opened. Dr. Haas emerged from the observation booth, bringing her a cup of coffee.

"Here, Regina. You'll feel better."

"Carl." She nearly spat the name.

"Don't look at me that way. There are a number of valuable uses for mutable proteases." He shrugged, "But only, apparently, in the private sector."

Haas held out the hot coffee. Snyder slapped his wrist, scalding him with a coffee cascade. He gasped and drew back, hurting, enraged.

"She was the same way with me," shrugged Threll. "Now, Doctor Snyder, why not give in to the inevitable? There's a database that was off-loaded from this facility. Gentry claimed only he knew the code needed to access it again, but I believe you know it, too. Don't you?"

"All you have to do is remember—and key it in on that terminal over there," said Threll, gesturing to a workstation near the diagonal corner of the lab room. Snyder nodded, acknowledging the presence of the computer, if nothing else. It was near the fire extinguisher, to the left, and a fire ax on the wall ... three to four feet away from the PC. Hm. A sudden lunge to the left—? Could this be a test?

Avery broke in over the lab's public address system, "Do the kid, Threll."

Haas looked annoyed. "Can we take the Major off-line, Dr. Threll?"

Threll sighed. "This is a delicate moment, Major. We have negotiations under weigh, thank you."

Avery, sitting in the monitor room with which he was so familiar, resentfully fell silent again. He knew Threll held the real inside ace. He hadn't gotten what he truly wanted, yet. When he did get it, it would be the last payoff he'd ever need. *Slow and steady wins the race,* he reminded himself.

"Look, we're offering you a partnership, Regina," wheedled Haas. Snyder looked at him dully. "In full sincerity," he went on. "Why *hang* yourself over Will Monday? We're not going to kill him, you know. Don't you realize, with the forces arrayed against him, we could have pumped him full of lead several times over by now."

"We had to make him think his life was in great danger," Threll added. He had to bear down enough to learn to use his remarkable psionic abilities. He's done so rather well. The possbilities are amazing.

"Certain members of our group want to study him," Threll added. "Surely, he's used to that. We'll fix him up, too. He wants to *live it up,* right? Well, we can easily fix him with girls, drugs, booze, whatever keeps him happy."

"But it's not enough to have Will to 'study'? You have to have the total data bank?"

"Doctor, you could make such a mark here. The pharmaceutical division estimates a $420 million profit increase the first year if they can access your cross-hybridizing technology. It grows from there. Strategically, he could be brokered over to many other groups, in time, and with the right experience," Threll added. It was like a board meeting in now as they contemplated the profitable possibilities. "I see two million in it for you personally, Doctor. More, in time." He winked like her kindly uncle passing on a stock tip.

"Don't hold your breath waiting for me to sign on," she said, stoically.

"Where is this misguided sense of dignity leading you, lady?" demanded Threll. "There is no 'dignity' in the desert. There's no *je nes ce faire* in the jungle. There's just a shirt sticking to you with sweat. Snakes closing in, with the vines hanging from the trees."

"She's still stubborn. Well, I can tell you, what comes next will be a true pleasure, Regina," said Haas, still rubbing tenderly on his scalded wrist.

A couple of hundred feet above them, beneath a catwalk in a dark, obscure corner of the nuclear plant, Gentry felt with his hand until he located a barely-perceptible seam in the wall.

"Here it is. This was our way out, if we ever lost power. Now it's our way in. Ready?"

Travers inhaled, then sighed, "Yeah."

Gentry continued to probe the wall until he got his fingernails between two bricks. One of them turned out to be a latch, as Gentry pulled it outward slightly, and a section of wall opened, just big enough for a man to step into.

A steel chamber with a sealed hatch lay within. It was through this hatch, down a steel ladder attached to the wall, that they had to descend into darkness.

45.

Will huddled within the glass chamber, the side of his head pressed against the glass, listening.

"Once more, Doctor. The data. The Wilderbeeks won't be kept waiting."

"Just who do you people think you are," demanded Snyder, near tears.

"We know who we are. We're global magnates in arms, chemicals, finance—!"

Avery sat at the monitor room control panel, impatient and feeling futile. The hatch behind him swung slowly open on well-oiled hinges. Gentry, gun drawn, entered the room.

Gentry's gun barrel jutted into the back of Avery's head as Gentry's left hand cupped over Avery's mouth. Panic leaped across Avery's face.

Travers plucked Avery's sidearm from its holster. She covered the mic with one hand until she could locate and verify Avery's audio broadcast and reception were switched off on the control panel. She cuffed his wrists as Gentry covered him. "Holy shit," complained Avery. "I told him you'd be trouble."

"You know me best," Gentry said, gingerly.

"Listen, General, I know what you think of me, but, you know, survivability's *out*," Avery whined, trying to "reason" with him. "You know what future war's gonna be like. Directed energy weapons that can turn a whole army's brains to jelly, for Chrissakes. Nobody's gonna 'survive.' The Joint Chiefs know it, the President knows it…"

"Save it for your day in court," Gentry snarled back.

Avery barked a laugh. "You crazy? *My day in court?* Do you realize what you're saying? I'm being inducted into the Wilderbeeks, General. They have the price list of every judge in this country."

"Go to hell."

"It doesn't have to be this way, ya know..."

Gentry hesitated, but said, "I want it all out there, now. Let the chips fall. Your paymasters obviously want to reveal Will's existence. 'Make known all that is hidden.' isn't that what they call it? Well, maybe somebody oughtta talk about them in public, too."

He and his protégé, Travers, looked over the situation on screen. "We can't cut off the air to the lab without including Will in the area," he fumed. Turning to Travers, he patted his weapon and said, "Let's go clean up, girly-girl. It's the only way."

Travers steeled herself, swallowing hard.

In the lab, Threll was finished with the tender approach. "You think you can thwart me? You're wrong. Your life ended with your presence at our ceremony. You are reborn only at our pleasure." He turned. "Vee. See that ax on the wall?"

Vee looked over to the wall at the fire ax Snyder noted earlier. He nodded. He retrieved the ax from the wall, carried it over to the table and lay it down.

To Snyder, Threll said, "There is an environmental test you never took to the furthest extreme. Now, we will. Once he's frozen solid—" he waved toward the ax—"I'll have Vee take it to the limit."

Dr. Haas had stalked back up the steps into the control booth. Threll nodded to the dark window. In the glass chamber, the gas jets pumped once more at full force. Inside the tank, Will disappeared in the cloud of white gas.

Snyder struggled desperately with the decision she must make. Within seconds, the glass had frosted over. There was no more sign of Will in the white, chaotic swirl.

"All right! If you want the data, I'll download it for you." This was her moment. If death was inevitable for both her and her son, this was the only way she could postpone it. Only if there was no more time would there be no more hope, she decided.

Inside the now-obscured tank, amidst the stark white gas, Will backed against the hatch. He was generating heat, so the skin of his fingertips would not stick, frozen to the dry ice covering the hatch. Shivering, he probed his hands over the hatch, tentatively, painfully from the cold.

If there were even someone in the maintenance hallway to see this, his effort was doomed. But it seemed like a chance. As Will's fingers probed, the hatch wheel began to twitch, to turn—an inch, another, counterclockwise.

In the lab, Haas burst from his control chamber.

"Regina? You'll restore the data to the computers here? Yes?"

"Yes, Carl."

Threll nodded.

Haas popped back inside his control chamber. The gas stopped shooting into the glass chamber, opposite. The view of the interior remained obscured by a frozen glaze. "Proceed, then, Doctor Snyder. Go on... you know it's the right thing to do."

"Will."

"Once you access the data bank for us, he'll go free."

Haas toddled down the steps from the control chamber riser, saying, "Okay, over here. I'll be watching." He pointed to the workstation.

Haas joined Snyder at the terminal, watching over her shoulder. She engaged in a dialogue with a remote mainframe, keying in a series of passwords penetrating deeper into the mysteries until the monitor showed them a banded screen which bore the message "ACCESS: PROTEUS. DATASET - BLUE MONDAY. PASSWORD:"

"Now. Release him, Threll. Let him go and I'm cooperating. But I won't enter this last sequence until he's out of there. And if I don't key it in, I guarantee you'll never hack it."

Threll shrugged. He spoke to Vee, "Go get the blue boy."

"Excellent," said Haas, pleased that it was all coming together at last. "One more password, and we download."

Threll slyly donned his headset. Murder lit his eyes as he studied the pair of scientists. He rested his hand just inside his coat lapel, ready for the end game.

46.

The door to the lab opened unexpectedly. Avery rounded the corner and entered slowly from the corridor. Gentry, holding a gun to his head, followed. Travers rounded the opposite side of the door, holding Avery's sidearm on the room at large.

Mouth poised to whisper a command into his microphone, Threll looked toward Vee, pretty much in shock for once.

Behind Vee, just inside the door, Gentry aimed a gun at Threll, and Travers covered Avery. Vee twitched, but Threll tensely raised his hand, signaling him to wait.

In the corridor beyond the temperature tank, the hatch wheel turned again, inch by inch. Eventually, the hatch opened, and Will tumbled out, stiffly, onto the floor, more gas escaping behind him. On his back, he kicked up against the hatch, closing it back.

He was covered with ice crystals. He slowly pushed himself up from the floor, back against a wall. He pushed himself up against the wall, torturously, by steps, by steps, came upright to his feet. He was shivering, trembling with the cold, numb but functioning.

"You're done, Threll," Gentry was saying, in the lab. "I hope, for your sake, Regina and Will are okay."

"You can see that your Dr. Snyder is just fine," Threll snarled. "In fact, she was just betraying your project's ultimate secrets to us."

"'Gina!" shouted Gentry.

"Too late! Shouted Haas across the lab back at him. He still held a gun over Snyder, as well. It looked like a Mexican standoff of sorts was in progress. Gentry's nightmare of how it might turn out.

Back in the corridor, Will twisted his wrists behind his back, involved in some effort for several long moments. At last, with a click, his cuffs opened and fell to the floor.

Will removed the bag from his head with trembling fingers. He staggered along the hallway like a terminal arthritic. Painfully, he climbed a short riser. Laboriously, he turned a hatch wheel, little by little.

In the lab, the directory to all the Proteus data Dr. Threll or the Wilderbeeks could ever want now lay open before Dr. Haas. He grabbed Dr. Snyder in a stranglehold. He pulled her away from the computer terminal, then twisted her arm behind her back. Using her as a shield, he dragged her up the riser steps until they were poised just outside the open hatch to the observation deck.

"Okay, Regina's right here with me, and Will Monday is in that tank, where I can kill him with the flip of a switch. Got that? So, lay down your guns."

Threll smiled, pleased at the turn of events. "Masterful, Doctor," he purred.

Haas also smiled, proud of himself. Across the control room which they had yet to enter, fifteen feet behind Haas, a hatch opened slowly. Will shuffled, not unlike some undead creature from the movies, toward Haas's back.

Gentry tried to counter Haas's move somehow. "I'm aiming at your head, Mister Threll. Tell 'em—how the CIA let you try your mind surgery on this guy—a contract agent who had a total nervous breakdown. They weren't pleased with the results, were they? They let him go."

"Jacob. Is that true?"

"Shut up!" Threll hissed at Gentry.

"But you don't give up easy. You put out feelers until you found your next chance at the big score. You bribed some contacts, and snagged some advanced weapons. At Haas's university, you found your ticket—into the Proteus Project. Tell me a good one, Haas. How much did he promise you? And you, Avery? Your rich uncle, the supplier for Advanced Projects, he get our friends here some of that portable hardware that took out my men's copters? You did help them get that stuff, didn't you?"

Avery knew he had the right to remain silent, and for once, he did so.

"Intelligence is a business of relationships, gentlemen. Lots of people owed me some favors. I called in a few. Got you checked out."

"How very gumshoe of you," smirked Threll. "Aren't you forgetting, we know you care about your Dr. Snyder—"

As all eyes turned toward Haas, a blue hand tapped his shoulder from behind. Haas, startled, slowly turned his head. Will's fist smashed his face. Haas staggered back into the steel railing lining the riser and collapsed, Snyder shrugging from his grip as he did so.

"All- ri-i-i-ight!" Said Snyder, as she realized what, or rather, who, had happened to Haas. Will, half-frozen, shook his smarting hand. Snyder turned to give him a big hug. He bent stiffly.

"Will. My God. You're so cold." She held him anyway.

"Never knew you cared."

They tottered down the steps to the lab floor.

Threll looked about, desperately, sensing imminent defeat.

"Vee! The ax."

That was all it took. In quick succession: Vee pulled his gun from its shoulder holster. Gentry turned his gun toward Vee, aiming for his head. Threll dove under the table.

Avery wheeled around, grabbing the distracted Travers' forearm, making her shoot into space. Gentry lurched into motion, shot for Vee's head, missed, and was missed in return by a hasty shot squeezed off by the man-mountain.

Vee then kicked the table, upending it, sending its contents flying. The table itself knocked Gentry to the floor.

Will tackled Vee, to keep him from advancing on Gentry. They hit the floor and grappled ferociously.

Threll, crawling on the floor, grabbed Travers's foot. She and Avery, clinging to her like a leech, tumbled to the floor. Avery rolled on top, slammed her viciously with his handcuffed fists. "Take-this-girl-*scout*!" he shouted.

Gentry staggered to his feet. A shot took him back down. Snyder screamed.

"You should've stayed home." Avery sneered, holding his smoking pistol in his hand. He stood and turned, aiming it next at the fallen Travers.

"Bye-bye."

Just then, Avery caught an office chair, swivel base first, across the skull. Snyder had charged him with the chair from behind. Snyder rammed the chair into Avery's back, staggering him. "You killed him!" she shrieked.

Threll gained his feet, taking in the sordid action.

Will sat atop Vee, clutching his wrists, one knee dug into Vee's throat. Smoke poured from both of Will's hands. He spared the giant nothing.

"Drop the gun, damn you! Choke!" Will appeared ready to keel over with the effort he was pouring forth.

Vee released the pistol at last. Will waved an arm swiftly, and the gun flew across the floor. He stood up, trembling. Vee coughed violently and gasped for air.

Avery dodged Snyder's next vicious swing of the chair, and caught the chair's shaft on the back swing. They struggled, tugging on the chair by turns.

"Give me a minute, bitch!"

He aimed at Snyder. The gun fired... into the ceiling, as Avery's arm jerked upward at the last second. Will glared at Avery. Desperation written on his face, Will gripped Avery's forearm via telekinesis.

Threll took advantage of the distraction to leap over Gentry's prone body and dash out the lab doors. Travers, having now somewhat recovered her senses, rose to her feet, and ran out after him.

"Avery." a voice croaked from the floor.

47.

Avery looked down...

Into the barrel of Gentry's upraised gun. The bloody general fired a slug into Avery's chest. Avery, in shock, sagged to the floor.

"Now *you* need a sick day," Will muttered, watching Avery keel over from the mortal wound. He leapt to the general's side.

"Come on, old man, you're gonna make it," he cried.

The General weakly shook his head. His chest was a puddle of blood.

Behind Will, Vee, on hands and knees, had regained his gun. But as he aimed, he struggled with it, his arm bending backward. Will had turned his attention back to the adversary just in time. He angrily used his telekinesis to wrestle Vee's gun back, toward his own head. Vee, feeling the tension of Will's etheric tentacle on him directly, mustered up all the hate and fury he could, in an effort at counteraction.

The effort began to cost Will. Vee clutched his own forearm, trying to control the tension. He saw that Will was straining to contain his movements, sensed the telekinetic connection could work both ways. He grinned, his warrior instincts undimmed by Threll's mind control implants..

He suddenly tensed every muscle, and flung himself backward. Will was, to his own surprise, pulled forward. He belly-flopped to the floor, winded. Vee leapt up, and jump-kicked him in the head.

Vee stood, gasping, glaring, looking around for Threll—who was nowhere to be seen. Suddenly, Vee looked lost. He uttered a pathetic cry of frustration and cast down his gaze. When he looked up again, his expression was one of sullen resentment. He looked at Regina Snyder. With utter psychosis written on his face, he aimed his gun at her.

"No!!" Will leapt, tackling Vee just as the gun fired.

The two men's bodies smacked the floor.

Vee's pistol slid beneath a cabinet.

Will sat up to see Dr. Snyder's dying form as she, too, lay bleeding on the floor, near the General.

"You're dead!" he snarled at Vee, diving for the back of the prone giant.

Will punched the back of Vee's head with the impact of a mortar shell. Vee lay completely prone after the blow. Will turned him over. Vee, nose shattered, teeth missing, lay still as though dead.

Will scurried to Snyder's side, to assess his mother's wounds.

"Mother... no."

Snyder bled profusely from the sternum. She emitted little coughs.

"Forgive—me?" she gasped.

"I—I forgive you. I—thank you. Thank you for giving me life."

Snyder mustered a brave smile, but she was already too far gone to say more. Will pulled her to his chest, now letting it go, crying profusely.

Her labored breathing finally stilled, he lay her lifeless body back against the floor. He gently extended his fingers to close his mother's eyelids.

The powerful arms of Vee grabbed Will in a choke hold, pulling him away from Snyder's body and subduing him with one hand, while he plucked up the fire ax from the table with the other.

On the floor, Morgan Gentry opened his eyes. The prone form of Regina Snyder lay straight across from him. His face twisted in pain, he gasped and shuddered. He began crawling, feebly, with his last strength, toward her.

"Gina."

Struggling, Vee dragged the now-smoldering Will across the room. He hurled him against the wall and took a savage swing with the ax. Will ducked, and the blow chopped a section of an electrical conduit open, sending sparks flying. One section broke loose from the wall.

Vee dropped the ax, closed in, grabbed Will's head in a choke hold. He grabbed a loose section of conduit, and pulled it down toward Will. Will grabbed Vee's wrist and burned him some more. He didn't seem to feel it, though it had to be hurting him. Their struggles redoubled as Vee bent Will's head down toward the deadly exposed wires.

On the riser, Dr. Haas pulled himself together, taking in the scene of carnage with dismay.

Vee snapped another section of steel conduit loose. The live wires now mere inches from Will's head, he marshalled his inner forces and directed an intense stare elsewhere—at Dr. Haas's lab coat. Its hem burst into flames. Haas panicked and rushed down the steps, smoke pouring off him. He shed the flaming, smoking coat and fled the lab. On came the high-pressure sprinkler system to douse the smoking coat-blaze.

Haas' panic provided just enough of a distraction for Vee to pause. Will reached up and gouged fingers right into Vee's eyes. One of them was soft, one was hard. At last, Will found live nerve endings on the giant. Vee, screaming, flung Will from him.

But he still grasped the electrical conduit. As the water struck him, electrical current arced from the wires. The current electrocuted him where he stood. His body jerked hard against the surging current for a moment, then expired, in glowing spasms.

Will, drenched like everything else in the lab, ambled over to the valve on the wall to shut off the sprinklers.

Gentry, crawling in an inch of water, trembling and wheezing, sloshed near the half-submerged head of Regina Snyder.

In a final reach, his dying fingers clutched her lifeless ones.

Their blood mingled in the swirling waters running down the floor drain.

Will, in tears and complete shock, surveyed the terrible tableaux.

He was not to have time to succumb to grief. Travers burst into the lab entrance behind him.

"Oh, my God," she gasped.

"This was my world. I always hated it. Now look..."

"Will. I followed Threll. He's climbing up—to the nuclear plant!"

Will seemed not to hear. "*They* did this, with their guns, and their greed."

"He's climbing to the nuclear plant, Will. Do you understand? Vee *worked* up there for months. There's no telling what he *did* in that place."

"I never knew what I had, Pam."

"I can't be your shrink right now, Will! Please! Threll is in the nuclear plant!"

Will, wild-eyed, in a whole new level of shock and dismay, walked unsteadily among the field of bodies before him, as if taking inventory. He arrived at the body of Vee. He looked at Travers. She saw madness twist Will's face.

To her dismay, he pounced ferociously on the lifeless body of Vee. She covered her eyes and sagged to her knees, in despair.

48.

The hidden section of wall opened in a corner of the plant, and Jacob Threll emerged. An observer might have caught a glimpse of an open steel hatch in the interior chamber, before the wall / door closed again.

Threll emerged from the dark corner of the plant, pausing beneath a catwalk to orient himself. Then he strode briskly, tensely through the plant. The third-shift crew operated the nuclear plant, going about their routine stations, unaware of the menace that stalked their midst.

The smoking security guard with whom Gentry had made momentary solidarity earlier in the dim night, spotted the wiry figure while on his rounds. Unable to identify the man, he moved to intercept.

"Excuse me. Could I see some identification."

Threll reached for his wallet. "I'm with the NRC."

"Huh? There's no inspection, is there?"

Threll opened his "wallet". A tiny dart sprang into the Security Guard's throat. The guard shook his head and looked at Threll in mute shock, before he sagged to the floor.

"It's a strong derivative of curare," he observed drily. Threll bent and heaved, dragging the guard around a corner.

Threll reappeared moments later, wearing the Security Guard's uniform, which fit him rather loosely. He strolled down a flight to the control room. Entering casually, he walked between rows of seated, bored technicians, manning panels of monitors, buttons, sliders, and digital readouts. They scarcely noticed him; to catch a glimpse of a patrolling security guard's uniform while they watched their panels was routine. He stopped at a corner of the deck.

"Hey. You smell anything?" Threll asked the corner tech.

"Huh? No, I don't." He turned and, taking his first good look at this "guard," said, "Huh. You're new here, aren't you?"

"Yeah, first night actually. Had to borrow a uniform." Threll went ahead and called attention to the bagginess of the shirt, pulling the loose belly out a few inches. "But, you ought to know, I saw smoke coming from under your panel, here." he nudged the corner gently with his toe. "Mind if we check it out?"

"You're kidding," the tech said. "I don't see anything." He sniffed. "There's no odor."

Threll impatiently motioned him back. "Still, gotta keep you guys safe," he said tersely.

The technician slid his chair back. Threll knelt and slid open the cabinet doors beneath the panel. He lay down on one shoulder and reached inside the dark, open space.

A small plastic detonator rested in the shadows. As Threll was aware, it had been surreptitiously planted by Vee in a pre-arranged plan during his stint as a "workman" in the plant.

This was to be a "do-or-die" mission. Threll had seen defeat snatched from the jaws of victory. Under the Brotherhood's rules, his life could now be forfeit, especially if there were survivors with inside information to speak of the Wilderbeeks' existence.

"Dusty down here," he coughed. He was sweating; his teeth, though they could not be seen by anyone else, were clenched. This was not an easy thing to do. But, it would clean the slate, destroying the Proteus Project utterly and in such a way that he would live to implement his schemes another day.

It had to be this way, he reminded himself. He had not achieved so much by being faint of heart. He reached inside. He wrapped his forefinger around that trigger. It rested there a few seconds.

"What's happenin' down there, ya find your fire or what?" he heard the technician say.

Threll squeezed the detonator trigger.

Inside the adjacent turbine building, six pipe lines ran out of turbines humming in the floor. One of these pipes exploded a second after Threll depressed that plunger. Deadly steam gushed from the rupture.

Workers on the catwalk broke out in panic, making a run for the exits.

In the reactor building, two fifty-foot tall steam generator towers dominated the interior, with catwalks accessing the middle and the top areas of the towers. At the midsection, each tower had an attached heat transport pump, standard in a light water nuclear reactor of this type.

One of these pumps also exploded. This was one more critical emergency than its human response teams could cope with. The tower ruptured, releasing a vast gust of scalding, radioactive steam. In this section, too, workers on the catwalks jumped into action, running for the exits before the mist could cook their flesh.

In the control room, the lights faded into blackness as the plant's main generator died.

Instantly, a babel arose in the room. "What the hell? Where's backup power? Holy shit, it's a meltdown."

In the reactor's cooling chamber, the level of hissing, boiling water dropped. The all-important damping mechanism, the automatic "scram" mechanism malfunctioned, dumping the control rods into a heap. They glowed red hot, their nuclear fuel now exposed to air, with less and less steam carrying off their heat as it normally did.

Realizations grew among some in the control room. As they tried to assess their situation, they knew the heat of those rods could quickly build into that of a radioactive mini-sun, burning its way into the earth, dooming virtually everyone underground as well as above.

Threll stood up, in the dark. It had taken three acts of sabotage committed in obscure, "routine maintenance" in the course of a year, to implement the contingency plan he had just set in motion. A pity, he thought, that he was actually having to resort to it. But it was all part of the clandestine world where stakes were high and the games were for keeps.

Overwhelmed, frustrated, and frightened, a knot of technicians rushed out of the now-useless control room.

"Crank the emergency generators! Get the panels back up!" their voices chattered.

Threll slipped out behind them. He found a catwalk and climbed for a better vantage, savoring the chaos he had caused. This was at least an exercise in raw power, and he felt, here at the end, like glorying in it for a few moments.

The secret door back in the rear corner shadows of the plant opened for the third time that night. Will's head peeked out. He saw the human cross-currents on the floor, panicked personnel scrambling to somehow regain control of the wounded Leviathan they normally shepherded through nuclear nights.

In the control room, technicians who had remained inside using flashlights, plugged panels into portable gasoline generators some of them wheeled into the room. The displays on their control panels lit up anew.

But the technicians emitted more frantic shouts when they got a look at the real-time data etching itself in colors onto the screens. "Oh, God, pressure's dropping in the number two tower. Emergency core coolant system failure. Got a break at the separator release. Oh, *shit! Scram* release failure!"

One technician spoke into a microphone which fed a public address system. "Core meltdown imminent. This is not a drill." The technician's voice reverberated through the complex. Personnel paused in whatever they were doing to try to hear clearly over the whine and roar of the stricken plant.

"Implement procedure N-E at once. Do not gather possessions. Estimated time to core meltdown, *ten* minutes."

49.

Personnel clad in radiation suits headed for the access chamber to the reactor building, located next to the control room. Theirs was to be a last-ditch, possibly suicidal mission to regain control over the heat of the rods in the reactor chamber.

Blue hands grabbed the last crew member amongst them from behind and spun him around. The nimble hands snatched off the astonished man's protective headgear.

"Where you going?" The blue man's voice demanded.

"I—uh- uh—"

"Where?!?" Will snarled at the crewman.

"A-a-access chamber!" he heard his own voice say. He pointed in the direction he meant, where the other crew members neared a hatch leading into the reactor tower.

Will's hands unstrapped the man's gloves.

"Give me your suit. Now!"

"Hey—!"

Will's hands now shoved the Crewman down, pulled off one of his boots as the man's feet flew up. Moments later, Will donned the visored headpiece, completing his protective suit. He ran after the other crewmen and entered the same hatch as they.

As Will had scrambled across the open ground to nab himself a suit, unnoticed high above, Threll stalked the catwalk. He had been taking in the melee with grisly satisfaction, which turned to a scowl as he turned a corner just in time to catch sight of Will donning the headpiece. The freak was still bent on thwarting him! Threll darted down steel stairs.

Blue Monday

The radiation crew, Will among them, were firmly shut inside the airlock. All but Will, who hadn't grabbed one and didn't need one anyway, activated their flashlights. They opened the inner hatch to confront the darkened gangways and apparatus of the nuclear reactor.

The crew leader pointed to the gangways and barked out orders to the others. "Get up to the dousing tank, now! Hit the manual release, *muy pronto!*" Another crewman clapped a temperature gauge onto the steam generator. Shining his light, he read from the gauge: "It's down to three hundred and fifty degrees, sir!"

"What does it need to be?" Will shouted. The other two men looked at him with their amazement hidden by the face masks.

"Six hundred and twenty!" barked the crew leader. You should know that!"

Will thrust out his arms dramatically. "Stay back!" He raised those hands high above him.

Slowly, incredibly, the rushing cloud of steam began to pause in mid-air. It still flowed from the tower accumulating, growing denser for a moment. Then, miraculously, it began finally to roll back within invisible boundaries, back even into the steam tower.

Will leaned into the tower itself with both hands.

To the other crewman, the leader yelled, "Holy hannah, it's a freakin' *miracle.*"

"Can't—last long," Will groaned. He had reached the upper volume limit that his "feelers" could contain.

The distant, muffled Public Address message continued. "Five minutes to core meltdown."

"Generator heat's up to three-sixty! And climbing!" the crewman read from the gauge.

"Hurry—do what you can." Will sagged to his knees.

An armed crewman—Threll, under an ill-gotten protective suit of his own—stalked forward at that moment, along the catwalk toward Will and the crew leader.

Meantime, Travers entered the plant through the secret door, a few minutes behind Will. She was still sobbing, feeling sick from the grisly slaughter scene she had witnessed in the secret world below. She made her way, dazed and confused, through the darkened plant she had glimpsed only once in the light.

After minutes of searching, she stepped into the control room at last. Seeing her in her overalls, one tech responded, "Maintenance? How's the patch coming on that secondary breach?"

"Uh, we're working on it. Ah, you didn't happen to see a young man, all blue, did you?"

"None of us is exactly cheerful right now," the tech retorted sarcastically.

"Estimate one minute to core meltdown," said the PA system.

"A minute!?" shouted Travers. "What happens then?"

"How'd you get your job?! Uranium-235 rods in there melt the floor of their tank. Burn into the earth. Radiation escapes. And we meet our Maker."

Travers staggered back out of the room, and there was McIntire, in his body cast, looking pathetically helpless. The sight broke her heart for him all over again. She tenderly embraced his unwounded side, laid her head on that manly shoulder.

"Those alarms. What's going on? What happened down there?" he demanded.

"I think everybody's dea—dead," Travers sobbed. "And it's all to *hell* up here—!"

"Pam. I think *this is it*," said McIntire. "That devil must have planted some bombs in here. He's going to ... wipe it *all* out if he can't have it himself."

In the reactor building, Threll raised his gun and fired at one of the crew members who stood near the dousing tank at the top. The stricken crewman buckled. Threll stalked a few steps up one of the catwalks. Drawing a bead, he felled another crewman walking another high catwalk with another expert shot.

The crew leader beside Will realized what was happening. Survival instinct kicked in.

"Oh, hell! *Run* for it!"

The crew leader and the crewman beside him ran for their lives as Threll approached, waving his gun hand around almost cavalierly. He stalked swiftly toward Will, who quivered with effort to contain the deadly, roiling gases Threll's sabotage had unleashed.

Threll stopped and took level aim.

"Remember what I promised you?" he shouted through the mask. "No more pain, Will Monday."

Threll fired for the heart.

Will crumpled to the catwalk. Above them, once more, the steam rushed freely.

Threll turned to make good his final escape. He had not strode far when gloved hands seized him from behind.

"Here's your pain."

The hands ripped off Threll's headgear. Threll screamed in agony, as the searing, radioactive steam scalded his exposed face.

Threll fell onto his back, writhing, gloved hands clutching his face. Will wobbled and collapsed to his knees, near Threll's feet.

The crew leader and crewman who had been with Will ran back up the catwalk. The crew leader bent over Threll.

Threll's face was a raw mass, all the flesh burned away. He weakly clutched the fabric of the Crew Leader's outfit, pulling him close. His hideous reflection grimaced in the Crew Leader's visor. It was a mass of red, subcutaneous flesh—hamburger with facial features.

With a shuddering moan, Threll's rolled his eyes back in their sockets. He fell back, dead.

50.

With a shudder, the crew leader pulled the clutching hands of the corpse from the front of his radiation suit. He and his crewman turned away, and proceeded to climb the catwalks above, toward the stations occupied by the men Threll had wounded.

At length, at the top of the tower, on the highest catwalk, the crew leader turned the release valve of the dousing water tank. A great gushing sound ensued as vast quantities of stored water flooded down the inside walls.

Inside the nuclear reactor coolant chamber, at that moment, fresh water flooded the hot rods. The sealed chamber flooded with instant radioactive steam. As much as it could dissipate the heat of the accumulated rods, it could delay the meltdown.

In the control room, the technician spoke into the public address system, announcing, "Emergency cooling system kicked in. Meltdown averted!"

"Thank God!" exclaimed the tech beside him. "I thought sure the rods would explode when that water hit 'em. But they kept enough steam circulating down there—somehow."

In sudden realization, outside that room, Travers and McIntire grabbed each other in fresh hugs. In a moment, they laughed and jumped for joy.

"Whew. You really take life for granted sometimes," McIntire exclaimed.

"Yes," Travers nodded.

"We better take inventory. If Threll's still around, he's capable of anything. Obviously."

Travers agreed, and they walked the plant until they found a knot of congregating techs uniformed in medical garb.

The hatch from the nuclear tower section opened. The radiation crew emerged in their briefs, dripping from decontamination showers. As they filed out, two supported wounded colleagues, who were quickly taken onto gurneys by medics standing by.

The crew leader stepped solemnly forward, hands folded.

"I don't know who he is. Hell, I don't even know what he is. But this young fellow bought us time—helped save us all. Come out here—Will Monday!"

Will stepped slowly out of the chamber, sheepish and exhausted. From one hand dangled Vee's bullet-proof vest.

His haggard gaze look over the stunned faces of the plant workers. In their midst, his eyes met those of Travers. Both faces gradully broke out in huge grins.

"Will!" she shouted.

"Pam!" Will dropped the vest. They surged to embrace one another in a passionate kiss. The other men and women, faces full of wonder, broke into spontaneous applause in the dream-like moment.

Fatigue mingled with relief as Will and Pam parted. They exchanged glances, then looked outward at the others. Both were suddenly thinking ahead, toward a vastly uncertain future. Joined by the bemused McIntire, the three took in the wild applause of the workers, survivors all.

The three knew their lives would never be the same – or like anyone else's.

THE END

ABOUT THE AUTHOR

Ron Brassfield was born in Detroit, Michigan and currently resides in Tennessee. He has lived life as a visual artist and writer since he first held a pencil at the age of four, an interest first sparked by the Fleischer Studios "Popeye" cartoons. Ron experienced enthusiasms from dinosaurs and the US Civil War to super heroes as a young child. He learned to play the guitar as a teen and listens to the Beatles and Radiohead as an adult. In high school he was elected newspaper editor, columnist and won prizes as a short story writer as well as a stage actor. He devoted himself to the art of painting as a college undergraduate and earned his Bachelor's Degree in Fine Art. He read classic literature, contemporary novels, science fiction and comic books as a child. Some of his favorite authors include Henry Miller, Thomas Pynchon, and Steve Erickson. He has also studied the political landscape as a concerned American citizen for more than a quarter century. Ron currently earns his living in an internet related computer field. **Blue Monday** is his first completed novel, adapted from his original screenplay written in various versions since early 1994 until it developed into its current novel format.

Printed in the United States
41637LVS00006B/182